The Cruise of the Land Yacht Wanderer

WILLIAM GORDON STABLES

Published in 1886

TABLE OF CONTENTS

PREFACE

I need, I believe, do little more herein, than state that the following pages were written on the road, on the coupé of my caravan, and from day to day. First impressions, it must be admitted, are not always infallible, but they are ever fresh.

I have written from my heart, as I saw and thought; and I shall consider myself most fortunate and happy if I succeed in making the reader think in a measure as I thought, and feel as I felt.

It is but right to state that many of the chapters have appeared in The Leisure Hour.

Some of the illustrations are from photographs kindly lent me by Messrs Valentine and Sons, of Dundee; others from rough sketches of my own; while the frontispiece, "Waiting till the Kettle Boils," is by Mr Eales, of Twyford.

Gordon Stables.
The "Wanderer" Caravan,
Touring in Yorkshire, August 1886.

INTRODUCTORY

No man who cannot live in his house on wheels, cook, eat, and sleep in, on, or under it, can say that he is cut out for a gipsy life. But to do this you require to have your temporary home well arranged—a perfect multum in parvo, a domus in minima. The chief faults of the old-fashioned caravan are want of space—two ordinary-sized adults can hardly move in it without trampling on each other's toes—general stuffiness, heat from sky or stove, or probably both combined, and a most disagreeable motion when on the road. This latter is caused by want of good springs, and errors in the general build.

"The man who is master of a caravan," says a writer, "enjoys that perfect freedom which is denied to the tourist, whose movements are governed by the time-table. He can go where he likes, stop when he lists, go to bed at the hour which suits him best, or get up or lie daydreaming, knowing there is not a train to catch nor a waiter's convenience to consult. If the neighbourhood does not suit the van-dweller, all he has to do is to hitch in the horses and move to more eligible quarters. The door of his hotel is always open. There is no bill to pay nor anybody to 'remember;' and, if the accommodation has been limited, the lodger cannot complain of the charges. In a caravan one has all the privacy of a private residence, with the convenience of being able to wheel it about with a facility denied to the western settler, who shifts his 'shanty' from the 'lot' which he has leased to the more distant one which he has bought. In the van may, for all the passer-by can discover, be a library and drawing-room combined, or it may be bedroom and dining-room in one, though, as the pioneers in this mode of touring sleep under canvas, we may presume that they find the accommodation indoors a little stuffy."

Now, this sounds very well, but at the present sitting I have my doubts if a gipsy's—even a gentle-man-gipsy's—life be altogether as independent and sunshiny as the sentences represent them to be.

About going where he likes, for instance? Are there not certain laws of the road that forbid the tarrying by the way of caravan folks, for a longer period than that necessary to water and feed a horse or look at his feet? By night, again, he may spy a delightfully retired common, with nothing thereon, perhaps, except a flock of gabbling geese and a superannuated cart-horse, and be tempted to draw up and on it, but may not some duty-bound police man stroll quietly up, and order him to put-to and "move on?"

Again, if the neighbourhood does not suit, then the caravan-master may certainly go elsewhere, if the horses be not too tired or dead lame.

To be sure, there is inside a caravan all the privacy to be desired; but immediately outside, especially if drawn up on a village common, it may be noisy enough.

As regards going to bed and getting up when he pleases, the owner of a caravan is his own master, unless he chooses to carry the ideas and customs of a too-civilised life into the heart of the green country with him, and keep plenty of company.

Methinks a gentleman gipsy ought to have a little of the hermit about him. If he does not love nature and quiet and retirement, he is unsuited for a caravan life, unless, indeed, he would like to make every day a gala day, and the whole tour a round of pleasurable excitement—in other words, a farce.

It is, however, my impression at the present moment that the kind of life I trust to lead for many months to come, might be followed by hundreds who are fond of a quiet and somewhat romantic existence, and especially by those whose health requires bracing up, having sunk below par from overwork, overworry, or over much pleasure-seeking, in the reckless way it is the fashion to seek it.

Only as yet I can say nothing from actual experience. I have to go on, the reader has to read on, ere the riddle be solved to our mutual satisfaction.

THE CARAVAN ITSELF

"A horse, a horse, my kingdom for a horse!"

Travelling through the romantic little village of Great Marlow one summer's day in a pony-trap, I came suddenly on a row of caravans drawn up on the roadside. Some flying swings were started just as I approached, and the unwonted sight, with the wild whooping and noise, startled my horse. He shied, and made a rather thoughtless but very determined attempt to enter a draper's shop. This resulted in damage enough to the trap to necessitate my staying an hour or two for repairs.

I would have a look at the caravans, at all events.

There was one very pretty little one, and, seeing me admire it, the owner, who stood by, kindly asked if I cared to look inside. I thanked him, and followed him up the steps. It proved to be a good thing of the class, but inside the space was limited, owing to the extraordinary breadth of the bed and size of the stove.

I asked the address of the builder, however, and wrote to him for an estimate. This was sent, but the penmanship and diction in which it was couched sent no thrill of pleasure through me. Here is a sentence: "Wich i can build you a wagon as ill cary you anyweres with 1 orse for eity pounds, i 'as built a power o' pretty wagons for gipsies, an' can refer you to lots on 'em for reference."

Well, to be sure, there is no necessity for a builder of caravans being a classical scholar, but there was a sad absence of romance about this letter; the very word "wagon" was not in itself poetic. Why could not the man have said "caravan"? I determined to consult a dear old friend of mine who knows everything, C.A. Wheeler, to wit (the clever author of "Sportascrapiana.")

Why, he said in reply, did not I go straight to the Bristol Waggon

Company? They would do the thing well, at all events, and build my caravan from my own drawings.

This was good advice. So I got a few sheets of foolscap and made a few rough sketches, and thought and planned for a night or two, and thus the Wanderer came into existence—on paper.

Now that the caravan is built and fitted she is so generally admired by friends and visitors, that I may be forgiven for believing that a short description of her may prove not uninteresting to the general reader.

Let us walk round her first and foremost and view the exterior.

A glance will show you (see illustration) that The Saloon Caravan "Wanderer" is by no means of small dimensions. From stem to stern, without shafts or pole, she measures nearly twenty feet, her height from the ground being about eleven feet, and her breadth inside six feet fully.

For so long a carriage you will naturally say the wheels seem low.

This is true; the hind wheels are little over four feet, but they are under the carriage. Had they been tall they must have protruded beyond her considerably, and this would have given the Wanderer a breadth of beam which would have been awkward on the road, and rendered it impossible to get her through many gateways.

I might have had a semicircle or hollow in the sides of the caravan, in which high wheels could have moved without entailing a broader beam, but this would have curtailed the floor space in the after-cabin, on which my valet has to sleep athwartships, and this arrangement was therefore out of the question.

But she must be very heavy? Not for her size and strength. Although solid mahogany all round outside and lined with softer wood, she scaled at Bristol but 30 hundredweight, and loaded-up she will be under two tons. The loading-up includes master, valet, coachman, and a large Newfoundland dog, not one of whom need be inside except "coachee" on a stiff hill.

Obeying my instructions, then, the builders made her as light as was consistent with strength. The wood too is of the best and best seasoned that could be had. A firm that builds Pullman cars, not only for England but for America, has always a good supply of old wood on hand.

But if the Wanderer does not look light she certainly looks elegant. Polished mahogany with black and gold mouldings and shutters—jalousies—leaves little to be longed for as regards outside show, neither does it give a gay appearance. The wheels and underworks are dark chocolate, picked out with vermilion. The only "ornament" about her is the device on the side, and this is simply a sketch of the badge of my uniform cap—crown, anchor, and laurel leaves,—with a scroll of ribbon of the Robertson tartan, my mother's plaid. This looks quite as pretty and costs less than armorial bearings.

In the illustration the fore part of the caravan is visible. There is a splashboard, an unusual luxury in carriages of this kind. The coupé is very roomy; the Newfoundland lies here when he likes, and a chair can be placed on it, or if rugs and a cushion are put down it forms a delightful lounge on a fine day, and this need in no way interfere with the comfort of either the driver or the great dog. The driver's seat is also the corn-bin, and holds two bushels. From the broad panel at the other side of the door a board lets down at pleasure, and this forms still another seat for an extra passenger besides myself.

It may also be noticed that the front part of the roof protrudes, forming ample protection against sun and rain. This canopy is about three feet deep.

The brake, which is handy to the driver, is a very powerful one, and similar to those used on tram-cars. There is also an iron skid to lock one wheel if required on going down hill, and a roller besides for safety in stopping when going up hill.

There is a door behind right in the centre, similar in appearance to the front door, with morsels of stained glass let in at the upper corners.

Both doors have light shutters that are put up at night.

Under the rear door the broad steps are shipped, and at each side is a little mahogany flap table to let down. These the valet finds very handy when washing up. Beneath each of these flaps and under the carriage is a drawer to contain tools, dusters, blacking-brushes, and many a little article, without which comfort on the road could hardly be secured.

Under the caravan are fastened by chain and padlock a light long ladder, a framework used in holding out our after-awning or tent, a spade, and the buckets. But there is also space enough here in which to hang a hammock.

Under the caravan shafts are carried, which may, however, never be much required.

In order to give some notion of the internal economy of the Wanderer I append a linear plan of her floor.

I may mention first that there is quite as much room inside for even a tall man to stand as there is in a Pullman car.

Entering from behind you may pass through A, the pantry or kitchen, into B, the saloon. Folding doors with nice curtains divide the caravan at pleasure into two compartments. C is the sofa, upholstered in strong blue railway repp. It is a sofa only by day. At night it forms the owner's bed. There are lockers under, which contain the bedclothes, etc, when not in use, as well as my wardrobe. D is the table, over which is a dainty little bookcase, with at each side a beautiful lamp on brackets. E is the cupboard, or rather the cheffonière, both elegant and ornamental, with large looking-glass over and behind it. It will be noticed that it juts out and on to the coupé, and thus not only takes up no room in the saloon, but gives me an additional recess on top for glove-boxes, hanging baskets for handkerchiefs, and nicknacks. The chiffoniere and the doors are polished mahogany and glass, the bulkheads maple with darker mouldings, the roof like that of a first-class railway carriage, the skylight being broad and roomy, with stained glass and ample means of ventilation.

The other articles of furniture not already mentioned are simple in the extreme, simple but sufficient, and consist of a piano-stool and tiny camp-chair, music-rack, footstool, dressing-case, a few artful cushions, pretty mirrors on the walls, with gilt brackets for coloured candles, a corner bracket with a clock, a guitar, a small harmonium, a violin, a navy sword, and a good revolver. There are gilded cornices over each window, with neat summer curtains, and also over the chiffoniere recess.

The floor is covered with linoleum, and a Persian rug does duty for a carpet.

The after-cabin contains a rack for dishes, with a cupboard above, a beautiful little carbon-silicated filter,—the best of filters made—a marble washstand, a triangular water-can that hangs above, complete with lid and tap, and which may be taken down to be filled at a well, a rack for hats and gloves, etc, neat pockets for tea and other towels, a box—my valet's, which is also a seat—and a little flap table, at which he can take his meals and read or write. Also the Rippingille cooking-range. This after-cabin is well-ventilated; the folding doors are shot at night, and the valet makes his bed athwartships, as I have already said. The bed is simply two long soft doormats, with above these a cork mattress. The latter, with the bedding, are rolled up into an American cloth cover, the former go into a Willesden canvas bag, and are placed under the caravan by day.

No top-coat or anything unsightly hangs anywhere; economy of space has been studied, and this goes hand-in-hand with comfort of fittings to make the gipsy's life on the road as pleasant as ever a gipsy's life can be. A glance at the illustrations of our saloon and pantry will give a still better idea of the inside of the Wanderer than my somewhat meagre description can afford. These are from photographs taken by Mr Eales, of Twyford. (The frontispiece to this book is also by Mr Eales.)

The Rippingille cooking-range is a great comfort. On cool days it can be used in the pantry, on hot days—or, at pleasure, on any day—it can be placed under our after-tent, and the chef's work got through expeditiously with cleanliness and nicety. Our caravan menu will at no time be a very elaborate one. I have long been of opinion, as a medical man and hygienist, that plain living and health are almost synonymous terms, and that intemperance in eating is to blame for the origin of quite as many diseases as intemperance in drinking.

On Getting Horsed.

A correct knowledge of horseflesh is not one of those things that come intuitively to anybody, though I have sometimes been given to think it did.

It is a kind of science, however, that almost every one, gentle or simple, pretends to be at home in. Take the opinion of even a draper's assistant about some horse you happen to meet on the road, and lo! he begins to look knowing at once, and will strain a nerve, or even two, in order to give you the impression that he is up to a thing or two.

But let a young man of this kind only see the inside of a stable a few times, then, although he can hardly tell the heel from the knee in the genus equus, how glibly does he not begin to talk, till he almost takes your breath away, about capped hocks, side-bones, splints, shoulders, knees, fetlocks, and feet, and as he walks around a horse, feeling him here or smoothing him there, he verily seems to the manner born.

Ladies are seldom very far behind men in their knowledge of hippology. What young girl fresh from school can be found who cannot drive? "Oh, give me the reins, I'm sure I can do it." These are her words as often as not. You do not like to refuse, badly as a broken-kneed horse would look. You sit by her side ready for any emergency. She is self-possessed and cool enough. She may not know her own side of the road, but what does that matter? If a man be driving the trap that is meeting her, is it not his duty to give place to her? To be sure it is. And as for the reins, she simply holds them; she evidently regards them as a kind of leathern telephone, to convey the wishes of the driver to the animal in the shafts.

But a man or woman either may be very clever at many things, and still know nothing about horses. It is their want of candour that should be condemned. Did not two of the greatest philosophers the world ever saw attempt to put their own nag in the shafts once? Ah! but the collar puzzled them. They struggled to get it on for half an hour, their perseverance being rewarded at last by the appearance on the scene of the ostler himself. I should have liked to have seen that man's face as he quietly observed, suiting action to his words,—

"It is usual, gentlemen, to turn the collar upside down when slippin' it hover the 'orse's 'ead."

But what must the horse himself have thought of those philosophers?

Now I do not mind confessing that riding is not one of my strong points. When on horseback there ever prevails in my mind an uncertainty as regards my immediate future. And I have been told that I do not sit elegantly, that I do not appear to be part and parcel of the horse I bestride. My want of confidence may in some measure be attributed to the fact that, when a boy of tender age, I saw a gentleman thrown from his horse and killed on the spot. It was a terrible sight, and at the time it struck me that this must be a very common method of landing from one's steed. It seems to me the umbra of that sad event has never quite left my soul.

It is due to myself, however, to add that there are many worse whips than I in single harness. Driving in double harness is harder work, and too engrossing, while "tandem" is just one step beyond my present capabilities. The only time ever I attempted this sort of thing I miserably failed. My animals went well enough for a time, till all at once it occurred to my leader to turn right round and have a look at me. My team was thus "heads and tails," and as nothing I could think of was equal to the occasion, I gave it up.

Notwithstanding all this, as far as stable duties are concerned, I can reef, steer, and box the compass, so to speak. I know all a horse needs when well, and might probably treat a sick horse as correctly as some country vets. No, I cannot shoe a horse, but I know when it is well done.

It is probably the want of technicality about my language when talking to real professed knights of the stable, which causes them to imagine "I don't know nuffin about an 'orse." This is precisely what one rough old farmer, with whom I was urging a deal, told me.

"Been at sea all your life, hain't you?" he added.

"Figuratively speaking," I replied, "I may have been at sea all my life, but not in reality. Is not," I continued, parodying Shylock's speech—"Is not a horse an animal? Hath not a horse feet, organs, dimensions, senses, affections, passions? Fed with good oats, oftentimes hurt by the whip? Subject to the same diseases, healed by the same means, warmed and cooled by the same winter and summer as a Christian is?"

The man scratched his head, looked puzzled, and we did not deal.

But, dear reader, were I to tell one-tenth part of the woes I endured before I got horsed and while still tossed on the ocean of uncertainty and buffeted by the adverse winds of friendly advice, your kindly heart would bleed for me.

I believe my great mistake lay in listening to every body. One-half of the inhabitants of our village had horses to sell, the other half knew where to find them.

"You'll want two, you know," one would say.

I believed that I would need two.

"One large cart-horse will be ample," said another.

I believed him implicitly.

"I'd have a pole and two nags," said one.

"I'd have two nags and two pair of shafts," said another.

"I'd have two nags," said another; "one in the shafts and the other to trace."

And so on ad nauseam till my brains were all in a whirl, and at night I dreamt I was a teetotum, and people were playing with me. Perhaps they were.

A friend to whom I appealed one day in my anguish cut the Gordian knot.

"You've got a nut on you?" he remarked (he meant my head). "Well," he said, "make use of that."

I took his advice.

FIRST EXPERIENCES OF GIPSY LIFE

"Now rings the woodland loud and long,
The distance takes a lovelier hue,
And drown'd in yonder living blue
The lark becomes a sightless song.
"Now dance the lights on lawn and lea,
The flocks are whiter down the vale,
And milkier every milky sail,
On winding stream or distant sea."
Tennyson.

It was to be our first outing—our trial trip, "by the measured mile," as navy sailors call it. Not so much a trial, however, for the caravan itself, as for a certain horse that was to be attached thereto; and, considering the weight of our house upon wheels, I thought it at least doubtful if any one horse would be sufficient to do the work.

The horse in this instance was—a mare. A splendid powerful dark bay draught mare, with small head, strong, shapely, arching neck, good shoulders, and long enough in body not to look cloddy. Her tail, about two yards long, had been specially plaited and got up for the occasion.

Matilda, as she was named, had never done anything except ploughing before, unless it were an occasional visit to the railway station with a load of wheat or hay. But she appeared quiet, and took the situation in at a glance, including the caravan and its master. We put-to, and after as much manoeuvring as would have sufficed to bring a P. and O. steamer away from a Southampton pier, we cleared the gate and got fairly under way.

In the matter of provisions the Wanderer was amply furnished. We had edibles for the day, and enough for a week, my wife having been steward and caterer for the occasion.

My companion voyageurs were the two eldest members of my family—Inez (aetat 7), Lovat (aetat 10), their summer dresses and young beauty making them look quite gay. Besides these, I had Hurricane Bob, my champion Newfoundland, who looked as though he could not quite understand any part of the business.

Very slowly at first walked that mare, and very solemnly too—at a plough-pace, in fact,—and the farmer's man walked soberly on at her neck. A rousing touch or two of the light gig whip mended matters considerably, and there was far less of the "Dead March in Saul" about the progress after this. Matilda warmed to her work; she neighed merrily, and even got into a kind of swinging trot, which, properly speaking, was neither trot nor tramp, only it took us over the ground at four knots an hour, and in pity I made the farmer's man—who, by the way, had his Sunday clothes all on—get up and sit down.

The morning was very bright and sunny, the road hard and good, but dusty. This latter was certainly a derivative from our pleasure, but then gipsies do not have it all their own way in this world any more than other people. The wind was with us, and was somewhat uncertain, both in force and direction, veering a little every now and then, and soon coming round again. But a select assortment of juvenile whirlwinds had been let loose from their cave, and these did not add to our delight.

Matilda had plenty of pluck, only she must have thought it an exceedingly long furrow, and at the end of two miles suddenly made up her mind to go about of her own accord. This determination on Matilda's part resulted in a deviation from the straight line, which nearly landed our fore wheels in the ditch; it also resulted in admonitory flagellation for Matilda.

Before we had gone three miles the perspiration was streaming down the mare's legs and meandering over her hoofs, so we pulled up to let her breathe. The day was young, it was all before us, and it is or ought to be in the very nature of every gipsy—amateur or professional—to take no note of time, to possess all the apathy of a Dutchman, all the drowsy independence of a garden tortoise.

The children begged for a cake, and Inez wanted to know what made the horse laugh so.

She might well put this question, for Matilda neighed nearly all the way.

"Why, pa," said Inie, "the horse laughs at everything; he laughs at the trees, he laughs at the flowers, and at the ponds. He laughs at every horse he meets; he laughed at the cows cropping the furze, and at the geese on the common, and now he is laughing at that old horse with its forefeet tied together. What are the old horse's forefeet tied together for, pa?"

"To keep him from running away, darling."

"And what does this horse keep on laughing for?"

"Why, he is so proud, you know, of being harnessed to so beautiful a caravan, that he can't help laughing. He wants to draw the attention of every creature he sees to it. He will be sure to dream about it to-night, and if he wakes up any time before morning he will laugh again."

"Oh!" said Inie, and went on eating her currant-cake thoughtfully.

In about a quarter of an hour we had started again. Lovat, who had been aft having a view at the back door window, came running forward and said excitedly,—

"Oh! pa, there is a gentleman with a carriage and pair behind us, making signs and shouting and waving his whip."

I pulled to the side at once, and the party in the waggonette passed, the gentleman who handled the ribbons scowling and looking forked lightning at us. No wonder, the idea of being stopped on the road by itinerant gipsies! Well, in driving a large caravan, as you cannot look behind nor see behind, it is as well to keep pretty near your own side of the road. This was a lesson I determined to lay to heart. But if seeing behind me was impossible, hearing was quite as much so, unless it had been the firing of a six-pounder. This was owing to the rattling of things inside the van, for, it being but our trial trip, things had not settled shipshape.

It is but fair to the builders of the Wanderer to say that an easier-going craft or trap never left Bristol. The springs are as strong and easy as ever springs were made. There is no disagreeable motion, but there is—no, I mean there was on that first day—a disagreeable rattling noise.

Nothing inside was silent; nothing would hold its tongue. No wonder our mare Matilda laughed. The things inside the sideboard jingled and rang, edged towards each other, hobnobbed by touching sides, then edged off again. The crystal flower-boat on the top made an uneasy noise, the crimson-tinted glass lampshades made music of their own in tremolo, and the guitar fell out of its corner on top of my cremona and cracked a string. So much for the saloon; but in the pantry the concert was at its loudest and its worse—plates and dishes, cups and saucers, tumblers and glasses, all had a word to say, and a song to sing; while as for the tin contents of the Rippingille cooking-range—the kettle and frying-pan, and all the other odds and ends—they constituted a complete band of their own, and a very independent one it was. Arab tom-toms would hardly have been heard alongside that range.

With bits of paper and chips of wood I did what I could to stop the din, and bit my lip and declared war à outrance against so unbearable a row. The war is ended, and I am victor. Nothing rattles much now; nothing jangles; nothing sings or speaks or squeaks. My auxiliaries in restoring peace have been—wedge-lets of wood, pads of indiarubber, and nests of cottonwool and tow; and the best of it is that there is nothing unsightly about any of my arrangements after all.

But to resume our journey. As there came a lull in the wind, and consequently some surcease in the rolling storm of dust, we stopped for about an hour at the entrance to Maidenhead Thicket. The children had cakes, and they had books, and I had proofs to correct—nice easy work on a day's outing!

Meanwhile great banks of clouds (cumulus) came up from the north-east and obscured the sun and most of the sky, only leaving ever-changing rifts of blue here and there, and the wind went down.

Maidenhead Thicket is a long stretch of wild upland—a well-treed moor, one might call it, and yet a breezy, healthful tableland. The road goes straight through it, with only the greensward, level with the road at each side, then two noble rows of splendid trees, mostly elm and lime, with here and there a maple or oak. But abroad, on the thicket itself, grow clumps of trees of every description, and great masses of yellow blossoming furze and golden-tasselled broom.

To our left the thicket ended afar off in woods, with the round braeland called Bowsy Hill in the distance; to the right, also in woods, but finally in a great sweep of cultivated country, dotted over with many a smiling farm and private mansion.

Maidenhead Thicket in the old coaching days used to be rather dreaded by the four-in-hands that rolled through it. Before entering it men were wont to grasp their bludgeons and look well to their priming, while ladies shrank timorously into corners (as a rule they did). The place is celebrated now chiefly for being a meeting-place for "'Arry's 'Ounds."

How have I not pitied the poor panting stag! It would be far more merciful, and give more real "sport," to import and turn down in the thicket some wild Shetland sheep.

Some few weeks ago the stag of the day ran for safety into our wee village of Twyford; after it came the hounds in full cry, and next came pricking along a troop of gallant knights and ladies fair. Gallant, did I say? Well, the stag took refuge in a coal-cellar, from which he was finally dragged, and I am thankful to believe that, when they saw it bleeding and breathless, those "gallant" carpet-knights were slightly ashamed of themselves. However, there is no accounting for taste.

Sometimes even until this day Maidenhead Thicket is not safe. Not safe to cyclists, for example, on a warm moonlit summer's night, when tramps lie snoozing under the furze-bushes.

But on this, the day of our trial trip, I never saw the thicket look more lovely; the avenue was a cloudland of tenderest greens, and the music of birds was everywhere around us. You could not have pointed to bush or branch and said, "No bird sings there." It was the "sweet time o' the year."

Where the thicket ends the road begins to descend, and after devious and divers windings, you find yourself in the suburbs of Maidenhead, two long rows of charming villas, with gardens in front that could not look prettier. The pink and white may, the clumps of lilac, the leafy hedgerows, the verandahs bedraped with mauve wistaria, the blazes of wallflower growing as high as the privet, and the beds of tulips of every hue, and beds of blood-red daisies in the midst of green lawns—it was all a sight, I can assure you! It made Matilda laugh again, and the children crow and clap their tiny hands with glee.

We passed through the town itself, which is nice enough, and near the bridge drew to the side and stopped, I walking on and over the bridge to find a place to stand for a few hours, for Matilda was tired and steaming, and we all looked forward to dinner.

The river looks nowhere more lovely and picturesque than it does at Maidenhead in summer. Those who cross it by train know this, but you have to stand on the old bridge itself and look at it before you can realise all its beauty. The Thames here is so broad and peaceful, it seems loth to leave so sweet a place. Then the pretty house-boats and yachts, with awnings spread, and smart boats laden with pleasure-seekers, and the broad green lawns on the banks, with their tents and arbours and bright-coloured flower vases, give this reach of the Thames quite a character of its own. How trim these lawns are to be sure! almost too much so for my ideas of romance; and then the chairs need not be stuck all in a row, nor need the vases be so very gaudy.

I found a place to suit me at last, and the Wanderer was drawn up on an inn causeway. Matilda was led away to the stable, the after-steps were let down, and the children said, "Isn't it dinner-time, pa?"

Pa thought it was. The cloth was spread on this soft carpet, and round it we all squatted—Hurricane Bob in the immediate rear—and had our first real gipsy feed, washed down with ginger-ale procured from the adjoining inn.

I wondered if the Wanderer really was an object of curiosity to the groups who gathered and walked and talked around us?

Younger ladies, I know, were delighted, and not slow to say so.

But I do not think that any one took us for hawkers or cheap-Jack people.

"If I had that caravan, now, and a thousand a year," we heard one man observe, "I'd kick about everywhere, all over the country, and I wouldn't call the king my cousin."

Soon after we had returned from a walk and a look at the shops a couple of caravans with real gipsies crossed the bridge.

"Stop, Bill, stop!" cried one of the tawny women, who had a bundle of mats for a chest protector. "Stop the 'orses, can't yer? I wouldn't miss a sight o' this for a pension o' 'taters."

The horses were stopped. Sorry-looking nags they were, with coffin heads, bony rumps, and sadly swollen legs.

"Well I never!"

"Sure there was never sich a wan as that afore on the road!"

"Why, look at her, Sally! Look at her, Jim! Up and down, and roun' and roun', and back and fore. Why, Bill! I say, that wan's as complete as a marriage certificate or a summons for assault."

We people inside felt the compliment.

But we did not show.

"Hi, missus!" cried one; "are ye in, missus? Surely a wan like that wouldn't be athout a missus. Will ye buy a basket, missus? Show your cap and your bonny face, missus. Would ye no obleege us with just one blink at ye?"

They went away at last, and soon after we got Matilda in and followed.

With her head towards home, and hard, level road, Matilda trotted now, and laughed louder than ever.

But soon the road began to rise; we had to climb the long, steep Maidenhead hill.

And just then the storm of rain and hail broke right in our teeth. At the middle of the hill it was at its worst, but the mare strode boldly on, and finally we were on fairly level road and drew up under some lime-trees.

The distance from Twyford to Maidenhead is nine miles, so we took it as easy going: as we had done coming.

We had meant to have tea in the thicket, but I found at the last moment I had forgotten the water. There was nothing for it but to "bide a wee."

We stopped for half-an-hour in the thicket, nevertheless, to admire the scenery. Another storm was coming up, but as yet the sun shone brightly on the woods beyond the upland, and the effect was very beautiful. The tree masses were of every colour—green elms and limes, yellowed-leaved oaks, dark waving Scottish pines, and black and elfin-looking yews, with here and there a copper beech.

But the storm came on apace. The last ray of sunlight struck athwart a lime, making its branches look startlingly green against the dark purple of the thundercloud.

Then a darting, almost blinding flash, and by-and-bye the peal of thunder.

The storm came nearer and nearer, so that soon the thunder-claps followed the flashes almost instantly.

Not until the rain and hail came on did the blackbirds cease to flute or the swallows to skim high overhead. How does this accord with the poet Thomson's description of the behaviour of animals during a summer thunderstorm, or rather the boding silence that precedes it?—

"Prone to the lowest vale the aerial tribes
Descend. The tempest-loving raven scarce
Dares wing the dubious dusk. In rueful gaze
The cattle stand," etc.

Our birds and beasts in Berkshire are not nearly so frightened at thunder as those in Thomson's time must have been, but then there were no railway trains in Thomson's time!

The poet speaks of unusual darkness brooding in the sky before the thunder raises his tremendous voice. This is so; I have known it so dark, or dusk rather, that the birds flew to roost and bats came out. But it is not always that "a calm" or "boding silence reigns." Sometimes the wind sweeps here and there in uncertain gusts before the storm, the leaf-laden branches bending hither and thither before them.

We came to a part of the road at last where the gable end of a pretty porter's lodge peeped over the trees, and here pulled up. The thunder was very loud, and lightning incessant, only it did not rain then. Nothing deterred, Lovat, kettle in hand, lowered himself from the coupé and disappeared to beg for water. As there was no other house near at hand it was natural for the good woman of the lodge, seeing a little boy with a fisherman's red cap on, standing at her porch begging for water, to ask,—

"Wherever do you come from?" Lovat pointed upwards in the direction of the caravan, which was hidden from view by the trees, and said,—

"From up there."

"Do ye mean to tell me," she said, "that you dropped out of the clouds in a thunderstorm with a tin-kettle in your hand?"

But he got the water, the good lady had her joke, and we had tea.

The storm grew worse after this. Inez grew frightened, and asked me to play.

"Do play the fiddle, pa!" she beseeched. So, while the "Lightning gleamed across the rift," and the thunder crashed overhead, "pa" fiddled, even as Nero fiddled when Rome was burning.

TWYFORD AND THE REGIONS AROUND IT

"I heard a thousand blended notes
While in a grove I sat reclined
In that sweet moor, when pleasant thoughts
Bring sad thoughts to the mind.
"One moment now may give us more
Than fifty years of reason;
Our minds shall drink at every pore
The spirit of the season."
Wordsworth.

Not to say a word about Twyford—the village that has given me birth and bield for ten long years—would be more than unkind, it would be positively ungrateful.

I must hasten to explain, however, that the Twyford referred to is THE Twyford—Twyford, Berks. About a dozen other Twyfords find their names recorded in the Postal Guide, from each and all of which we hold ourselves proudly aloof. Has Twyford the Great then, it may reasonably enough be asked, anything in particular to boast of? Well, methinks to belong to so charming a county as that of Berks is in itself something to be proud of. Have we not—

"Our forests and our green retreats,
At once the monarch's and the muse's seats,
Our hills and dales, and woods and lawns and spires,
And glittering towns and silver streams?"

Yes, and go where you will anywhere round Twyford, every mile is sacred to the blood of warriors spilt in the brave days of old. Not far from here Pope the poet lived and sang. The author of "Sandford and Merton" was thrown from his horse and killed at our neighbouring village of Wargrave, the very name of which is suggestive of stirring times. Well, up yonder on the hillhead lived the good old Quaker Penn, the founder of Pennsylvania. Yet, strange to say, no Americans are ever known to visit the spot. There is at Ruscombe (Penn's parish) a pretty and rustic-looking church, and not far off is the cosy vicarage of redbrick, almost hidden in foliage. On a knoll behind it, and in the copse at one side, is quite a forest of waving pines and larches and oaks. Hidden in the centre of this forest is a rude kind of clearing; in reality it has been a quarry or gravel-pit, but it is now charmingly embanked with greensward, with here and there great patches of gorse and bramble.

This place all the livelong summer I made my everyday retreat, my woodland study. But it is not of myself I would speak. At one side of this clearing stands a great oak-tree. It rises from a flat grassy eminence, and affords an excellent shelter from showers or sun. At the foot of this tree sometimes, on moonlight midnights, a tall and aged figure, in a broad-brimmed hat, may be seen seated in meditation. It, or he, ever vanishes before any one is bold enough to approach. Can this be the ghost of Penn? Mind, I, myself, have never seen it or him, and the apparition may be all fancy, or moonshine and flickering shadow, but I give the story as I got it.

Twyford the Great is not a large place, its population is barely a thousand; there is a new town and an old. The new town is like all mushroom villages within a hundred miles of the city—a mere tasteless conglomeration of bricks and mortar, with only two pretty houses in it.

But old Twyford is quaint and pretty from end to end—from the lofty poplars that bound my orchard out Ruscombe way, to the drowsy and romantic old mill on the Loddon. This last is worth a visit; only, if you lean over the bridge and look at this old mill for any length of time, you are bound to fall asleep, and I am bound to tell you so.

Twyford in summer, as well as the neighbourhood all round, may be seen at their best. The inhabitants of Twyford are at their best any day. I have strong reasons for believing the village must have been founded by some philosophical old Dutchman, or Rip van Winkle himself. And the peace of Penn seems to rest for ever around it.

The amusements in my wee village are few, rural, and primitive. Amateur cricket in summer, amateur concerts in winter, sum up the enjoyments of "Twyford at home."

But the most delightful time of all in our Twyford is the season from March to June. Concerts are over, cricket has not commenced, and therefore dulness and apathy might now be reasonably supposed to prevail among us. Perhaps; but the lover of nature is now quite as happy as the birds and the early flowers and budding trees.

So many lightning-tipped pens have written about spring and its enjoyments, that I shall not here attempt to sing its praises. I may be excused for saying, however, that while the inhabitants of towns and cities like, as a rule, to have their spring all ready-made when they pay a visit to rural districts, the orchards all in full bloom, the may all out, and the nightingales turned down, we simple-minded "country bodies" delight in watching and witnessing the gradual transformation from leafless tree to glittering leaf; from bare brown fields, o'erswept by stormy winds, to daisy-covered leas, cowslip meads, and primrose banks.

To me—and, no doubt, to many—there is far more of beauty in a half-blown floweret of the field, say the mountain-daisy, Burns's "Wee modest crimson-tippèd flower," than there is in a garden favourite full outspread—take the staring midday tulip as a familiar example.

Down here in bird-haunted Berkshire spring begins in February even, whatever it may do in Yorkshire. Now noisy rooks begin to build; the mavis or thrush, perched high on some swaying tree, sings loud and sweet of joys in store; on sunny days I've known an invalid-looking hedgehog or dormouse wriggle out from his hibernal grave, look hungrily around, sun himself, shiver, and wriggle back again. But the sly snake and the sage old toad stick close to bank until the days are longer. Even thus early an occasional butterfly may be seen afloat, looking in vain for flowers. He cannot be happy; like the poet, he is born before his time.

But soon after big humble bees appear about gardens and woodland paths, flying drowsily and heavily. They are prospecting; they get into all kinds of holes, and I may say all kinds of scrapes, often tumbling helplessly on their backs, and getting very angry when you go to their assistance with a straw.

Did it ever strike the reader that those same great velvety bees are republicans in their way of thinking? It is true. One humble bee is just as good as another. And very polite they are to each other too, and never unsheath their stings to fight without good occasion. Just one example: Last summer, in my woodland study, I noticed one large bee enter a crimson foxglove bell. Presently round came another—not of the same clan, for he wore a white-striped tartan, the first being a Gordon, and wearing the yellow band. The newcomer was just about to enter the bell where bee Number 1 was. Bee Number 1 simply lifted his forearm and waved the intruder back. "I really beg pardon," said bee Number 2. "I didn't know there was any one inside." And away he flew.

In February, down with us, the hazel-trees are tasselled over with catkins. Every one notices those, but few observe the tiny flower that grows on the twig near those drooping catkins. Only a tuft of green with a crimson tip, but inexpressibly beautiful. At the same time you will find the wild willow-bushes all covered with little flossy white cocoons.

There will be also a blaze of furze blossom here and there in the copse, but hardly a bud yet upon the hedgerows, while the great forest trees are still soundly wrapped in their winter sleep.

But high up on yonder swaying bough the thrush keeps on singing. Spring and joy are coming soon.

"It is the cuckoo that tells us spring is coming," some one may say. The man who first promulgated that notion ought to have been tried by court-martial. The cuckoo never comes till leaves are out and flowers in bloom. Nor the noisy wryneck nor melodious nightingale. These are merely actors and musicians, and they never put in an appearance till the carpet has been spread on the stage, and the scenery is perfect.

A cherry orchard is lovely indeed when its trees are snowed over with the blossoms that cluster around the twigs like swarms of bees, their dazzling whiteness relieved by just the faintest tinge of green. An apple orchard is also beautiful in the sunshine of a spring morning when the bloom is expanded. I grant that, but to me it is far more to be admired when the flowers are just opening and the carmine tint is on them.

Probably the pink or white may looks best when in full unfolded bloom; but have you ever noticed either of these just before they open, when the flowerets look like little balls of red or white wax prettily set in their background of green leafage? The white variety at this stage presents an appearance not unlike that of lily-of-the-valley bloom, and is just as pretty.

The ordinary laurel too is quite a sight when its flowers are half unfolded. The Portuguese laurel blooms later on; the tree then looks pretty at a distance, but its perfume prevents one from courting a too close acquaintance with it.

But there is the common holly that gives us our Christmas decorations. Has my city reader noticed it in bloom in May? It is interesting if not beautiful. All round the ends of the twiglets, clustering beneath last year's leaves, is first seen an excrescence, not unlike that on the beak of a carrier pigeon. This opens at last into a white-green bunch of blossom, and often the crimson winter berries still cling to the same twiglet. This looks curious at least—May wedded to bleak December, Christmas to Midsummer.

The oak and the ash are among the last trees to hear the voice of spring and awaken from their winter's sleep. Grand, sturdy trees both, but how exceedingly modest in their florescence! So too is the plane or maple-tree.

The first young leaves of the latter are of different shades of brown and bronze, while those of the stunted oaks that grow in hedgerows are tinted with carmine, making these hedges gay in May and June even before the honeysuckle or wild roses come out.

The oak-trees when first coming into leaf are of a golden-green colour, and quite a feature of the woodlands. The tall swaying poplars are yellow in leaf at first, but soon change to darkest green.

But in this sweet time of the year every tree is a poem, and the birds that hide among their foliage do but set those poems to music.

It is interesting to note the different kinds of showers that fall from the trees. Here in Twyford I live in a miniature wilderness, partly garden, partly orchard, partly forest. Very early in the year the yew-tree yonder sheds its little round blossoms, as thick as hail; soon after come showers of leaf scales or chaff from the splendid lime-trees; and all kinds of showers from the chestnuts. Anon there is a perfect snowstorm of apple-blossom, which continues for more than a week; and early in June, when the wind blows from the east, we are treated to a continued fall of the large flat seeds of the elms. They flutter downwards gently enough, but they litter the ground, cover the lawns and flower-beds, and lie inches deep on the top of the verandah.

A drive from Twyford to Henley-on-Thames is very enjoyable on a summer's day; a journey thither in a great caravan like the Wanderer is still more so. The first two miles of the road might be termed uninteresting, because flat and monotonous, but it is uninteresting only to those who have no eye for the beauty of the wild flowers that line the banks, no ear for the melody of birds.

Wargrave, just two miles on the road, lies among its trees pretty close to the river's bank. I should not like to call it a health resort all the year round, owing to the killing fogs that bury it at times, but in the season it is a pleasant spot at which to spend a week. Wyatt's is the inn, a well-known river house indeed—old-fashioned, clean, and comfortable. There is a sign on a pole outside which is worth taking a look at. Mr Leslie and Mr Hodson (the well-known artists) were sojourning here once upon a time, taking their ease at their inn. Perhaps it was raining, and the time felt long. Anyhow, between them they painted that sign, and there it hangs—Saint George on one side engaged in deadly combat with a monster dragon; on the other side the dragon lying dead, and Saint George dismounted, and engaged refreshing himself with a tankard of foaming ale.

From Wargrave to Henley the scenery is sweetly pretty, and the river never leaves your side, though at times it hides behind and beneath the spreading trees.

As every one has heard or read about or been at Henley Regatta, so every one knows something of Henley itself. It is a charming little town, and the wooded hills about, with, even on their summits, the white mansions peeping through the trees, the river—broad and sweeping—the fine old bridge, and the church, combine to form not one picture only, but a picture in whichever direction you choose to look.

From the top of the church steeple the views on all sides are delightful.

I recommend this plan of seeing scenery to my American friends at present visiting England, and to every one else; never miss a chance of visiting the churches and getting up into the steeple. By this means I have oftentimes found refreshment both for mind and body.

If it were not that I wish to wander and roam through my native land, and actually feel from home, I could write a book on Berkshire alone. Even in the immediate neighbourhood of Twyford there are hundreds of beautiful spots, which those in search of health and quiet pleasure would do well to visit.

Marlow is a delightful village; all round Maidenhead, up and down the river, it is even more so. One might say of the country hereabouts, especially in summer and autumn,—

"A pleasing land of drowsy head it is,
Of dreams that wave before the half-shut eye
Of gay castles... And soft delights that witchingly
Instil a wanton sweetness thro' the breast."

A FIRST WEEK'S OUTING

"From the moist meadow to the withered hill,
Led by the breeze, the vivid verdure runs
And swells and deepens to the cherished eye;
The hawthorn whitens; and the juicy groves
Put forth their buds, unfolding by degrees,
Till the whole leafy forest stands displayed
In full luxuriance to the sighing gales,
Where the deer rustle through the twining brake,
And the birds sing concealed."
Thornton's "Seasons."

Early in May I left my village to enjoy a taste of gipsy life in earnest—a week on the road.

Matilda is a splendid mare, and a very handsome one. Strong and all though she be, there was in my mind a doubt as to whether she could drag the Wanderer on day after day at even the rate of ten miles in the twenty-four hours.

It had been raining the night before, and as the road from our yard leads somewhat up hill, it was no wonder that the immense caravan stuck fast before it got out of the gate. This was a bad beginning to a gipsy cruise, and, as a small concourse of neighbours had assembled to witness the start, was somewhat annoying. But a coal-carter's horse came to the rescue, and the start was finally effected.

Matilda took us through Twyford at a round trot, and would fain have broken into a gallop, but was restrained. But the long hill that leads up from the Loddon bridge took the extra spirit out of her, and she soon settled down to steady work.

There is a pretty peep of Reading to be caught from the top of the railway bridge. No traveller should miss seeing it.

Rested at Reading, our smart appearance exciting plenty of curiosity. It was inside that the crowd wanted to peep—it is inside all crowds want to peep, and they are never shy at doing so.

The town of Reading is too well-known to need description; its abbey ruins are, however, the best part of it, to my way of thinking.

The day was as fine as day could be, the sky overcast with grey clouds that moderated the sun's heat.

Our chosen route lay past Calcot Park, with its splendid trees, its fine old solid-looking, redbrick mansion, and park of deer. This field of deer, I remember, broke loose one winter. It scattered in all directions; some of the poor creatures made for the town, and several were spiked on railings. The people had "sport," as they called it, for a week.

It was almost gloomy under the trees that here overhang the road. Matilda was taken out to graze, the after-tent put up, and dinner cooked beneath the caravan. Cooked! ay, and eaten too with a relish one seldom finds with an indoor meal!

On now through Calcot village, a small and straggling little place, but the cottages are neat and pretty, and the gardens were all ablaze with spring-flowers, and some of the gables and verandahs covered with flowering clematis.

The country soon got more open, the fields of every shade of green—a gladsome, smiling country, thoroughly English.

This day was thoroughly enjoyable, and the mare Matilda did her work well.

Unhorsed and encamped for the night in the comfortable yard of the Crown Inn.

When one sleeps in his caravan in an inn yard he does not need to be called in the morning; far sooner than is desirable in most instances, cocks begin to noisily assert their independence, dogs bark or rattle their chains, cows moan in their stalls, and horses clatter uneasily by way of expressing their readiness for breakfast. By-and-bye ostlers come upon the scene, then one may as well get up as lie a-bed.

Though all hands turned out at seven o'clock am, it was fully eleven before we got under way, for more than one individual was curious to inspect us, and learn all the outs and ins of this newest way of seeing the country. The forenoon was sunny and bright, and the roads good, with a coldish headwind blowing.

Both road and country are level after leaving Theale, with plenty of wood and well-treed braelands on each side. This for several miles.

Jack's Booth, or the Three Kings, is a long, low house-of-call that stands by the wayside at cross roads: an unpleasant sort of a place to look at. By the way, who was Jack, I wonder, and what three kings are referred to? The name is suggestive of card-playing. But it may be historical.

The fields are very green and fresh, and the larks sing very joyfully, looking no bigger than midges against the little fleecy cloudlets.

I wonder if it be more difficult for a bird to sing on the wing than on a perch. The motion, I think, gives a delightful tremolo to the voice.

My cook, steward, valet, and general factotum is a lad from my own village, cleanly, active, and very willing, though not gifted with too good a memory, and apt to put things in the wrong place—my boots in the oven, for instance!

He sleeps on a cork mattress, in the after-compartment of the Wanderer, and does not snore.

A valet who snored would be an unbearable calamity in a caravan.

Hurricane Bob, my splendid Newfoundland, sleeps in the saloon on a morsel of red blanket. He does snore sometimes, but if told of it immediately places his chin over his fore-paw, and in this position sleeps soundly without any nasal noise.

On our way to Woolhampton—our dining stage—we had many a peep at English rural life that no one ever sees from the windows of a railway carriage. Groups of labourers, male and female, cease work among the mangolds, and, leaning on their hoes, gaze wonderingly at the Wanderer. Even those lazy workaday horses seem to take stock of us, switching their long tails as they do so, in quite a businesslike way. Yonder are great stacks of old hay, and yonder a terribly-red brick farm building, peeping up through a cloudland of wood.

We took Matilda out by the roadside at Woolhampton. This village is very picturesque; it lies in a hollow, and is surrounded by miniature mountains and greenwood. The foliage here is even more beautiful than that around Twyford.

We put up the after-tent, lit the stove, and prepared at once to cook dinner—an Irish stew, made of a rabbit, rent in pieces, and some bacon, with sliced potatoes—a kind of cock-a-leekie. We flavoured it with vinegar, sauce, salt, and pepper. It was an Irish stew—perhaps it was a good deal Irish, but it did not eat so very badly, nor did we dwell long over it.

The fresh air and exercise give one a marvellous appetite, and we were hungry all day long.

But every one we met seemed to be hungry too. A hunk of bread and bacon or bread and cheese appears to be the standing dish. Tramps sitting by the wayside, navvies and roadmen, hawkers with barrows—all were carving and eating their hunks.

A glorious afternoon.

With cushions and rugs, our broad coupé makes a most comfortable lounge, which I take advantage of. Here one can read, can muse, can dream, in a delightfully lethargic frame of mind. Who would be a dweller in dusty cities, I wonder, who can enjoy life like this?

Foley—my valet—went on ahead on the Ranelagh Club (our caravan tricycle) to spy out the land at Thatcham and look for quarters for the night. There were certain objections to the inn he chose, however; so, having settled the Wanderer on the broad village green, I went to another inn.

A blackish-skinned, burly, broad-shouldered fellow answered my summons. Gruff he was in the extreme.

"I want stabling for the night for one horse, and also a bed for my driver." This from me.

"Humph! I'll go and see," was the reply.

"Very well; I'll wait."

The fellow returned soon.

"Where be goin' to sleep yourse'f?"

This he asked in a tone of lazy insolence.

I told him mildly I had my travelling saloon caravan. I thought that by calling the Wanderer a saloon I would impress him with the fact that I was a gentleman gipsy.

Here is the answer in full.

"Humph! Then your driver can sleep there too. We won't 'ave no wan (van) 'osses 'ere; and wot's more, we won't 'ave no wan folks!"

My Highland blood got up; for a moment I measured that man with my eye, but finally I burst into a merry laugh, as I remembered that, after all, Matilda was only a "wan" horse, and we were only "wan" folks.

In half an hour more both Matilda and my driver were comfortably housed, and I was having tea in the caravan.

Thatcham is one of the quietest and quaintest old towns in Berkshire. Some of the houses are really studies in primeval architecture. I could not help fancying myself back in the Middle Ages. Even that gruff landlord looked as if he had stepped out of an old picture, and were indeed one of the beef-eating, bacon-chewing retainers of some ancient baronial hall.

It was somewhat noisy this afternoon on the village green. The young folks naturally took us for a show, and wondered what we did, and when we were going to do it.

Meanwhile they amused themselves as best they could. About fifty girls played at ball and "give-and-take" on one side of the green, and about fifty boys played on the other.

The game the boys played was original, and remarkable for its simplicity. Thus, two lads challenged each other to play, one to be deer, the other to be hound. Then round and round and up and down the green they sped, till finally the breathless hound caught the breathless deer. Then "a ring" of the other lads was formed, and deer and hound had first to wrestle and then to fight. And vae victis! the conquered lad had no sooner declared himself beaten than he was seized and thrown on his back, a rope was fastened to his legs, and he was drawn twice round the ground by the juvenile shouting mob, and then the fun began afresh. A game like this is not good for boys' jackets, and tailors must thrive in Thatcham.

Next day was showery, and so was the day after, but we continued our rambles all the same, and enjoyed it very much indeed.

But now on moist roads, and especially on hills, it became painfully evident that Matilda—who, by the way, was only on trial—was not fit for the work of dragging the Wanderer along in all countries and in all weathers. She was willing, but it grieved me to see her sweat and pant.

Our return journey was made along the same route. Sometimes, in making tea or coffee, we used a spirit-of-wine stove. It boiled our water soon, and there was less heat. Intending caravanists would do well to remember this. Tea, again, we found more quickly made than coffee, and cocoatina than either.

As we rolled back again towards Woolhampton the weather was very fine and sunny. It was a treat to see the cloud shadows chasing each other over the fields of wind-tossed wheat, or the meadows golden with buttercups, and starred with the ox-eyed daisies.

The oldest of old houses can be seen and admired in outlying villages of Berkshire, and some of the bold Norman-looking men who inhabit these take the mind back to Merrie England in the Middle Ages. Some of these men look as though they could not only eat the rustiest of bacon, but actually swallow the rind.

On our way back to Theale we drew up under some pine-trees to dine. The wind, which had been blowing high, increased to half a gale. This gave me the new experience—that the van rocked. Very much so too, but it was not unpleasant. After dinner I fell asleep on the sofa, and dreamt I was rounding the Cape of Good Hope in a strong breeze.

There is a road that leads away up to Beenham Hill from Woolhampton from which, I think, one of the loveliest views in Berks can be had. A long winding avenue leads to it—an avenue.

"O'erhung with wild woods thickening green," and "braes" clad in brackens, among which wild flowers were growing—the sweet-scented hyacinth, the white or pink crane's-bill, the little pimpernel, and the azure speedwell.

The hill is wooded—and such woods!—and all the wide country seen therefrom is wooded.

Surely spring tints rival even those of autumn itself!

This charming spot is the home par excellence of the merle and thrush, the saucy robin, the bold pert chaffie, and murmuring cushat.

Anchored at Crown Inn at Theale once more.

A pleasant walk through the meadows in the cool evening. Clover and vetches coming into bloom, or already red and white. A field of blossoming beans. Lark singing its vesper hymn. I was told when a boy it was a hymn, and I believe it still.

After a sunset visit to the steeple of Theale Church we turned in for the night. Bob has quite taken up his commission as caravan guard. By day he sleeps on the broad coupé, with his crimson blanket over his shoulders to keep away the cold May winds; and when we call a halt woe be to the tramp who ventures too near, or who looks at all suspicions!

On leaving the Crown Inn yard, Matilda made an ugly "jib," which almost resulted in a serious accident to the whole expedition. Matilda has a mind of her own. I do not like a horse that thinks, and I shall not have much more of Matilda. To be capsized in a dogcart by a jibbing horse would be bad enough, but with our great conveyance it would mean something akin to shipwreck.

The last experience I wish to record in this chapter is this; in caravan travelling there is naturally more fatigue than there would be in spending the same time in a railway carriage. When, therefore, you arrive in the evening at one village, you have this feeling—that you must be hundreds of miles from another.

(One soon gets used to caravan travelling, however, and finds it far less fatiguing than any other mode of progression.)

"Is it possible," I could not help asking myself, "that Thatcham is only ten or twelve miles from Theale, and that by train I could reach it in fifteen minutes? It feels to me as if it were far away in the wilds of Scotland."

People must have felt precisely thus in the days before railways were invented, and when horses were the only progressive power.

OUR LAST SPRING RAMBLE

"The softly warbled song
Comes from the pleasant woods, and coloured wings
Glance quick in the bright sun, that moves along
The forest openings.

"And the bright sunset fills
The silver woods with light, the green slope throws
Its shadow in the hollows of the hill,
And wide the upland glows."
Longfellow.

It is now well into the middle of June. Like the lapwing in autumn, I have been making short flights here, there, and everywhere within a day's march previous to the start on my "journey due north."

Whatever it might be to others, with longer and wiser heads, to me the greatest difficulty has been in getting horses to suit. I have tried many. I have had jibbers, bolters, kickers; and one or two so slow, but so sore, that an eighty-one-ton gun fired alongside them would not increase their pace by a yard to the mile.

To get horsed may seem an easy matter to many. It might be easy for some, only it ought to be borne in mind that I am leaving home on a long journey—one, at all events, that will run to weeks and mayhap months; a journey not altogether unattended with danger—and that; my horses are my motor power. If they fail me I have nothing and no one to fall back upon. Hence my anxiety is hardly to be wondered at.

But here let me say that caravanning for health and pleasure had better not be undertaken with a single carriage, however well horsed. There ought to be two caravans at least. Then, in the event of coming to an ugly hill, there is an easy way of overcoming it—by bending all your horse-power on to one carriage at a time, and so trotting them over the difficulty.

To go all alone as I am about to do is really to go at considerable risk; and at this moment I cannot tell you whether I am suitably horsed or not.

But in the stable yonder stand quietly in their stalls Pea-blossom and Corn-flower, of whom more anon. Pea-blossom is a strong and good-looking dark bay mare of some fifteen hands and over; Corn-flower is a pretty light bay horse. They match well; they pull together; and in their buff leather harness they really look a handsome pair.

They are good in the feet, too, and good "doers," to use stable phraseology. Corn-flower is the best "doer," however. The rascal eats all day, and would deprive himself of sleep to eat. Nothing comes wrong to Corn-flower. Even when harnessed he will have a pull at anything within reach of his neck. If a clovery lea be beneath his feet, so much the better; if not, a "rive" at a blackthorn hedge, a bush of laurels, a bracken bank, or even a thistle, will please him. I'm not sure, indeed, that he would not eat an old shoe if nothing else came handy. But Pea-blossom is more dainty. It is for her we fear on the march. She was bought from a man who not only is a dealer, but is not ashamed to sign himself dealer; whereas Corn-flower was bought right off farm work.

Well, time will tell.

Yes, spring is waning, though hardly yet has summer really come, so backward and cold has the season been.

We have had our last day's pleasant outing en famille. Mamma went, and even baby Ida, who is old enough to ask questions and make queer remarks. A clear sky and the brightest of sunshine, though not distressingly hot. We crossed country for Wokingham. The trees very beautiful, though the leaves are already turning more crisp; in spring time, city reader mine, as the wind goes whispering through the trees, it seems as if every leaf were of softest silk; in summer the sound is a soughing or rustling one; but in winter the breeze moans and shrieks among the bare branches, and "blows with boisterous sweep."

We unlimbered in the market square at Wokingham. The English are a novelty-loving people. This was well shown to-day, for streets and pavements were speedily lined to look at us, and even windows raised, while Modesty herself must needs peep from behind the curtains. In the afternoon a regiment of artillery came into the town, and popular attention was henceforth drawn to them, though our visitors were not few.

On our way home we passed the lodges of Haines Hill, the residence of the well-known T. Garth, Esq, a country squire of the true English type—a man who, although over sixty, almost lives in the saddle, and in the season follows his own hounds five days a week. The narrowness of the avenues and plenitude of the drooping limes forbade a visit to the manor, of which, however, as we went slowly along the road we caught many a glimpse red-glimmering through the green.

Great banks of pink and crimson rhododendrons gave relief to the eye. Looking to the right the country was visible for miles, richly-treed as the whole of Berkshire is, and with many a farmhouse peeping up through clouds of foliage.

The cottages by the roadside at this time of the year are always worth looking at. They vie with each other in the tidiness of their gardens, their porches, and verandahs.

They cultivate roses, all kinds and colours; standards and half-standards and climbers, crimson, white, yellow, pink, and purple. Stocks and wallflowers are also very favourite flowers. Even those cottages that cannot boast of a morsel of garden have the insides of every window all ablaze with flowering geraniums.

The memorable features of this pleasant day's gipsying were flowers, foliage, and the exceeding brightness of the sunshine.

At Malta and in Africa I have seen stronger lights and deeper shadows, but never in England before. The sky was cerulean, Italian, call it what you like, but it was very blue. The sunshine gave beauty and gladness to everything and every creature around us. Birds, butterflies, and shimmering four-winged metallic-tinted dragon-flies flew, floated, and revelled in it. It lay in patches on the trees, it lent a lighter crimson to the fields of clover, a brighter yellow to the golden buttercups; it changed the ox-eye daisies to glittering stars, and gave beauty-tints innumerable to seedling grasses and bronzy flowering docks.

Under the trees it was almost dark by contrast. So marked, indeed, was this contrast that when a beautiful young girl, in a dress of white and pink, came suddenly out of the shadow and stood in the sunshine, it appeared to us as if she had sprung from the earth itself, for till now she had been invisible.

Before we reached home a blue evening haze had fallen on all the wooded landscape, making distant trees mere shapes, but hardly marring the beauty of the wild flowers that grew on each side of our path and carpeted the woodlands and copses.

This was our last spring outing, and a happy one too. From this date I am to be a solitary gipsy.

Solitary, and yet not altogether so. My coachman is, I believe, a quiet and faithful fellow, and eke my valet too. Then have I not the companionship of Hurricane Bob, one of the grandest of a grand race of jetty-black Newfoundlands, whose coats have never been marred by a single curly hair? Nay, more, have I not also my West Australian cockatoo to talk to me, to sing with me, and dance when I play? Come, I am not so badly off. Hurrah! then, for the road and a gipsy's life in earnest.

A START FOR THE FAR NORTH

"O spires of Oxford! domes and towers,
Gardens and groves;
I slight my own beloved Cam to range
Where silver Isis leads my wandering feet."
Wordsworth.

"A curious Gothic building, many gabled,
By flowering creepers hidden and entangled."

There is to my way of thinking a delicious uncertainty in starting on a long caravan tour, without being aware in the least what you are going to do or see, or even what route you are going to take.

As regards a route, though, I did throw up a pebble with a black tick on it before the horses pulled out at the gate, and twice running the spot pointed to the north-west.

So we steered for Reading, and on without stopping as far as the Roebuck Hotel at Tilehurst. Nine years ago this hotel was a very small one indeed, but all gables, thickest thatch, and climbing roses and honeysuckle. The thatch has given place to red tiles, and an addendum of modern dimensions has been built. The old most ever give place to the new. But what lovely peeps there are from this hotel, from the balcony and from the bedrooms. It is a river house now in every sense of the word, though not old as a hotel of the kind, and all day long, and far into the night, the bar and passages and the coffee-rooms are crowded in summer with men in snowy flannels, and with some in sailor garb and with artificial sailor swagger.

The road leads onwards through a cool elm avenue towards Pangbourne. The copses here are in earlier spring carpeted with wild hyacinths. On the hilltop the scenery opens out again, the tree-clad valley of the Thames, fields of green grain, with poppies here and there, or wild mustard, and fields crimson with blossoming trefoil. Surely milk and butter must be good when cows are fed on flowers.

"Lay till the day" in the great inn yard of the George. Rather too close to the railway embankment, for the trains went roaring past all night long. This did not make sleeping impossible, for a gipsy, even an amateur one, can sleep anywhere; but the earth shook and the lamps rattled every time a train rolled by. Some villas are built right beneath the embankment, which is far higher than their roofs. Facilis descensus Averni. What a strange and terrible accident it would be were one of those trains to leave the line and run through a roof! An old lady of the nervous persuasion, who lives here, told me that she oftentimes trembled in her bed when she thought of this dread possibility.

Pangbourne is a well-known haunt for those who love boating and fishing. It is quiet, and so well shaded as to be cool on the warmest summer day. But Pangbourne is not a hackneyed place, and never, I believe, will be so.

Left about nine o'clock on June 19th. It had been raining just enough to lay the dust and give a brighter colouring to the foliage.

Ivy leaves, when young, are, as my country readers know, of a very bright green. There are on a well-kept lawn by the riverside, and just outside Pangbourne, a coach-house and a boathouse. Both are well-built and prettily shaped. They are thatched, and the walls are completely covered in close-cropped ivy, giving them the look of houses built of green leaves.

Two miles from Pangbourne a nice view of the Thames valley is obtained, round wooded hills on the right bank, with farms here and there, and fields now covered with waving wheat, some of them flooded over with the rich red of the blossoming sainfoin.

We reach the village of Lower Basildon. Spring seems to linger long in this sweet vale. Here is a lofty spruce, each twiglet pointed with a light green bud; here a crimson flowered chestnut; yonder a row of pink mays and several laburnums, whose drooping blooms show no symptoms yet of fading or falling.

At the grotto we pass through a splendid avenue of beeches.

Just at the top of a steep hilltop we meet a girl and a boy on the same tricycle. How happy they look! We warn them of the steepness of the descent. They smilingly thank us, put on their brake, and go floating away and finally disappear among the beeches.

Every one has rushed through Goring and Streatley by train, and some may have thought the villages pretty. So they are indeed, but you must go by road to find this out. Look at them from Grotto Hill, for instance, just after you emerge from the lane.

Here is a pretty bit of road. On the left is a high bank covered with young beech-trees, a hedge on the right, then a green field sweeping down the hill to the river's edge. The Thames is here bordered with willow-trees and flowering elders. That hedgerow is low and very wild. It may be blackthorn at heart, but it is quite encanopied by a wealth of trailing weeds and flowers, and by roses and honeysuckle all in bloom, while the roadsides are laid out by nature's hand in beds of yellow trefoil and blue speedwell. The pink marsh-mallow, too, is growing in every grassy nook by the hedge-foot.

I wonder how far on my journey north will hedgerows accompany me. I shall feel sorry when they give place to unsightly wooden fences or walls of rugged stone.

High up yonder is a green grassy tableland or moor, through which goes the ancient ridge-way or cattle-road to Wales. Unused now, of course, but the scene of many a strange story in bygone times.

A little very old man gets out from under a tree and stands as straight as he can to gaze at us. Surely the oldest inhabitant of these regions. His dress is peculiar—a cow-gown worn beneath and protruding like a kilt from under a long blue coat, and a tall black hat. He bobs his wrinkled face, grins, and talks to himself as we pass. A queer old man indeed.

We stopped on Moulsford Hill to water horses. A fine open country, and breezy to-day. Rather too breezy, in fact, for hardly had we started again before the wind got in under the great awning which covers the roof from stem to stern. It ripped the cloth from the hooks that held it, but I caught it in time, else it would have blown over the horses' heads, and might have given rise to a very serious accident.

It was market-day at Wallingford, and busy and bustling it was in the little town. The place is close to the Thames. It boasts of a bridge with nineteen arches, a very ancient history, and the remains of an old castle, which, it is said, was at one time considered impregnable. It was besieged by King Stephen, and defied him.

It held out against Cromwell too, I am told, and was one of the last places to surrender. The remains of its ancient walls are visible enough in the shape of mounds, turf-clad, and green as a grave.

Did Wallingford not hold out against the Danes also? I believe it did. I have already had so much of Oliver Cromwell and the Danes dinned into my ear, that I am heartily tired of both. If I can credit current traditions, the Danes must have been very badly handled indeed, and must have bitterly repented ever setting a foot on English shores.

The country after leaving Wallingford is exceedingly picturesque; one is inclined to deem every peep of scenery prettier than that which preceded it, and to pity from the heart people who travel by train.

Shillingford, in our route, is a little village which, as far as I could see, consists mostly of public-houses. Near here are the Whittingham Clumps, which do not look of much account, merely two round green hills with a tuft of trees on the top of each. Yet they can be seen for many miles—almost, indeed, from every part of Berkshire.

Dorchester, some miles farther on, is quiet and pretty, and evidently an old village—its cottages look old, its inns look old, and eke the church itself. Just the spot for an artist to while away a month in summer, while an author might do worse than lay the scene of a tale in a place like this.

We stopped in front of the mansion house of Burcot, and made coffee under the chestnuts. The house lies off the road, but there is no fence around the park; we could rest in the shade therefore. Here are some splendid pine-trees (Scotch) and elms. What a noble tree an elm is, if its branches are spared by the billhook of pruner or axe of woodman! The most of our English trees are spoiled in appearance by injudicious interference.

We reached Abingdon in the evening, having done twenty miles and spent a delightful day. But the horses were tired of their long drag. There is to be a great fair here to-morrow. It is only natural, therefore, that the people should take us for real gipsies.

We have stabled our steeds, and the Wanderer lies snug in the back yard of a wealthy corn merchant, and within the precincts of the old gaol. The place was built at an expenditure of 36,000 pounds, but Abingdon being no longer the county town, it has been sold and turned into a granary. The town is all en gala, and the young folks, at all events, are enjoying the sights and sounds.

Visited to-night by a group of gipsies of the true type. They came, they said, to admire our "turnout." They had never seen so grand a caravan on the road, and so on and so forth.

Abingdon is a cosy little town, a neighbourly, kindly sort of a place that any one fond of country life must enjoy living in. Abingdon should be visited by tourists in summer far more than it is.

We started early, and had some difficulty in getting through the town, so narrow are the streets and so crowded were they to-day. On the road we met droves of horses and traps or conveyances of every sort and size taking country folks to the fair. The weather was wondrous cold for June, but endurable nevertheless, albeit clouds hid the sun and showers were not unfrequent.

We reached a hilltop about noon, and all at once a landscape burst upon our view which is hardly surpassed for quiet beauty in all England.

People who journey by rail miss this enchanting scene. Just beneath us, and in the centre of the plain, lay Oxford.

We dined by the roadside, gipsy-fashion, for there was no meadow we could draw our caravan into. Started about two pm, and rattled through Oxford, only stopping here and there to do our shopping. There is no better verb than "rattled" to convey the notion of our progress. Oxford is vilely paved for either carriage or cycle.

With the bumping and shaking we received, the saloon of the Wanderer soon looked like that of a yacht in a rough sea-way.

Poor Polly, my cockatoo, the pet of the ship, is sadly put about when there is much motion. I gave her a morsel of meat to-day when passing through Oxford. To stand on one leg and eat it as usual from her other claw was out of the question, but Polly was equal to the occasion. She put the choice morsel under her feet on the perch, and so quietly rent and devoured it.

We were all of us glad to get away from Oxford, where there is no rest for the soles of the feet of a caravanite. Hurricane Bob, though he dearly loves to travel, enjoys his morsel of meadow in the evening, his mode of enjoyment being to roll on the greensward, with all four legs waved aloft.

When he gets on to a bit of clovery sward by the wayside it really is a treat to see him.

"I wouldn't miss this, master," he says to me, "for all the world, and I only wonder you don't come and tumble as I do."

June, 22nd (Monday).—A village of grey limestone houses, thatched and tiled, many with charmingly antique roofs, a village built on ground that is level, a village embowered in orchards and trees, and with so many lanes and roads through it that a stranger could not be expected to know when he was in it or when he was out of it I have said "a village built," but rather it seems like a village that has grown, house by house, each in its own garden or orchard, and each one different in appearance from the others. Altogether English, however, is Kidlington, and the work-a-day people are thoroughly English too, very rustic, good-natured, and simple. I do not believe they ever brawl and fight here at pothouses on Saturday nights, or that the conversation ever advances much beyond "turmuts" and cattle.

I do not suppose that Kidlington ever looked much better than it does on this bright summer's morning. The breeze that blew all night, making the Wanderer rock like a ship at sea, has fallen; there is just sufficient left to sough through the ash-trees and whisper among the elms; cloudlets float lazily in the sky's blue and temper the sunshine. I am writing on the coupé, in the meadow where we have lain since Saturday afternoon. There is silence all round, except that cocks are crowing and a turkey gobbling; there is a rustic perched on the stile-top yonder, wondering at my cockatoo, and at Bob, who wears a scarlet blanket to keep the early morning chill away; another rustic is driving a herd of lazy cows along the lane. That is the scene, and that is about all. But what a quiet and pleasant Sabbath we spent yesterday in this meadow and at the village church!

It is now eight o'clock, and time to get the horses in. I wonder what the world is doing—the outside world, I mean. I have not seen a newspaper for three days, nor had a letter since leaving home. Now hey! for Deddington.

Somewhat pretty is the country for a mile or two out of Kidlington, rising ground all the way to Sturdy's Castle, four miles and a half. This is a solitary inn, of grey limestone, Sturdy by name and sturdy by nature, and if it could tell its story it would doubtless be a strange one. But what a wide, wild country it overlooks! It is wide and wild now. What, most it have been one hundred years ago? Found a carpet-hawker encamped with her caravan behind the castle. She travels all alone with her two children throughout the length and breadth of England. Seems very intelligent, and gives a terrible account of the difficulties to be encountered on ahead of us in getting in at night. We'll see.

We are at present in the Blenheim country, and the Dashwood estate lies east—away yonder. I make no détour to visit the palace. Every one knows it by heart.

A kind-hearted carter man has told me a deal about the scenes around us, which I daresay the jolting over these rutty roads will soon drive out of my head.

On we go again.

Hopcroft's Holt is an old-fashioned quiet inn close by intersecting roads that to the right branch off to Bicester. Stayed here to cook and eat.

Densely wooded and well hedged country all round, quiet and retired. It must be healthy here in summer.

Blacksmith has neatly mended my tricycle, which had broken down, so that I am able to make little excursions down by-roads. The village of Upper Heyford, about two miles from here, is as quaint and ancient-looking as if some town in the Orkneys.

June 23rd.—It needed all the strength of Corn-flower and Pea-blossom to get us into Deddington, for the hills are long and steep. We are furnished with a roller that drags behind the near after wheel, in case of accident or sudden stopping on a hill, and now for the first time we needed it.

New experiences come on this tour of mine every day, though adventures are but few, or have been hitherto. At Oxford and places en route from there we were reported to be the Earl of E—. At Deddington the wind changed, and we were taken for Salvationists on a pilgrimage. Salvationists are not liked in Deddington, and our arrival in the market-place, an ugly piece of rocky ground in the centre of the town (population about three thousand), was the occasion of a considerable deal of excitement. We had the horses out nevertheless, and prepared to spend the night there. We pulled blinds down, and I was about to batten down, as sailors say—in other words, get on the shutters—for the boys had taken to stoning each other, when the arrival of kindly Dr T— and an invitation to come to his grounds gave us relief and surcease from riot.

As the mob chose to follow and hoot, my Highland blood got up, and I got out with Hurricane Bob, the Newfoundland. The street was narrow, and further advance of those unmannerly louts was deemed by them indiscreet.

The change from the lout-lined street to the pleasant grounds of Dr T—'s old house at Deddington was like getting into harbour from off a stormy sea, and I shall never forget the kind hospitality of the kindly doctor and his family.

To be taken for an earl in the morning and a captain of the Salvation Army in the evening is surely enough for one day.

This morning I visited the fine old church, and, as usual, got up into the steeple. If ever you go to Deddington, pray, reader, do the same. The town stands on a hill, and the steeple-top is one hundred feet higher; you can see for many miles. The country round is fertile, rolling hill and dale and valley, and densely treed. There are villages to the right, villages to the left, and mansions peeping from the woods wherever you turn your eye.

The steeple-head is covered with lead, and it is the custom of visitors to place a foot on the lead and cut a mark round it. Inside this they write their initials and the date. Here are footmarks of every size. You can even tell the age and guess the sex. Among them are those of children, but looking at some of the dates those babes must have grown men and women long ago, grown old and died. There is food for thought in even this.

We pass the village of Adderbury on our way to Banbury. From an artistic as well as antiquarian point of view it is well worth a visit. See it from the Oxford side, where the stream winds slowly through the valley. The village lies up yonder on the ridge among grand old trees, its church as beautiful as a dream. Looking in the opposite direction to-day a thoroughly English view meets my gaze. On one bank of the valley is a broad flat meadow, where cattle are wading more than ankle-deep in buttercups and grass; on the other merry haymakers are busy; away beyond are sunny braelands with a horizon of elms.

Delayed for a time after leaving Adderbury by the collapse of a traction engine on the road. We are now cooking dinner outside Banbury, the horses grazing quietly by the roadside.

June 24th.—We went quickly through Banbury, pretty though the place be. We stayed not even to have a cake. Truth is, we were haunted by our greatest foe, the traction engine fiend, which twice yesterday nearly brought us to grief and my narrative to a close.

The country 'twixt Banbury and the little village of Warmington, which lies in a hollow—and that hollow is a forest of fine trees—is beautiful. The soil in many of the fields a rich rusty red. There is what may well be called a terrible hill to descend before you reach the road that leads to Warmington. Once here, we found ourselves on a spacious green, with ample room for a hundred caravans. The village is primitive in the extreme—primitive and pretty. Are we back in the middle ages, I wonder?

Here is no hotel, no railway, no telegraph, no peep at a daily paper, and hardly stabling for a horse.

"I can only get stabling for one horse," I said to a dry, hard-faced woman who was staring at me.

I thought she might suggest something.

"Humph!" she replied; "and I ain't got stabling e'en for one horse. And wot's more, I ain't got a 'orse to stable!"

I felt small, and thought myself well off.

The people here talk strangely. Their patois is different from Berkshire, even as the style of their houses is, and the colour of the fields. Wishing yesterday to get a photograph of the old church at Adderbury, I entered an inn.

The round-faced landlord was very polite, but when I asked for a photographer,—

"A wot, sir?" he said.

"A photographer," I replied, humbly.

"I can't tell wot ye means, sir. Can you tell wot the gemman means, 'Arry?"

"'Arry" was very fat and round, wore a cow-gown, and confronted a quart pot of ale.

I repeated the word to him thrice, but 'Arry shook his head. "I can't catch it," he said, "no 'ow."

When I explained that I meant a man who took pictures with a black box,—

"Oh, now I knows," said the landlord; "you means a pott-o-graffer."

But the children here that came down from their fastnesses in the village above are angels compared to the Deddington roughs. I was so struck with the difference that I asked four or five to come right away into the pantry and look at the saloon.

It rained hard all the afternoon and night, the dark clouds lying low on the hills—real hills—that surrounded us, and quite obscuring our view.

'Twixt bath and breakfast this morning, I strolled down a tree-shaded lane; every field here is surrounded by hedges—not trimmed and disfigured—and trees, the latter growing also in the fields, and under them cows take shelter from sun or shower. How quiet and still it was, only the breeze in the elms, the cuckoo's notes, and the murmur of the unseen cushat!

We are near the scene of the battle of Edgehill. For aught I know I may be sitting near a hero's grave, or on it. The village can hardly, have altered since that grim fight; the houses look hundreds of years old. Yonder quaint stone manor, they tell me, has seen eight centuries go by.

I don't wonder at the people here looking quiet and sleepy; I did not wonder at the polite postmistress turning to her daughter, who was selling a boy "a happorth of peppercorns," and saying, "Whatever is the day of the month, Amelia? I've forgot."

Warmington may some day become a health resort. At present there is no accommodation; but one artist, one author, or one honeymooning pair might enjoy a month here well enough.

Started at nine for Warwick—fourteen miles. For some miles the highway is a broad—very broad—belt of greensward, with tall hedges at every side. Through this belt the actual road meanders; the sward on each side is now bathed in wild flowers, conspicuous among which are patches of the yellow bird's-foot trefoil.

Hills on the right, with wooded horizons; now and then a windmill or rustic church, or farm or manor. A grey haze over all.

We come to a place where the sward is adorned with spotted lilac orchids.

Conspicuous among other wild flowers are now tall pink silenes, very pretty, while the hedges themselves are ablaze with wild roses.

Midday halt at cross roads, on a large patch of clovery grass. Here the Fosse, or old Roman road, bisects our path. It goes straight as crow could fly across England.

There is a pretty farm here, and the landlady from her gate kindly invited Hurricane Bob and me in, and regaled us on the creamiest of milk.

We shall sleep at Warwick to-night.

LEAMINGTON AND WARWICK

"... Evening yields
The world to-night...
... A faint erroneous ray,
Glanced from th' imperfect surfaces of things,
Flings half an image on the straining eye;
While wavering woods, and villages and streams,
And rocks and mountain-tops, that long retained
Th' ascending gleam, are all one swimming scene,
Uncertain if beheld."

Strange that for twelve long miles, 'twixt Warmington and the second milestone from Warwick, we never met a soul, unless rooks and rabbits have souls. We were in the woods in the wilds, among ferns and flowers.

When houses hove in sight at last, signs of civilisation began to appear. We met a man, then a swarm of boarding-school girls botanising, and we knew a city would soon be in sight. At Leamington, the livery stables to which we had been recommended proved too small as to yard accommodation, so we drove back and put up at the Regent Hotel. But there is too much civilisation for us here. Great towns were never meant for great caravans and gipsy-folk. We feel like a ship in harbour.

Rain, rain, rain! We all got wet to the skin, but are none the worse.

The old ostler at the Regent is a bit of a character, had been on the road driving four-in-hands for many a year. He was kindly-loquacious, yes, and kindly-musical as well, for he treated me to several performances on the coach-horn, which certainly did him great credit. He was full of information and anecdotes of the good old times, "when four-in-hands were four-in-hands, sir, and gentlemen were gentlemen." He told us also about the road through Kenilworth to Coventry. It was the prettiest drive, he said, in all England.

Beautiful and all though Leamington be, we were not sorry to leave it and make once more for the cool green country.

The horses were fresh this morning, even as the morning itself was fresh and clear. We passed through bush-clad banks, where furze and yellow-tasselled broom were growing, and trees in abundance. Before we knew where we were we had trotted into Kenilworth. We stabled here and dined, and waited long enough to have a peep at the castle. This grand old pile is historical; no need, therefore, for me to say a word about it.

After rounding the corner in our exit from Kenilworth, and standing straight away for Coventry, the view from the glen at the bridge, with the castle on the left, a village and church on the rising ground, and villas and splendid trees on the right, made a good beginning to the "finest drive in all England."

There is many a pretty peep 'twixt Kenilworth and Coventry.

The road is broad and good, and so tree-lined as often to merit the name of avenue. Especially is this the case at the third milestone, from near which the straight road can be seen for folly a mile and a half, shaded by the grandest of trees. This is a view not easily forgotten.

With all the beauty of this drive, however, it is too civilised to be romantic. The hedges are trimmed, and we actually noticed a man paring the grass on the edge of the footpath.

June 26th.—We are up very early this morning, for in Coventry the road-fiend rides rampant and in all his glory. They have steam-trams, which not only go puffing through the town, but for five miles out through the coal district itself. We must avoid them, get the start of them. So we are up and away long before seven.

We arrived here last night, and through the kindness of the editor of the Tricyclist got permission to draw in for the night into the large cricket and sports ground. The gates were closed at nine, and we had the keys. I was lord, therefore, of all I surveyed.

On the cinder-path last night a weary-looking but strong old man of over sixty was walking. He is doing or trying to do 1,000 miles in a shorter time than the pedestrian Weston. It is said that if he succeeds the brewers will pay him 1,000 pounds, and give him a free public-house, because he trains on beer instead of on tea, as did Weston!

The road leading northward from Coventry is terribly rough and rutty, and cut up with the trams from the mines, but being lined with trees, among which are many copper-beeches, it is not devoid of interest.

It is cold, bitterly cold and raw, with a strong north wind blowing, and we are obliged to wear top-coats on the coupé. Fancy top-coats at midsummer!

The country becomes unpleasant-looking even before the trams end. At

Redworth, where I drew up for a short time to make purchases, swarms of rough, dark, and grimy men surrounded us, but all were polite and most civil.

On the hilltop we again draw up in front of an inn. The panting horses want water, and we ourselves have till now had no breakfast.

"Good beds for travellers round the corner." This was a ticket in a window. I go round the corner. Here is a little show of some kind and a caravan. But the show business cannot be much of a success in this Black Country, for these caravanites look poverty-stricken. From a rude picture on a ragged screen I learn that this caravan is devoted to a horse-taming or Rarey show. The dramatis personae consist of a long, lean, unwholesome-looking lad with straggling yellow hair, a still longer and still leaner lad without any visible hair, and a short man with grey moustache. But this latter comes to the gate bearing in his arms a boy-child of ten years, worn to a skeleton, sickly, and probably dying. The boy shivers, the short man speaks soothingly to him, and bears him back into a dingy tent. I do not relish my breakfast after this sad sight.

We are not sorry when we are away from the immediate vicinity of the mines, and unlimbered by the roadside near the old Red Gate Inn. We have been following the ancient Roman road for many miles, and a good one it is, and very obliging it was of the Romans to make us such a road.

The inn is altogether so quiet and cosy that I determine to stable here for the night, and pass the day writing or strolling about.

So we cross the road and draw the Wanderer up beneath a lordly oak. In crossing we pass from Warwick into Leicestershire.

Pea-blossom is coughing occasionally. It is not a pleasant sound to have to listen to. She may be better to-morrow, for it will be Saturday, and a long and toilsome day is before us.

It is evening now; a walk of a mile has brought me to a hilltop, if hill it can be called. The view from here is by no means spirit-stirring, but quiet and calming to the mind. What a delightful difference between lying here and in that awful bustling inn yard at Leamington!

It is a country of irregular green fields, hedge-bounded, and plentifully sprinkled with oak and ash-trees and tall silver-green aspens; a country of rolling hills and flats, but no fens, with here and there a pretty old-fashioned farm peeping through the foliage.

There is not a cloud in the sky, the sun is sinking in a yellow haze, the robin and the linnet are singing beside me among the hawthorns, and down in the copse yonder a blackbird is fluting.

A pheasant is calling to its mate among the ferns; it is time apparently for pheasants to retire. Time for weasels too, for across the road runs a mother-weasel with a string of young ones all in a row. The procession had been feeding in that sweetly-scented beanfield, and is now bound for bed, and I myself take the hint and go slowly back to the Wanderer. But Hurricane Bob has found a mole, and brings that along. It is not dead, so I let it go. How glad it must feel!

At nine o'clock the sun had set, but left in the north-west a harbinger of a fine morning. What delicious tints! What delicate suffusion of yellows, greens, and blues! Just as the sun was sinking red towards the horizon uprose the moon in the east, round and full, and in appearance precisely like the setting sun. The trees on the horizon were mere black shapes, the birds had ceased to sing, and bats were flitting about. At eleven o'clock, it was a bright clear night with wavy dancing phosphorescent-like gleams of light in the north—the Aurora!

June 11th.—Started at eight o'clock en route by cross roads for Ashby-de-la-Zouch. Shortly afterwards passed a needle-shaped monument to George Fox, founder of the Society of Friends. It is a very humble one, and stands in a wooded corner almost surrounded by hawthorn. Went through the village of Fenny Drayton. Why called "Fenny," I wonder? It is a little hamlet, very old, and with a pretty and very old church, but I had no time to get up to the steeple.

Road narrow but good. A glorious morning, with a blue sky and delicious breeze.

Greensward at each side of the road, with ragged hedges and stunted oaks and ashes; roses in the hedgerows, golden celandine on the sward, and tall crimson silenes everywhere. By-and-bye the country opens, and we come upon a splendid view; and here is a sight—a hedgerow of roses nearly a mile long! Here are as many of these wildly beautiful flowers as would drape Saint Paul's Cathedral, dome and all.

We pass Sibson, with its very quaint old inn and little ivy-covered church surmounted by a stone cross; and Twycross, a most healthy and pretty rural village. There we unlimbered to dine, and in the afternoon went on towards our destination. Past Gopsal Park, with its quaint old lodge-gates and grand trees, on through dark waving woods of beech, of oak, and ash, on through lanes with hedgerows at each side, so tall that they almost meet at the top. We cross the railway now to avoid a steep bridge. Meesham is far away on the hill before us, and looks very romantic and pretty from the bridge. Its ancient church rears its steeple skyward, high over the houses that cluster round it, giving the place the appearance of a cathedral city in miniature. The romance vanishes, though, as soon as we enter the town. One long, steep street leads through it, its houses are of brick and most uninteresting, and the public-houses are so plentifully scattered about that thirst must be a common complaint here.

Ashby-de-la-Zouch lies above us and before as at last, and strangely picturesque it looks. Bows of queer-shaped trees are on each side of us; up yonder, in front, is a graveyard on a braeland; farther to the right a tall church spire, and flanking all, and peeping through the greenery of trees, is the ruined castle.

Market-day in Ashby, and we are mobbed whenever we stop to do some shopping.

The church here is well worthy of a visit; so too is the castle, but tourists ought to refresh their minds before spending a few days here by once more reading "Ivanhoe."

It was hard, uphill work from Ashby; drag, drag, drag; horses tired, Peablossom limping, and all weary.

At the hilltop we came into quite a Highland country, and thence we could catch glimpses of lovely scenery and far-off blue hills.

The effects of the sunlight on the green oak woods and the yellow ashes were very charming.

Lount at last; a humble inn, quiet, kindly people, and a little meadow.

A QUIET SUNDAY AT LOUNT

"How still the morning of this hallowed day!
Hushed is the voice of rural labour,
The ploughboy's whistle and the milkmaid's song."
June 28th.

The country is indeed a Highlands in miniature. I might describe the scenery in this way: Take a sheet of paper and thereon draw irregular lines, across and across, up and down, in any conceivable direction. These lines, then, shall represent blackthorn hedges bounding fields of flowering grass and hay. Place trees in your picture anywhere, and, here and there, a wood of dwarfed oak, and dot the field-nooks with picturesque-looking cattle-huts. In the centre let there be a cluster of irregularly-built brick-tiled houses and the domes of a pottery works. This, then, is Lount and its surroundings, where we are now bivouacked. But to complete the sketch there must be footpaths meandering through the meadows, with gaps in the hedges for rustic stiles. Nor must the cattle be forgotten.

And all the country visible from this point is broken up into round hills, and each field is a collection of smaller hills, shaped like waves of a storm-tossed ocean.

How still and quiet it is! And above the green of fields and woods is a blue, blue sunny sky. Larks are singing up yonder, their songs mingling sweetly with the chiming of the church bells that comes floating over the hills, rising and falling as the breeze does, now high and clear, now soft and far-away like.

I had the caravan half-filled this morning with bright-eyed, wondering children. A parent brought me a red cotton handkerchief.

"T'missus," he explained, "was makin' oop a pie, and I thought upon thee loike."

It was kindly, and I couldn't refuse the gift, though gooseberry pies form no part of the Wanderer's menu.

Ten o'clock pm.—The full moon has just risen over the dark oak woods; a strangely white dense fog has filled all the hollows—a fog you can almost stretch out your hands and touch. The knolls in the fields all appear over it, looking like little islands in the midst of an inland sea.

The corncrake is sounding his rattle in the hayfields—a veritable voice of the night is he—and not another sound is to be heard.

Passed a garden a few minutes ago while walking out. Such a sight! Glowworms in thousands; far more lovely than fireflies in an Indian jungle.

To bed.

June 29th.—We got under way by 8:30, after a brief visit to the Coleorton Pottery. This place has an ugly enough appearance outside, but is very interesting internally. The proprietor kindly showed my coachman and me over the works. We saw the great heaps of blue clay that had been dug from the hillside and left exposed for weeks to the weather, the tanks in which it is mixed with water, the machinery for washing and sifting it, the clay being finally boiled to the consistency of putty. An old man took dabs of this putty and cast them on a revolving table, smiling as he did so as he watched our wondering looks, for lo! cups and saucers and teapots seemed to grow up under his fingers, and a whole tea-set was produced more quickly than one could have brewed a cup of tea.

A somewhat misty morning, but roads good though hilly, and scenery romantic. But at Castle Donington, a long brick town, the scene changes. Away go hill and dale, away goes all romance, and we pass through a flat country, with nothing in it to enlist sympathy save the trees and rose-clad hedges.

But soon again comes another change, and we cross the broad and silvery Trent, stopping, however, on the bridge to admire the view.

We arrive at Long Eaton, and encamp by the roadside to cook dinner. Rows of ugly brick houses, a lazy canal with banks black with coal dust; the people here look as inactive as does their canal. Took the wrong turning and went miles out of our way.

We were stormed on our exit from Long Eaton by hordes of Board School children. They clustered round us like locusts, they swarmed like bees, and hung to the caravan in scores. No good my threatening them with the whip. I suppose they knew I did not mean much mischief, and one score was only frightened off to make room for another.

At Beeston, near Nottingham, I got talking to a tricyclist; a visit to a caravan followed, and then an introduction to a wealthy lace merchant. The latter would not hear of my going two miles farther to an inn. I must come into his grounds. So here in a cosy corner of the lawn of Beeston Hall lies the

Wanderer, overshadowed by giant elms and glorious purple beeches, and the lace manufacturer and his wife are simply hospitality personified.

Such is the glorious uncertainty of a gentleman gipsy's life—one night bivouacked by a lonely roadside in a black country, another in a paradise like this.

July 2nd.—A broiling hot day—almost too hot to write or think. At present we are encamped on the road, two miles from Worksop to the south. Tired though the horses were, we pushed on and on for miles, seeking shade but finding none; and now we have given up, and stand in the glaring sunshine. Roads are of whitest limestone, and, though there is little wind, every wheel of every vehicle raises a dust and a powder that seem to penetrate our very pores. We are all languid, drowsy, lethargic. Polly the parrot alone appears to enjoy the heat and the glare. The haymakers in yonder field are lazy-looking, silent, and solemn—a melting solemnity; the martins on that single telegraph-wire rest and pant open-mouthed, while the cattle in the meadow, with tails erect, go flying from end to end and back again in a vain attempt to escape from the heat and the flies.

But the flowers that grow by the wayside and trail over the hedges revel in the sunshine—the purple vetches, the red clover, the yellow wild-pea, and the starry Margueritas. Roses in sheets are spread over the hawthorn fences, and crimson poppies dot the cornfields. The white clover is alive with bees. This seems a bee country; everybody at present is either drumming bees or whitewashing cottages.

Got up to-day and had breakfast shortly after six. The kindly landlord of the Greyhound, Mr Scothern, and genial Mr Tebbet, one of his Grace the Duke of Portland's head clerks, had promised to drive me through the forest grounds of Welbeck.

As the day is, so was the morning, though the sun's warmth was then pleasant enough.

Our drive would occupy some two hours and a half, and in that time we would see many a "ferlie," as the Scotch say. The bare impossibility of giving the reader anything like a correct account of this most enjoyable ride impresses me while I write, and I feel inclined to throw down my pen. I shall not do so, however, but must leave much unsaid. If any one wishes to see the country around here as I have seen it this morning, and wander in the forest and enjoy Nature in her home of homes, he must come to Welbeck in summer. Never mind distance; come, you will have something to dream pleasantly about for many a day.

A visit to the great irrigation canal, by which all the drainage from Mansfield is carried along, and utilised by being allowed to flood meadows, might not appear a very romantic way of beginning a summer morning's outing. But it was interesting nevertheless. The meadows which are periodically flooded are wondrously green; three crops of hay are taken from each every season. They are on the slope, the canal running along above. The pure water that drains from these meadows finds its way into a river or trout stream that meanders along beneath them, and is overhung by rocks and woodland. Fish in abundance are caught here, and at present are being used to stock ponds and lochs on the duke's estate.

We soon crossed this stream by a Gothic bridge, and plunged into what I may call a new forest. There are fine trees here in abundance, but it is a storm-tossed woodland, and much of the felled timber is so twisted in grain as to be useless for ordinary purposes.

We saw many trees that had been struck by lightning, their branches hurled in all directions. Up a steep hill after leaving this forest, and stopping at an old-fashioned inn, we regaled ourselves on ginger-ale. The landlord pointed with some pride to the sign that hung over the door.

"The duke himself—the old duke, sir, his Grace of the leathern breeches—brought that sign here himself—in his own hands and in his own carriage, and it isn't many real gentlemen that would have done that, sir!"

The memory of the old duke is as much reverenced here, it appears to me, as that of Peter the Great is in Russia. The stories and anecdotes of his life you hear in the neighbourhood would fill a volume. People all admit he was eccentric, but his eccentricity filled many a hungry mouth, soothed the sorrows of the aged, and made many and many a home happy.

The tunnel towards Warsop is about two miles long, lighted by gas at night, and from windows above by day; there are a riding-school and wonderful stables underground, ballroom, etc, etc. I am writing these lines within a quarter of a mile of the open-air stables. The place looks like a small city.

Just one—only one—anecdote of the old duke's eccentricity. It was told me last night, and proves his Grace to have been a man of kindly feeling. A certain architect had finished—on some part of the ground—a large archway and pillared colonnade, at great expense to the duke, no doubt. It did not please the latter, however, but he would not wound the architect's feelings by telling him so. No, but one evening he got together some two hundred men, and every stone was taken away and the ground levelled before morning. The architect must have stared at the transformation when he came next day, but the matter was never even referred to by the duke, and of course the architect said nothing.

The country through which we went after passing the duke's irrigation works was a rolling one, hill and dale, green fields, forest, loch, and stream. There are wild creatures in it in abundance. Yonder are two swans sailing peacefully along on a little lake; here, near the edge of the stream, a water-hen with a brood of little black young ones. She hurries them along through the hedge as our trap approaches, but the more hurry the less speed, and more than one poor little mite tumbles on its back, and has to be helped up by the mother. Yonder on the grass is a brace of parent partridges; they do not fly away; their heads are together; they are having a loving consultation on ways and means, and the young brood is only a little way off. Before us now, and adown the road, runs a great cock pheasant; he finally takes flight and floats away towards the woods. Look in the stream, how the glad fish leap, and the bubbles escaping from the mud in that deep dark pool tell where some fat eel is feeding. We pause for a moment to admire the trees, and the music of birds and melancholy croodling of the cushat fall upon our ears, while young rabbits scurry about in all directions, and a cuckoo with attendant linnet flies close over our horse's head.

Not far from the little inn where we stopped we saw the ruins of King John's palace. But little is left of it now, the stones having been put to other purposes, and it looks as like the ruins of an old barn as those of a palace.

We leave the road and pass into the forest proper—the old Sherwood Forest, sacred to the memory of Robin Hood and Little John and the merry monks of the olden time.

We enter Birkland. Saving those wondrous and ancient oaks that stand here and there, and look so weird and uncanny as almost to strike the beholder with awe, the forest is all new. Long straight broad avenues go in all directions through it. The ground on these is as level as a lawn, and just as soft and green. Here is the Shamble Oak. Its weirdlike arms are still green, though it is said to be 1,700 years old, and may be more. The trunk, round which twelve good strides will hardly take you, is sadly gutted by fire. Some boys set it alight in trying to smoke out a hornet's hive. Here, in this oak, it is said, Robin Hood hung his slaughtered deer, and, in more modern times, keepers and poachers used it as a larder.

A quaint and pretty log-hut à la Russe has recently been erected near the Shamble Oak. It is not yet furnished, but we found our way inside, the keeper in attendance here giving us great and impressive injunctions to wipe our feet and not step off the canvas. I wonder he did not bid us remove our shoes.

From the balcony of this log-hut one could have rabbit-shooting all day long, and pigeon-shooting in the evening. I hope no one ever will though.

We went home a different way, Mr Tebbet opening the double-padlocked gates for us. We passed the Parliament Tree, as it is called, where they tell us King John used to assemble his councillors. It is an oak still, a skeleton oak hung together by chains.

From the brow of a hill which we soon reached, we enjoyed a panorama, the like of which is not elsewhere to be seen in all broad England. From Howitt's "Rural Life in England" I cull the following:

"Near Mansfield there remains a considerable wood, Harlowe Wood, and a fine scattering of old oaks near Berry Hill, in the same neighbourhood, but the greater part is now an open waste, stretching in a succession of low hills and long winding valleys, dark with heather. A few solitary and battered oaks standing here and there, the last melancholy remnants of these vast and ancient woods, the beautiful springs, swift and crystalline brooks, and broad sheets of water lying abroad amid the dark heath, and haunted by numbers of wild docks and the heron, still remain. But at the Clipstone extremity of the forest, a remnant of its ancient woodlands remains, unrifled, except of its deer—a specimen of what the whole once was, and a specimen of consummate beauty and interest. Birkland and Bilhaghe taken together form a tract of land extending from Ollerton along the side of Thoresby Park, the seat of Earl Manvers, to Clipstone Park, of about five miles in length, and one or two in width. Bilhaghe is a forest of oaks, and is clothed with the most impressive aspect of age that can perhaps be presented to the eye in these kingdoms... A thousand years, ten thousand tempests, lightnings, winds, and wintry violence have all flung their utmost force on these trees, and there they stand, trunk after trunk, scathed, hollow, grey, and gnarled, stretching out their bare sturdy arms on their mingled foliage and ruin—a life in death. All is grey and old. The ground is grey beneath—the trees are grey with clinging lichens—the very heather and fern that spring beneath them have a character of the past.

"But Bilhaghe is only half of the forest-remains here; in a continuous line with it lies Birkland—a tract which bears its character in its name—the land of birches. It is a forest perfectly unique. It is equally ancient with Bilhaghe, but it has a less dilapidated air. It is a region of grace and poetry. I have seen many a wood, and many a wood of birches, and some of them amazingly beautiful, too, in one quarter or another of this fair island, but in England nothing that can compare with this... On all sides, standing in their solemn steadfastness, you see huge, gnarled, strangely-coloured and mossed oaks, some riven and laid bare from summit to root with the thunderbolts of past tempests. An immense tree is called the Shamble Oak, being said to be the one in which Robin Hood hung his slaughtered deer, but which was more probably used by the keepers for that purpose. By whomsoever it was so used, however, there still remain the hooks within its vast hollow."

But it is time to be up and off. We lay last night in Mr Tebbet's private meadow. Had a long walk before I could secure a suitable place. But the place was eminently quiet and exceedingly private, near lawns and gardens and giant elms. The elm that grows near the pretty cemetery, in which haymakers were so busy this morning, is, with the exception of the oak at Newstead Abbey gates, the finest ever I have seen; and yet an old man died but recently in Mansfield workhouse who remembered the time he could bend it to the ground.

Warsop, which we reached over rough and stony roads and steepish hills, is a greystone village, the houses slated or tiled blue or red, a fine church on the hilltop among lordly trees, a graveyard on the brae beneath with a white pathway meandering up through it to the porch.

At the sixth milestone we reached a hilltop, from which we could see into several counties. Such a view as this is worth wandering leagues to look at. We watered the horses here, at the last of the Duke of Portland's lodges.

Thou down hill again. How lovely the little village of Cuckney looks down there, its crimson houses shimmering through the trees! We bought eggs at the inn called the Greendale Oak. There is a story attached to this oak which my reader has doubtless heard or read.

This is the land of oaks, and a smiling land too, a land of wealth and beauty, a great garden-land.

DONCASTER

"Was nought around save images of rest,
Sleep-soothing groves, and quiet lawns between,
And flowery beds, that slumberous influence kest,
From poppies breathed, and beds of pleasant green."

It is the morning of the 4th July, and a bright and beautiful morning it is. The storm clouds that yesterday lowered all around us have cleared away and the sun shines in an Italian sky. We are encamped in a delightful little level meadow close to the worthy brewer and farmer to whom it belongs. How did we come here? Were we invited? No, reader, we invited ourselves. Not quite liking the accommodation recommended to us by a villager, I called on Mr E—, and coyly—shall I say "coyly?"—stated my case. Though good Mr E— has a wife to please, and the gentle, kindly lady is an invalid, he granted me the desired permission, and when we were fairly on the lawn and...

stunted than the giants we have left behind us. Mulberry-trees have now made their appearance, and splendid acacias, tasselled over with drooping blooms. But the maple or plane-trees are also a sight; they are now in seed, and the hanging bunches of pods are tinted with carmine and brown.

Large elder-bushes, like enormous white-rose trees, brighten the dark-green of the hedgerows; beds of yellow sweet-pea, beds and patches of the blue speedwell, the purple tapering stachys, solitary spikes of crimson foxglove, roses, and honeysuckle meet the eye wherever I look. In some places the sward is covered as with snow by the lavish-spreading fairy-bedstraw.

At the little cosy town of Askern, with its capital hotels and civilised-looking lodging-houses, on stopping to shop, we were surprised at being surrounded by hosts of white-haired cripples—well, say lame people, for every one had a staff or a crutch.

But I soon found out that Askern is a watering-place, a kind of a second-class Harrogate, and these people with the locks of snow had come to bathe and drink the waters; they are sulphureous. There is here a little lake, with a promenade and toy stalls. The lake has real water in it, though it looks somewhat green and greasy, and a real boat on it, and real oars to pull it. There are fish in the lake too. This is evident from the fact that a twenty-pound pike was lately landed. On being opened, his stomach was found to contain a roach and two copper coins of the reign of our present blessed Majesty the Queen. It is evident that this pike was laving up against a rainy day.

But Askern is really a good resort for the invalid. Things are cheap, too, and the place would soon flourish if there were abundance of visitors.

We have halted to dine in the centre of a Yorkshire wold. The road goes straight through the hedge-bound sward, and can be seen for miles either way.

A wold means a wood—a wild wood. I like the word, there is a fine romantic ring about it. This wold has been cleared, or partially so, of trees, and fields of waving grain extend on all sides of us. Very delightful is this wold on a sweet summer's day like this, but one can easily imagine how dreary the scene must be in winter, with the road banked high with snowdrifts, and the wind sweeping over the flats and tearing through the leafless oaks.

The horses are enjoying the clover. Hurricane Bob and I are reclining among our rugs on the broad coupé. Foley is cooking a fowl and a sheep's heart; the latter for Bob's dinner. There are rock-looking clouds on the horizon, a thunderstorm is within a measurable distance.

How pretty those purple trailing vetches look! How sweet the song of yonder uprising lark! There is an odour of elder-flowers in the air. I hear a hen cackling at a distant farm. Probably the hen has laid an egg. Hurricane Bob is sound asleep. I think I shall read. Burns is by my elbow:

"Oh, Nature! a' thy shows and forms
To feeling pensive hearts hae charms!
Whether the summer kindly warms
  Wi' life and light,
Or winter howls in gusty storms,
  The lang dark night."

How lovely those dog-roses are, though! They are everywhere to-day; roses in clusters, roses in garlands, wreaths and wind-tossed spray, white, crimson, or palest pink roses—roses—

"The dinner is all on the table, sir."

"Aw—right."

"The dinner is quite ready, sir."

"To be sure, to be sure. Thank you, Foley."

"Why, you have been sound asleep, sir."

We are once more settled for the night and settled for the Sabbath, in a delightful clovery meadow near a fine old Yorkshire farm, round which blue-rock pigeons are flying in clouds.

A herd of fine shorthorn cows have arranged themselves in a row to look at us. A healthful, "caller" country lassie is milking one. Her name is Mary; I heard a ploughboy say "Mary" to her. Mary is singing low as she milks, and the sleek-sided cow is chewing her cud and meditating.

Yonder is a field of white peas all in bloom, and yonder a field of pale-green flax.

It must be a great satisfaction for those pigeons to see those peas in bloom.

"Good-night, Mary."

"Good-night, sir."

Away marches Mary, singing, "Tra, la, lalla, la lah."

What a sweet voice the little maiden has!

A DAY IN THE LIFE OF A GENTLEMAN GIPSY

"He journeyed on like errant-knight the while,
While sweetly the summer sun did smile
On mountain moss and moor."

It has occurred to me that a slightly more detailed account of the internal economy of our land-yacht, the Wanderer, might not prove devoid of interest to the reader, and I cannot give this in an easier way to myself, nor more completely, than by describing a day in the life of a gentleman gipsy.

It is the ninth of July, and early morning. The belfry-clock, which we can see from the meadow in which we have been lying all night, will presently chime out the quarter-past six. Foley is busy erecting the after-tent under which I have my bath every morning, as sure as sunrise. In a few minutes, ere ever I have finished my toilet, our coachman will be here for oats and beans for Corn-flower and Pea-blossom. No fear that John will neglect his horses, he is quite as kind to them as I myself am to Bob and Polly, and now that Pear-blossom's fetlock is slightly strained, it is three times a day most carefully bandaged and rubbed with healing liniment.

The bed which is made every night on the sofa is not yet taken up, but as soon as I emerge from the back door and enter the tent my valet enters by the saloon front door, the bedclothes are carried outside, carefully shaken and folded, and finally stowed away under the lockers. The saloon is then brushed and dusted and the cloth laid for breakfast.

Bob sleeps on the driving apron in the corner of the saloon, Polly in her cage occupies another corner. The first thing I do every morning is to hang Polly under the balcony, and chain Bob on the coupé, wrapping him in his red blanket if the weather be chilly. He is there now; ominous warning growls are followed by fierce barking, for some one is nearing the caravan whose looks Bob does not like, or whose movements he deems suspicious. At every bark of the brave dog the van shakes and the lamp-glasses rattle.

I have finished shaving—water boiled by spirits-of-wine.

"The bath all ready? thank you, Foley."

Do not imagine that I carry an immense tin-ware bath in the Wanderer. No, a gipsy's bath is a very simple arrangement, but it is very delightful. This is the modus operandi. I have a great sponge and a bucket of cold water, newly drawn from the nearest well. This morning the water is actually ice-cold, but I am hungry before I have finished sponging, so benefit must result from so bracing an ablution.

Foley has laid the cloth. The kettle is boiling, the eggs and rashers are ready to put in the frying-pan, the Rippingille oil-stove is in a little tent made of mats under the caravan. There is nothing in the shape of cooking this stove will not perform.

Now Bob must have his early run, and while I am walking with him I call a bunch of the seedling grasses Polly loves so well, for I believe with Norman McLeod, D.D. "I think nothing of that man's religion," said that truly great and good man, "whose cat and dog are not the better for it."

We have not a caravan cat, but Polly is an excellent substitute.

I return and once more fasten Bob on the coupé, but he now insists on having the front door open that he may watch me at breakfast, and get the tit-bits. How bright, and clean, and pleasant the saloon looks! There are garden flowers in the crystal boat, and a splendid bouquet of wild flowers and ferns that I culled in the woods yesterday morning stands in the bracket beneath one of the windows; crimson foxgloves there are, rare and beautiful ox-eye daisies, and a score of others of every colour and shade.

The sun is streaming in through the panes and shimmering on the red lamp-glasses; the table is laid to perfection, the tea is fragrant, the eggs and bacon done to a turn, and the bread as white as snow. The milk, too, is newly from that very cow who was playing the trombone so noisily last night in the meadow near me, and the butter all that could be desired. And yet some of these dainties are wondrous cheap up here in Yorks; for that butter we paid but eleven pence a pound, fourteen new-laid eggs we secured for a shilling, the bacon cost but sixpence, while three halfpence buys me a jugful of the richest of milk. Who would not be a gipsy?

But breakfast is soon discussed and everything cleared away, the spoons and dishes are washed beneath the tent, the hind tables having been let down to facilitate matters. In half an hour or less the pantry is as bright and tidy as eye could wish to see. The tent itself is taken down and stowed away, the ladder is shipped and secured, buckets and mats, and nosebags and chains, fastened beneath the caravan, then the steps are put up, and the after-door closed and locked. The horses are now put-to; I myself have one last walk round the Wanderer to see that everything is in its place and no drawer left unlocked, then away we rattle right gaily O!

To-day the gate that leads to the meadow is narrow, it does not give us two inches to spare at each side. I have to walk backwards in front of the horses to guide the coachman in his exit. But John has a keen eye, and in a few moments we are in the road.

Nothing has been forgotten, and the landlord of the Stalled Ox gives us kindly good morning and wishes us bon voyage. More than one friendly hand is waved, too, and some hats are lifted, for the good people, having soon settled in their minds that we were neither in the Cheap-Jack line nor Salvation soldiers, have promoted me to the dignity of baronet. This is nothing new. Some scions of nobility are actually caravanning around somewhere, and I am often supposed to be one of them.

I travel incog, and do not care whom I am taken for, whether Cheap-Jack, noble earl, or political agent. I now let down the front seat, and Hurricane Bob withdraws to the quiet seclusion of the pantry, where he rests on cushions to fend him from the jolting.

Pea-blossom invariably nudges Corn-flower with her nose before starting. This is to make him straighten out and take the first pull at the caravan. He never refuses, and once it is in motion they both settle soberly down to their work.

Foley is on ahead with the tricycle—some hundred yards. This is a judicious and handy arrangement. We hardly know how we should have done without our smart and beautiful Ranelagh Club machine.

The day will be a warm one. It is now eight o'clock, the road is level and firm, and we hope to reach Darlington—sixteen miles—to-night.

The country is flat again, but the landscape is bounded by far-off blue hills.

The roses still accompany us in the hedgerows. There is even a greater wealth of them to-day than usual, while the sward at each side of our path still looks like a garden laid out in beds and patches of brightest colours.

There is nothing of very special interest to view in this long town of Northallerton, not in the streets at all events. Last night, though, we were visited by hundreds of well-dressed people; many of these were really beautiful girls, though here the beauty is of a different type from that you find far south. More of the Saxon probably, and a sprinkling of the auburn-haired Dane.

For weeks I have cared but little how the world wagged. With an apathy and listlessness born of bracing air and sunshine, I have troubled myself not at all about foreign wars or the fall of governments, but to-day I have invested in a Yorkshire Post. I arrange my rags on the coupé, and lying down, dreamily scan my paper as the horses go trotting along. I have plenty of work to do if I choose, bundles of proofs to correct from my publishers, but—I'll do it by-and-bye. By-and-bye is a gipsy's motto. There is no news in this day's paper. What care I that Oko Jumbo has departed, or that there has been a royal visit to Leeds? Bah! I fold the thing up and pitch it to a cow-boy. Had it fallen in that cow-boy's mouth it would hardly have filled it.

The road is silent and almost deserted, so we see but few people saving those who run to their garden gates, or peep from behind the geraniums in windows.

But it is most pleasant lolling here on such a glorious morning, and the veriest trifles that I notice in passing awaken a kind of drowsy interest in my mind.

In proof of this let me mention a few. A country boy playing with a collie puppy. Puppy nearly gets run over. Agony and anxiety of country boy. Red-tiled brick cottages peeping up through orchards. Red-tiled cottages everywhere, by hedgerows, by brook-sides, in meadows, on morsels of moorland. A sweep in full costume, brush and all, standing glaring from under a broad Scotch bonnet. A yellow-haired wee lassie standing in a doorway eating a slice of bread; she has not finished her toilet, for she wears but one stocking, the other shapely leg is bare. Great banks of elder-trees covered with snowy blossoms. A quiet and pretty farm-steading near the road, its garden ablaze with crimson valerian. Milch cows in the adjacent meadow, ankle-deep in yellow celandine and daisies. A flock of lambs in a field lying down under the shade of a great sycamore, the sycamore itself a sight worth seeing.

And now we are on the top of Lovesome Hill. What a charming name, by the way! Spread out before and beneath us is a large and fertile plain, fields and woodlands, as far as ever the eye can reach, all slumbering in the sweet summer sunshine. In the distance a train is speeding along, we can trace it by its trailing smoke. I had almost forgotten we lived in the days of railway trains. There is a redbrick village on the hilltop straight ahead of us.

That must be Smeaton. Smeaton? Yes, now I remember, and the lovely fertile plain yonder, that now looks so green and smiling, hides in its bosom the dust of an army. History tells us that ten thousand Scotchmen were there slain. I can fancy the terrible tulzie, I can people that plain even now in imagination with men in battle array; I see the banners wave, and hear the border slogan cry:

"And now at weapon-point they close,
Scarce can they hear or see their foes;
They close in clouds of smoke and dust,
With sword's-sway and lance's thrust;
And such a yell was there,
Of sudden and portentous birth,
As if man fought upon the earth,
And fiends in upper air.
Oh! life and death were in the shout,

And triumph and despair."

(The Battle of the Standard, fought in 1138, in which the Scottish army was routed, and the flower of the land left dead on the field.)

But here we are in Smeaton itself—grass or a garden at every cottage. This village would make a capital health resort. We stop to water the horses, and though it is hardly ten o'clock I feel hungry already.

Clear of the village, and on and on. A nice old lady in spectacles tending cows and knitting, singing low to herself as she does so. An awful-looking old man, in awful-looking goggles, breaking stones by the roadside. I address the awful-looking old man.

"Awful-looking old man," I say, "did ever you hear of the Battle of the Standard?"

"Naa."

"Did you never hear or read that a battle was fought near this spot?"

The awful-looking old man scratched his head.

"Coome ta think on't noo, there was summut o' th' kind, but it's soome years agone. There war more 'n a hoondred cocks. A regular main as ye might call it."

I pass on and leave the old man muttering to himself. Pinewoods on our right mingling with the lighter green of the feathery larches. A thundercloud hanging over a town in the plains far away. A duck-pond completely surrounded by trailing roses. Ducks in the pond all head down, tails and yellow feet up. Road suddenly becomes a lovers' lane, charmingly pretty, and robins are singing in the copses. We are just five miles from Darlington. We stable our horses at a roadside inn and Foley cooks the dinner.

How very handy sheets of paper come in! Look at that snow-white tablecloth—that is paper; so is the temporary crumb-cloth, and eke my table-napkin; but in fifty other ways in a caravan paper is useful.

The dinner to-day is cold roast beef and floury new potatoes; add to this a delightful salad, and we have a menu a millionaire might not despise.

I write up my log while dinner is cooking, and after that meal has been discussed comes the hour for reading and siesta.

Now the horses are once more put-to, and we start again for Darlington. We pass through the charming village of Croft; it lies on the banks of the Tees, and is a spa of some kind, and well worthy of being a better-frequented resort for the health or pleasure seeker.

The treescapes, the wood and water peeps, are fine just before you reach Darlington. This town itself is one of the prettiest in England. Fully as big but infinitely more beautiful even than Reading.

Wherever we stop we are surrounded by people, so we make haste to shake the dust of civilisation from our carriage-wheels, and are happy when we once more breathe country air, and see neither perambulators nor boarding-school girls.

At the top of a hill some two miles out of town we come upon a cosy wee hotel—the Harrogate Hill Hotel.

"A've little convenience," says the landlord, in his broad Durham brogue, "but A'll clear anoother stall, and A'll turn t'ould pony oot o' his. A'll mak' room."

And the Wanderer is steered up a narrow lane and safely landed in a tiny meadow, o'ergrown with rank green grass and docks and sheltered with fine elms and ashes. And here we lie to-night.

Supper will soon be ready. I shall have a ride on my tricycle; there is always something to see; then beds will be made, shutters put up. I will read and write, while Foley in his cabin will write up his road-log, and by eleven every one on board will be wrapped, we hope, in dreamless slumber.

This then is a true and faithful account of one day in the life of a gentleman gipsy. Quiet and uneventful, but very pleasant, almost idyllic.

Do you care for the picture, reader?

AT DURHAM

"March! march! Ettrick and Teviotdale,
Why, my lads, dinna ye march forward in order?
March! march! Eskdale and Liddesdale,
All the blue bonnets are over the border.
Many a banner spread flutters above your head;
Many a crest that is famous in story;
Mount and make ready then,
Sons of the mountain glen:
Fight for your Queen, and the old Scottish glory!"

July 11th.

A six-miles' drive, through some of the most charming scenery in England, brought us into Durham. The city looks very imposing from the hilltop; its noble old castle, and grand yet solemn looking cathedral. Eight hundred years of age! What a terrible story they could tell could those grey old piles but speak! It would be a very sad one to listen to. Perhaps they do talk to each other at the midnight hour, when the city is hushed and still.

It would take one a week, or even a fortnight, to see all the sights about Durham; he would hardly in that time, methinks, be tired of the walks around the town and by the banks of the winding Weir.

It is a rolling country, a hilly land around here. The people, by the way, call those hills banks. We had a hard day. John's gloves were torn with the reins, for driving was no joke. I fear, however, the horses hardly enjoyed the scenery.

The streets in Durham are badly paved and dangerously steep. We did not dare to bring the Wanderer through, therefore, but made a sylvan détour and got on the north road again beyond.

If we reckoned upon encamping last night in a cosy meadow once more we were mistaken, we were glad to get standing room close to the road and behind a little public-house.

Miners going home from their work in the evening passed us in scores. I cannot say they look picturesque, but they are blithe and active, and would make capital soldiers. Their legs were bare from their knees downwards, their hats were skull-caps, and all visible flesh was as black almost as a nigger's.

Many of these miners, washed and dressed, returned to this public-house, drank and gambled till eleven, then went outside and fought cruelly.

The long rows of grey-slab houses one passes on leaving Durham by road do not look inviting. For miles we passed through a mining district, a kind of black country—a country, however, that would be pleasant enough, with its rolling hills, its fine trees and wild hedgerows, were, it not for the dirt and squalor and poverty one sees signs of everywhere on the road. Every one and everything looks grey and grimy, and many of the children, but especially the women, have a woebegone, grief-stricken look that tells its own tale.

I greatly fear that intemperance is rampant enough in some of these villages, and the weaker members of the family have to suffer for it.

Here is an old wrinkled yellow woman sitting on a doorstep. She is smoking a short black clay, perhaps her only comfort in life. A rough-looking man, with a beard of one week's growth, appears behind and rudely stirs her with his foot. She totters up and nearly falls as he brushes past unheeding.

Yonder are two tiny girls, also sitting on a doorstep—one about seven, the other little more than a baby. An inebriated man—can it be the father?—comes along the street and stops in front of them. He wants to get in.

"Git oot o' t'way!" he shouts to the oldest.

His leg is half lifted as if to kick.

"And thou too,"—this to the baby.

One can easily imagine what sort of a home those poor children have. It cannot be a very happy one.

More pleasant to notice now a window brilliant with flowers, and a clean and tidy woman rubbing the panes.

On and on through beautiful scenery, with peeps at many a noble mansion in the distance. Only the landscape is disfigured by unsightly mine machinery, and the trees are all a-blur with the smoky haze that lies around them.

The country around the village of Birtley is also very pretty. A mile beyond from the hilltop the view is grand, and well worth all this tiring day's drag to look upon.

Everywhere on the roadside are groups of miners out of work, lying on the grass asleep or talking.

The dust is trying to the nerves to-day; such a black dust it is, too.

We stop at Birtley. I trust I shall never stop there again.

"No, there is no stabling here;" thus spoke a slattern whom I addressed.

"Water t' hosses. Dost think I'd give thee water? Go and look for t' well."

Some drunken miners crowded round.

"For two pins," one said, "I'd kick the horses. Smartly I would."

He thought better of it, however.

We pushed on in hopes of getting stabling and perhaps a little civility.

We pushed on right through Gateshead and Newcastle, and three miles farther to the pleasant village of Gosforth, before we found either.

Gosforth is a village of villas, and here we have found all the comfort a gipsy's heart could desire.

We are encamped on a breezy common in sight of the Cheviot Hills, and here we will lie till Tuesday morning for the sake of our horses if not ourselves.

I shall never forget the kindly welcome I received here from the Spanish Consul.

July 14th.—Down tumbled the mercury yesterday morning, and down came the rain in torrents, the rattling, rushing noise it made on the roof of the Wanderer being every now and then drowned in the pealing of the thunder.

But this morning the air is delightfully cool, the sky is bright, the atmosphere clear, and a gentle breeze is blowing.

Left Gosforth early. The country at first was somewhat flat, sparsely treed, well cultivated and clean.

The first village we passed through is called, I think, Three Mile Bridge. It is quite a mining place, far from wholesome, but the children looked healthy, a fact which is due, doubtless, to the bracing, pure air they breathe. All are bare-legged and shoeless, from the lad or lass of fifteen down to the month-old kicking baby.

Came to a splendid park and lodge-gates, the latter surmounted by two bulls couchant; I do not care to know to whom the domain belongs.

I find it is best not to be told who lives in the beautiful mansions I am passing every day in my journey due north. I can people them all in imagination. A name might banish every morsel of romance from the finest castle that peeps through the greenery of trees in some glen, or stands boldly out in the sunshine of some steep hill or braeland.

By eleven o'clock we had done ten miles and entered Morpeth.

Now, O ye health-seekers or intending honeymoon enjoyers! why not go for a month to Morpeth? It lies on the banks of the winding Wansbeck, it is but four miles from the ocean; it is quaint, quiet, curious, hills everywhere, wood and water everywhere; it has the remains of a grand old castle on the hill top, and a gaol that looks like one. Accommodation? did you say. What a sublunary thought, but Morpeth has capital lodging-houses and good inns, so there!

We caught our first glimpse of the sea to-day away on our right.

We had hoped to stay at Felton, a romantic little village on the river. Partly in a deep dell it lies, partly on a hill; rocks and wooded knolls with shady walks by the streamlet-side make it well suited for a summer resort, but it is hardly known. Not to Londoners, certainly.

Stabling we could have here, but so hilly is the place that a flat meadow was looked for in vain. After spending a whole hour searching for accommodation I returned to the glen where I had left the Wanderer, and our poor tired horses had to go on again.

Hills, hills, hills, that seemed as if they never would end; hills that take the heart, and life, and spirit out of the horses and make my heart bleed for them. The beauty of the scenery cannot comfort me now, nor the glory of the wild flowers, nor the blue sea itself. We but lag along, hoping, praying, that a hostelry of some sort may soon heave in sight.

I am riding on in front, having often to dismount and push my cycle before me.

All at once on a hilltop, with a beautiful green valley stretching away and away towards the sea, I come upon the cosiest wee Northumbrian inn ever I wish to see. I signal back the joyful tidings to the weary Wanderer.

Yee, there is stabling, and hay, and straw, and everything that can be desired.

“Hurrah! Come on, Bob, I feel as happy now as a gipsy king.”

July 15th.—The drag began this morning in earnest. We were among the banks of Northumbria. (Bank—a stiff hill.) With a light carriage they are bad enough, but with a two-ton waggon, small in wheel and long ’twixt draughts, the labour, not to say danger, reaches a maximum. The country here is what a cockney would term a mountainous one, and in some parts of it even a Scotchman would feel inclined to agree with him. At one time we would be down at the bottom of some gloomy defile, where the road crossed over a Gothic bridge, and a wimpling stream went laughing over its rocky bed till lost to sight among overhanging trees.

Down in that defile we would eye with anxious hearts the terrible climb before us.

“Can we do it?” That is the question.

“We must try.” That is the answer.

The roller is fastened carefully behind a back wheel, and “Hip!” away we go, the horses tearing, tottering, scraping, almost falling.

And now we are up, and pause to look thankfully, fearfully back while the horses stand panting, the sweat running in streamlets over their hoofs.

The short banks are more easily rushed. It is a long steep hill that puts us in danger.

There is hardly probably a worse hill or a more dangerous hollow than that just past the castle gate of Alnwick.

It needed a stout heart to try the descent. Easy indeed that descent would have been had a horse fallen, for neither the brake, which I now had sole charge of, nor the skid, could have prevented the great van from launching downwards.

But the ascent was still more fraught with danger. It was like climbing a roof top. Could the horses do it this time?

Impossible. They stagger half way up, they stagger and claw the awful hill, and stop.

No, not stop, for see, the caravan has taken charge and is moving backwards, dragging the horses down.

The roller and a huge stone beneath the wheels prevented an ugly accident and the complete wreck of the Wanderer. Twelve sturdy Northumbrians went on behind and helped us up. The road ascends higher and higher after we pass Alnwick, until at last we find ourselves on the brow of a lofty hill. There is an eminence to the right covered with young firs; near it is a square tower of great strength, but only a ruin. The traveller who does not see the country from this knoll misses one of the grandest sights in England. From the lone Cheviot mountains on the left to the sea itself on the far-off right round and round it is all beautiful.

I had stayed long enough in Alnwick to see the town and "sights;" the latter is a hateful word, but I have no better ready.

I was greatly impressed by the massive grandeur of the noble old castle, the ancient home of the Percys. The figures of armed men on the ramparts, some holding immense stones above the head, as if about to hurl them on an assailant, others in mail jackets with hatchet and pike, are very telling. I could not help thinking as I passed through the gloomy gateways and barbican of the many prisoners whose feet had brushed these very stones in "the brave days of old."

THE CREW OF THE WANDERER

"His hair, his size, his mouth, his lugs,
Showed he was nane o' Scotland's dogs."
Burns.

While perusing these memoirs of my gipsy life, I should be more than delighted if my readers could to some extent think as I thought, and feel as I felt.

In an early chapter I gave a sketch of the Wanderer herself; let me now give a brief account of its occupants by day. Why I say by day is this: my coachman does not sleep in the caravan, but takes his ease at his inn wherever the horses are stabled. Doubtless, however, when we are far away in the wilder regions of the Scottish Highlands, if it ever be our good fortune to get there safely, John G, my honest Jehu, will have sometimes to wrap himself in his horse rugs and sleep upon the coupé. And we have so many awnings and so much spare canvas that it will be easy enough to make him a covering to defend him from the falling dew.

Having mentioned John G, then, it is perhaps but right that I should give him the preference even to Hurricane Bob, and say a word about him first.

My Jehu John.

When I advertised for a coachman in the Reading Mercury I had no lack of replies. Among these was one from a certain Major B, recommending John. He gave him an excellent character for quietness, steadiness, and sobriety, adding that when I had done with him he would be happy to take him back into his employment.

This was virtually offering me John on loan, and having a soft side for the Queen's service, I at once sent for John G.

When John returned that forenoon to Mapledurham he was engaged. If

John could speak Latin, he might have said,—

"Veni, vidi, vici."

But, with all his other good qualities, John cannot talk Latin.

I was naturally most concerned to know whether my coachman was temperate or not, and I asked him. "I likes my drop o' beer," was John's reply, "but I know when I've enough."

John and myself are about ages, ie, we were both born in her Majesty's reign. John, like myself, is a married man with young bairnies, of whom he is both proud and fond.

John and I have something else in common. We are both country folks, and therefore both love nature. I do not think there is a shrub or tree anywhere about that is not an old friend, or a bird or wild creature in meadow or moorland or wood that we do not know the name and habits of. If we see anything odd about a tree or come to one that seems somewhat strange to us, we stop horses at once, and do not go on again until we have read the arboreal riddle.

John is very quiet and polite, and thoroughly knows his place.

Finally, he is fond of his horses, most careful to groom them well and to see to their feet and pasterns, and if ever the saddle hurts in the least on any particular spot, he is not content until he has eased the pressure.

Next on the list of our crew all told comes—

Alfred Foley.

Foley has reached the mature age of twenty, and I have known him for eight years. To put it in broad but expressive Scotch, Foley is just "a neebour laddie." He has done many odd jobs for me at home as my librarian, clerk, and gardener, and having expressed a wish to follow my fortunes in this long gipsy tour of mine, I have taken him.

Both John and he have regularly signed articles, shipshape and sailor fashion, for the whole cruise; and I mean to be a good captain to both of them.

As Foley at home is in fairly good circumstances of life, and has a kind and religious mother, it is needless to say much about his character. I could trust him with untold gold—if I had it. But here is a greater proof of my trust in his integrity—I can trust him with Hurricane Bob, and Hurricane Bob is more to me than much fine gold.

On board the Wanderer, Foley fills the position of my first lieutenant and secretary; with this he combines the duties of valet and cook, I myself sometimes assisting in the latter capacity. He is also my outrider—on a tricycle—and often my agent in advance.

On the whole he is a good lad. I do not believe he ever flirts with the maids at the bars of the village inns when we buy our modest drop of beer or secure our ginger-ale. And I am certain he reads the Book, and says his prayers every night of his life.

So much for the crew of the Wanderer. Now for the live stock, my companions.

I have already said a word about my horses, Corn-flower and Pear-blossom. We know more about their individual characters now.

Nothing then in the world would annoy or put Corn-flower out of temper. Come hills or come valleys, on rough road and on smooth, walking or at the trot, he goes on with his head in the air, straight fore and aft, heeding nothing, simply doing his duty.

There is far more of the grace and poetry of motion about Pea-blossom. She bobs and tosses her head, and flicks her tail, looking altogether as proud as a hen with one chicken.

If touched with the whip, she immediately nibbles round at Corn-flower's head, as much as to say, "Come on, can't you, you lazy stick? There am I getting touched up with the whip all owing to you. You're not doing your share of the work, and you know it."

But Corn-flower never makes the slightest reply. Pea-blossom is a thorough type of the sex to which she belongs. She is jealous of Corn-flower, pretends not to like him. She would often kick him if she could, but if he is taken out of the stable, and she left, she will almost neigh the house down.

If in a field with Corn-flower, she is constantly imagining that he is getting all the best patches of grass and clover, and keeps nagging at him and chasing him from place to place.

But the contented Corn-flower does not retaliate. For Corn-flower's motto is "Never mind."

Polly—The Cockatoo.

I want my friends—the readers—to know and appreciate my little feathered friend, so far as anyone can to whom she does not grant a private interview. I want them to know her, and yet I feel how difficult it is to describe her—or rather him, though I shall continue to say her—without writing in a goody-goody or old-maidish style. "Never mind," as Corn-flower says, I'll do my best.

Polly's Birth and Parentage.—The bird came about five years ago from the wilds of West Australia, though she has been in my possession but little more than a year. She belongs to the great natural family Psattacidae, and to the soft-billed species of non-crested cockatoos. As regards the softness of her bill, however, it is more imaginary than real, for though she cannot crack a cocoa-nut, she could slit one's nose or lay a finger open to the bone.

I daresay Polly was born in some old log of wood in the bosh, and suffered, as all parrots do coming to this country, from vile food, close confinement, and want of water.

Polly's Personal Appearance.—Having no crest—except when excited—she looks to the ordinary eye a parrot and nothing else. Pure white is she all over except for a garland of crimson across her breast, a blue patch round her wondrous eyes, and the red of the gorcock over the beak. This latter is a curious apparatus; so long and bent is it that the dealers usually call this species of cockatoo "Nosey," which is more expressive than polite.

Polly's Tricks and Manners.—These are altogether very remarkable and quite out of the common run.

No cockatoo that ever I saw would beat a well-trained red-tail grey parrot at talking, but in motion-making and in tricks the latter is nowhere with Nosey.

I place no value on Polly's ordinary tricks, for any cockatoo will shake hands when told, will kiss one or ask to be kissed or scratched, or even dance. This last, however, if with a musical accompaniment, is a very graceful action. Polly also, like other cockatoos, stands on her head, swings by head or feet, etc, etc. But it is her extreme love for music that makes this bird of mine so winning.

When she first came to me she was fierce, vindictive, and sulky. It was the guitar that brought her round. And now when I play either guitar or violin she listens most attentively or beats time with her bill on the bars of the cage.

This she does when I am playing quadrille or waltz, but the following I think very remarkable: Polly cannot stand a Scotch strathspey, and often, when I begin to play one, she commences to imitate a dog and cat fighting, which she does to perfection. Again, if I play a slow or melancholy air on the violin, Polly seems entranced, and sits on her perch with downcast head, with one foot in the air, slowly opening and shutting her fist in time to the music.

Polly plays the guitar with her beak when I hold it close to her cage, ie, she touches the strings while I do the fingering.

I am teaching her to turn a little organ, and soon she will be perfect. Heigho! who knows that when, after a lapse of years, my pen and my gigantic intellect fail me, Polly may not be the prop of my declining years—Polly and the fiddle?

Another of Polly's strange motions is moving her neck as if using a whip. This she always does when she sees boys, so I daresay she knows what boys need.

Her words and sayings are too numerous to mention. She calls for breakfast, for food, for sugar, for supper, etc. She calls Bob and the cat, and imitates both. She calls hens, imitates their being killed, puts them up to auction, and sells them for half-a-crown. She laughs and she sings, words and music both being her own composition.

She drinks from cup, or bottle, or spoon, milk, coffee, or tea, but no beer or ginger-ale.

Her water is merely used to float and steep her seeds or crusts in. When frozen one day last winter, I found her throwing the seeds on top of the ice, and saying, "Poor dear Polly?" in a most mournful tone of voice.

In conclusion, Polly is most affectionate and loving to me, and—

"If to her lot some human errors fall,
Look in her face, and you'll forget them all."

Hurricane Bob.

He is the caravan dog, a noble fellow, straight in coat, and jetty-black, without one curly hair. He is the admired of all beholders.

He has gained prizes enough to entitle him to be dubbed champion according to the older rules. His real or bench name is Theodore Nero the Second. In his day his father was known all over the world.

As to pedigree, Bob's father, grandfather, great-grandfather, and great-great-grandfather were all champions, and he is himself the father of a champion, Mr Farquharson's, MP, celebrated Gunville.

(Vide "Aileen Aroon," by the same author. Published by Messrs Partridge and Co, 9 Paternoster Row, EC.)

In character, Bob—NB: We call him Robert on the Sabbath Day and on bank-holidays—is most gentle and amiable. And though, like all pure Newfoundlands, he is fond of fighting, he will never touch a small dog.

Wherever Bob is seen he is admired, and neither children nor babies are ever afraid of him, while—

"His locked and lettered braw brass collar
Shows him the gentleman and scholar."

The words of North and the Shepherd, in the "Noctes Ambrosianae," come into my head as I write:—

"A dog barks. Shepherd. Heavens! I could hae thocht that was Bronte.

"North. No bark like his, James, now belongs to the world of sound.

"Shepherd. Purple black was he all over, as the raven's wing. Strength and sagacity emboldened his bounding beauty, but a fierceness lay deep down within the quiet lustre o' his een that tauld ye, had he been enraged, he could hae torn in pieces a lion.

"North. Not a child of three years old and upwards in the neighbourhood that had not hung by his mane, and played with his paws, and been affectionately worried by him on the flowery greensward."

Such was Bronte.

Such is Hurricane Bob, only more so.

LETTERS HOME

"Come listen to my humble friends.
Nor scorn to read their letters,
The faithfulness of horse and dog
Oft-times makes us their debtors.
Yet selfish man leads folly's van,
The thought is food for laughter.
He admits all virtues in his 'beast,'
But—denies him a hereafter."

Letter from Polly Pea-Blossom to a Lady-Friend.

NOW fulfil my promise of writing to you, my dear, which you remember I made long ago, saying I should do so at the earliest opportunity. By the way, poor Corn-flower, my pole-mate, spells opportunity with one 'p.' It is quite distressing, my dear, to think how much Captain Corn-flower's education has been neglected in many ways. He is only called 'Captain' by courtesy you know, having never been in the army. Heigho! what a deal of ups and downs one does see in one's life to be sure. Why, it is not more than three years since you and I, my dear, resided in the same big stable, and used to trot great fat old Lady C— to church in that stupid big yellow chariot of hers. And now heigho! the old lady has gone to heaven, or wherever else old ladies do go, and you and I are parted. But often and often now, while housed in some sad unsavoury den, I think of you, my dear, and olden times till tears as big as beans roll over my halter. And I think of that old stable, with its tall doors, its lofty windows, its sweet floors and plaited straw, and the breath of new-mown hay that used to pervade it! Heigho! again.

"I was telling Corn-flower only last night of how I once kicked an unruly, unmannerly nephew of my ladyship's out of the stable door, because he tried to pull hairs out of my tail to make a fishing line. Poor Corn-flower laughed, my dear, and said,—

"'Which ye was always unkimmon ready to kick, Polly, leastways ever since I has a-known ye.'

"He does talk so vulgarly, my dear, that sometimes my blood boils to think that a mare of my blood and birth should be—but there! never mind, Corn-flower has some good points after all. He never loses his temper, even when I kick him and bite him. I only wish he would. If he would only kick me in return, oh, then wouldn't I warm him just! I gave him a few promiscuous kicks before I commenced this letter. He only just sighed and said, 'Ye can't help it, Polly—that ye can't. You're honly a mare and I be a feelosopher, I be's.'

"On the whole, though, I have not much to complain of at present; my master is very kind and my coachman is very careful, and never loses his temper except when I take the bit in my teeth and have my own way for a mile.

"When we start of a morning we never know a bit where we are going to, or what is before us; sometimes it is wet or rainy, and even cold; but bless you, my dear, we are always hungry, that is the best of it, and really I would not change places with any carriage-horse ever I knew. Travelling does improve one's mind so, though heigho! I don't think it has done much yet for the gallant Captain Corn-flower.

"The greatest bother is getting a nice stable. Sometimes these are cool and comfortable enough, but sometimes so close and stuffy one can hardly breathe. Sometimes they smell of hens, and sometimes even of pigs. Isn't that dreadful, my dear? I hate pigs, my dear, and one day, about a month ago, one of these hateful creatures struck my near hind leg with such force that he was instantly converted into pork. As regards bedding, however, John—that is our coachman—does look well out for us, though on more than one occasion we could get nothing better than pea-straw. Now pea-straw may be good enough for Corn-flower, my dear, but not for me; I scorn to lie on it, and stand all night!

"I dearly love hay. Sometimes this is bad enough, but at other times a nice rackful of sweetly-scented meadow hay soothes me, and almost sends me to sleep; it must be like eating the lotus leaf that I hear master speak about.

"Perhaps you would not believe this, my dear—some innkeepers hardly ever clean out their stables. The following is a remark I heard only yesterday. It was a Yorkshireman who made it—

"'Had I known you'd been coming, I'd ha' turned th' fowls out like, and cleaned oop a bit. We generally does clean oop once a year.'

"Sometimes, my dear, the roads are very trying, and what with big hills and thousands of flies it is a wonder on a warm day how I can keep my temper as well as I do.

"But there, my dear, this letter is long enough. We must not grumble, must we, my dear? It is the lot of horses to work and toil, and there may be rest for us in some green hereafter, when our necks are stiffened in death, and our shoes taken off never to be nailed on again.

"Quien sabe? as master says. Quien sabe?

"Your affectionate old friend and stable-mate,—

"Polly Pea-blossom."

II.

From Captain Corn-Flower to Old Dobbin, a Brewer's Horse.

"Dear old Chummie,—Which i said last time i rubbed noses with you At the wagon and hosses, as 'ow i'd rite to you, and which i Now takes the Oportunity, bein' as 'ow i would ha' filled my Promise long Ago, If i was only arf as clever as Polly pea-blossom.

"My shoes! old chummie, but Polly be amazin' 'cute. She is My stable-mate is polly, likewise my pole-companion As you might say. Which her name is polly pea-blossom, all complete. Gee up and away you goes!

"And which I considers it the completest 'onor out to be chums along o' polly, anyhow whatsoever. Gee up and away you goes!

"'You're a lady, polly,' i says, says i, 'and i ain't a gentleman—no, beggar me if i be's.'

"'You sometimes speak the truth,' says polly, she says.

"Which that was a kind o' 2-handed compliment, dear dobbin. Gee up and away you goes!

"Which polly is unkimmin clever, and I allers appeals to polly.

"Which polly often amooses i like, while we Be a-munchin' a bit o' meadow hay, arter we've been and gone and 'ad our jackets brushed, and our Feet washed, and got bedded-up like; Polly allers tells me o' the toime when she were a-pullin' of a big chariat and a-draggin' of a duchess to church, and what a jolly nice stable she lived In, and what fine gold-plated 'arness she used to put on, and Lots else I don't recomember, dobbin, and all in such Fine english, dobbin, as you and i couldn't speak with our bits out. Yes, polly be's unkimmin clever. Gee up and away you goes!

"But 1 nite, dobbin, i says to myself, says i, i'll tell polly summit o' my younger days, so I hits out as follers: 'When i were a-livin' wi' farmer Frogue, polly,' says i, which he were a farmer in a small way, and brew'd a drop o' good beer for the publics all round like, there were me and my mate, a boss called dobbin; and bless your old collar, polly, dobbin were a rare good un, and he'd a-draw'd a tree out by the roots dobbin would. Gee op and away ye goes! And there were old Garge who drov us like, which he Had a fine temper, polly, 'ceptin' when he got a drop too much, then it was whip, whip, whip, all day, up hill and down, and my shoulders is marked till this day. But Old farmer frogue, he comes to the stable once upon a time, which a very fat un were farmer frogue, wi' no legs to speak of like. Well, polly, as I were a sayin', he comes to the stable, and he says to Garge, 'Garge,' says he—

"But would you believe it, dear dobbin? I never got further on with my story like.

"'Oh! bother you,' cries polly, a-tossin o' her mane that proud like. 'Do you imagine for a moment that a born lady like me is interested in your Dobbins, and your Garges, and your fat old farmer Frogues? You're a vulgar old horse, Corn-flower.'

"Gee op, says i, and away ye goes!

"And polly ups wi' her hind foot and splinters the partition, and master had to pay for that, which polly is amazin' clever at doin' a kick like.

"But I likes polly unkimmon, and polly likes i, and though she bites and kicks she do be unhappy when i goes away to be shoed. Which I never loses my temper, dobbin, whatsomever. Gee up and away ye goes!

"Which we never funks a hill though, neither on us. When we Comes to a pertikler stiff un like i just appeals to polly.

"'Pull up,' says Polly, says she, 'every hill has a top to it; pull up, you old hass, pull op!'

"Sometimes the hay we gets ain't the sweetest o' perfoomery, dobbin, old chummie; then I appeals to polly, cause you see if polly can eat it so kin i.

"Sometimes we meet the tractive hengine; i never liked it, and what's more i never will. It seems unnatural like, so i appeals to polly.

"'What's the krect thing to do, polly?' i says, says i; 'shall us kick or shall us bolt?'

"'Come straight on, ye hold fool,' says polly pea-blossom, says she.

"Gee up, says i, and away ye goes!

"Which i must now dror to a klose, dobbin, and which i does hope you'll allers have a good home and good shoes, dobbin, till you're marched to the knacker's. Gee up and away ye goes!—

"Good-bye, dobbin, polly's gone to sleep, and master is a-playin' the fiddle so soft and low like, in the meadow beyant yonder, which it allers does make me think o' what the parson's old pony once told me, dobbin, o' a land where old hosses were taken to arter they were shot and their shoes taken off, a land o' green meadows, dobbin, and a sweet quiet river a-rollin' by, and long rows o' wavin' pollards like, with nothing to do all day, no 'arness to wear, no bit to hurt or rein to gall. Think o' that, dobbin. Good-bye, dobbin—there goes the moosic again, so sweet and tremblin' and sobbin'-like. i'm goin' to listen and dream.

"Yours kindly,—

"Poor old Corn-flower."

III.

From Polly the Cockatoo to Dick the Starling.

"Dear Dick,—If you weren't the cleverest starling that ever talked or flew, with a coat all shiny with crimson and blue, I wouldn't waste a tail feather in writing to you.

"You must know, Dick, that there are two Pollys on this wandering expedition, Polly the mare, Polly Pea-blossom, and Polly the pretty cockatoo, that's me, though however master could have thought of making me godmother to an old mare, goodness only knows. Ha! ha! ha! it makes me laugh to think of it.

"They do say that I'm the happiest, and the prettiest, and the merriest bird, that ever yet was born, and I won't be five till next birthday, though what I shall be before I am a hundred is more than I can think.

"Yes, I'll live to a hundred, cockatoos all do; then my body will drop off the perch, and my soul will go into something else—ha! ha! ha! Wouldn't you laugh too, if you had to live for a hundred years?

"All that time in a cage, with only a run out once a day, and a row with the cat! Yes, all that time, and why not? What's the odds so long as you're happy? Ha! ha! ha!

"I confess I do dream sometimes of the wild dark forest lands of Australia, and I think at times I would like to lead a life of freedom away in the woods yonder, just as the rooks and the pigeons do. Dash my bill! Dick, but I would make it warm for some of them in the woods—ha! ha! ha!

"Sometimes when the sparrows—they are cheeky enough for anything—come close to my cage, I give vent to what master calls my war-cry, and they almost drop dead with fright.

"'Scray!' that's my war-cry, and it is louder than a railway whistle, and shriller than a bagpipe.

"'Scray! Scray! Scray—ay—ay!'

"That's it again.

"Master has just pitched a 'Bradshaw' at my cage. I'll tear that 'Bradshaw' to bits first chance I have.

"Master says my war-cry is the worst of me. It is so startling, he says.

"That's just where it is—what would be the use of a war-cry if it weren't startling? Eh, Dick?

"Now out in the Australian jungles, this war-cry is the only defence we poor cockatoos have against the venomous snakes.

"The snakes come gliding up the tree.

"'Scray! Scray!!' we scream, and away they squirm.

"A hundred years in a cage, or chained by a foot to a perch! A hundred years, Dick! It does seem a long time.

"But the other day, when master put my cage on the grass, I just opened the fastening, and out I hopped. Ha! ha! ha! There were butterflies floating about, and bees on the flowering linden trees, and birds singing, and wild rabbits washing their faces with their forefeet among the green ferns, and every creature seemed as happy as the summer day is long. I did have an hour's good fun in the woods, I can tell you. I caught a bird and killed it; I caught a mouse and crunched it up; and I scared some pigeons nearly to death, for they took me for an owl. Then an ugly man in a velvet jacket fired a gun at me, and I flew away back to my cage.

"I wouldn't have got much to eat in the woods, and there is always corn in Egypt.

"But hanging up here in the verandah of the Wanderer is fine fun. I see so many strange birds, and so many strange children. I dote on children, and I sing and I dance to them, and sometimes make a grab at their noses.

"Hullo! Dick. Why, the door of my cage is open! Master has gone out.

"I am going out too, Dick.

"I've been out, Dick. I have had a walk round the saloon. I've torn 'Bradshaw' all to pieces. I made a grab at Hurricane Bob's tail, and the brute nearly bit my head off. Just as if his tail was of any consequence! I've been playing the guitar, and cut all the strings in two. I've pitched a basket of flowers on the carpet, and I've spilt the ink all over them, and I've danced upon them; and torn master's letters up, and enjoyed myself most thoroughly. Ha! ha! ha! Master's face will be as long as his fiddle when he comes back.

"'Scray! Scray! Scray—ay—ay!'

"Well, no more at present, Dick my darling. I never tried to pull your tail off, did I? I don't think I have done very much harm in this world, and I never say naughty words, so, perhaps, when my hundred years are over, and my body drops off the perch, my soul will go into something very nice indeed.

"Ha! ha! ha!

"Scray! Scray!! Scray!!!

"Poor Polly."

IV.

From Hurricane Bob to his Kennel-Mate Eily.

"You said in your last, dear Eily, that you wanted to know how I enjoyed my gipsy life, and the answer is, 'out and out,' or rather, 'out and in,' outside the caravan and inside the caravan. If there be a happier dog than myself in all the kingdom of kenneldom, let him come right up and show himself, and the probability is we'll fight about it right away.

"Well, you see, I don't take many notes by the way, but I notice everything for all that.

"First thing in the morning I have my breakfast and a trot out.

"It pains me though to see so many poor dogs muzzled. I am sure that Carlyle was right, and that most men—especially magistrates—are fools. Wouldn't I like to see some of them muzzled just?—the magistrates, I mean.

"Every dog on the street makes room for me, and if they don't—you know what I mean, Eily.

"The other day a Scotch collie—and you know, Eily, you are the only Scotch collie I could ever bear—walked up to me on the cliff-top at Filey, and put up his back. As he did not lower his tail, I went straight for him, and it would have done you good to see how I shook him. There was a big dandy on me too, and as soon as I had quietened the collie I opened the dandy up. My bites are nearly well, and I am quite prepared for another fight. I won't allow any dog in the world to come spooning round my master.

"We travel many and many a long mile, Eily, and I am generally tired before the day is done, but at night there is another long walk or a run behind the tricycle. Then a tumble on the greensward; sometimes it is covered all over with beautiful flowers, prettier than any carpet you ever lay upon.

"Everybody is so kind to me, and the ladies fondle me and say such pretty things to me. I wonder they don't fondle master and say pretty things to him. I wish they would.

"Good-bye, Eily. There is a tramp coming skulking round the caravan, and I don't like his looks.

"'R-r-r-r-bow! Wow-w!'

"He is gone, Eily. Good-bye, take care of master's children till we all come back.

"Yours right faithfully,—

"Hurricane Bob."

V.

From the Author to his Good Friend C.A.W.

(C.A. Wheeler, Esq, of Swindon, the clever author of "Sports-scrapiana," etc, etc.)

"The Wanderer Caravan,—

"Touring in Notts,—

"July 28, 1886.

"My dearly-beloved Caw,—For not writing to you before now I must make the excuse the Scotch lassie made to her lover—'I've been thinkin' aboot ye, Johnnie lad.' And so in my wanderings I often think of thee and thine, poor old Sam included; and my mind reverts to your cosy parlour in Swindon, Nellie in the armchair, Sam on the footstool, my Hurricane Bob on the hearth, and you and I viewing each other's smiling faces through the vapour that ascends from a duality of jorums of real Highland tartan toddy.

"Yes, I've been thinking of you, but I have likewise been busy. There is a deal to be done in a caravan, even if I hadn't my literary connection to keep up, and half-a-dozen serieses to carry on. You must know that a gentleman gipsy's life isn't all beer and skittles. Take the doings of one day as an example, my Caw. The Wanderer has been lying on the greensward all night, we will say, close by a little country village inn. Crowds gathered round us last night, lured by curiosity and the dulcet tones of your humble servant's fiddle and valet's flute, but soon, as we loyally played 'God save the Queen,' the rustics melted away, our shutters were put up, and soon there was no sound to be heard save the occasional hooting of a brown owl, and the sighing of the west wind through a thicket of firs. We slept the sleep of gipsies, or of the just, the valet in the after-cabin, I in the saloon, my faithful Newfoundland at my side. If a step but comes near the caravan at night, the deep bass, ominous growl that shakes the ship from stem to stern shows that this grand old dog is ready for business.

"But soon as the little hands of the clock point to six, my eyes open mechanically, as it were, Bob gets up and stretches himself, and, ere ever the smoke from the village chimneys begins to roll up through the green of the trees, we are all astir. The bath-tent is speedily pitched, and breakfast is being prepared. No need of tonic bitters to give a gipsy an appetite, the fresh, pure air does that, albeit that frizzly ham and those milky, newborn eggs, with white bread and the countriest of country butter, would draw water from the teeth of a hand-saw. Breakfast over, my Caw, while I write on the coupé and Bob rolls exultant on the grass, my valet is carefully washing decks, dusting, and tidying, and the coachman is once more carefully grooming Captain Corn-flower and Polly Pea-blossom.

"It will be half-past eight before the saloon and after-cabin are thoroughly in order, for the Wanderer is quite a Pullman car and lady's boudoir, minus the lady. Then, my old friend, visitors will begin to drop in, and probably for nearly an hour I am holding a kind of levée. It is a species of lionising that I have now got hardened to. Everybody admires everything, and I have to answer the same kind of questions day after day. It is nice, however, to find people who know me and have read my writings in every village in the kingdom. Hurricane Bob, of course, comes in for a big share of admiration. He gets showers of kisses, and many a fair cheek rests lovingly on his bonnie brow. I have to be content with smiles and glances, flowers and fruit, and eggs and new potatoes. The other day a handsome salmon came. It was a broiling hot day. The salmon said he must be eaten fresh. I was equal to the occasion. The lordly fish was cooked, the crew of the Wanderer, all told, gathered around him on the grass, and soon he had to change his tense—from the present to the past.

"The other day pigeons came. My valet plucked them, and the day being windy, and he, knowing no better, did the work standing, and, lor! how the feathers flew. It was a rain of feathers, and a reign of terror, for the ladies passing to the station had to put up their umbrellas.

"But the steps are up, the horses are in, good-byes said, hands are waved by the kindly crowd, and away we rattle. My place is ever on the coupé, notebook in hand.

"'A chiel's among ye,' etc.

"My valet is riding on ahead on the tricycle. This year it is the charming 'Marlborough,' which is such a pleasant one to ride. On and on, now we go, through the beautiful country; something to attract our attention at every hundred yards. Heavens! my dear Caw, how little those who travel by train know of the delights of the road. We trot along while on level roads, we madly rush the short, steep hills at a glorious gallop, we crawl up the long, bad hills, and carefully—with skid and chain on the near hind wheel—we stagger down the break-neck 'pinches.' The brake is a powerful one, and in bad countries is in constant use, so that its brass handle shines like gold, and my arm aches ere night with putting it on and off.

"Well, there is a midday halt after ten miles, generally on the roadside near water. We have a modest lunch of hard-boiled eggs, milk, beer, cheese, bread, and crushed oats and a bit of clover. Then on and on again. By five we have probably settled for the night, when dinner is prepared. We hardly need supper, and what with the rattling along all day, and the hum of the great van—with running and riding, and studying natural history and phenomena, including faces—I am tired, and so are we all, by nine o'clock.

"But we generally have music before then. I have a small harmonium, a guitar, and a fiddle, and my valet plays well on the flute.

"'Then comes still evening on.'

"The bats and owls come out, and we retire.

"Of weather we have all varieties—the hot and the cool, the rain that rattles on the roof, the wind that makes the Wanderer rock, and the occasional thunderstorm. One dark night last week—we were in a lonely place—I sat out on the coupé till one o'clock—'the wee short hoor ayont the twal'—watching the vivid blue lightning, that curled like fiery snakes among the trees. By the way, I had nothing on but my night-shirt, and a dread spectre I must have appeared to anyone passing, seen but for a moment in the lightning's flash, then gone. I marvelled next day that I had caught a slight cold.

"I love little, quiet meadows, Caw. I dote on rural villages, and hate big towns. If the caravan is not lying on the grass there is no comfort.

"I lay last night in the cosiest meadow ever I have been in. The very rural hamlet of Bunny, Notts, is a quarter of a mile away, but all the world is screened away from me with trees and hedges. I have for meadow-mates two intelligent cows, who can't quite make us out. They couldn't make Bob out either, till in the zeal of his guardianship he got one of them by the tail. There is in this hamlet of three hundred souls one inn—it is tottering to decay—a pound, a police-station, and a church. The church is ever so old, the weather-cock has long been blown down, and the clock has stopped for ever. The whole village is about as lively and bright as a farthing candle

stuck in an empty beer bottle.
"But here come the horses. Good-bye till we meet.
"Gordon Stables,—
"Ye Gentleman Gipsy."

THE HUMOURS OF THE ROAD

"I am as free as Nature first made man,
Ere the base laws of servitude began,
When wild in woods the noble savage ran."
Dryden.

Madly dashing on through the country as cyclists do, on their way to John o' Groats or elsewhere, probably at an average rate of seventy miles a day, neither scenery nor anything else can be either enjoyed or appreciated.

The cyclist arrives in the evening at his inn, tired, dusty, and disagreeably damp as to underclothing. He has now no other wish except to dine and go to bed. Morning sees him in the saddle again, whirring ever onwards to the distant goal.

He is doing a record. Let him. For him the birds sing not in woodland or copse; for him no wild flowers spring; he pauses not to listen to hum of bee or murmur of brooklet, nor to admire the beauties of heathy hills, purple with the glorious heather, or bosky dells, green with feathery larch or silvery birch; nor does he see the rolling cloudscapes, with their rifts of blue between. On—on—on—his way is ever on.

But gipsy-folks, like myself, jogging along at a quiet six-or-seven-miles-an-hour pace, observe and note everything. And it is surprising what trifles amuse us.

Although I constantly took notes from the coupé, or from my cycle saddle, and now and then made rough sketches, I can in these pages only give samples from these notes.

A volume could be written on public-house or inn signs, for example.

Another on strange names.

A third on trees.

A fourth on water—lakes, brooklets, rivers, cataracts, and mill-streams.

A fifth upon faces.

And so on, ad libitum.

As to signs, many are curious enough, but there is a considerable amount of sameness about many. You meet Red Lions, White Harts, Kings' Arms, Dukes' Arms, Cricketers' Arms, and arms of all sorts everywhere, and Woolpacks, and Eagles, and Rising Suns, ad nauseam.

The sign of a five-barred gate hung out is not uncommon in the Midland Counties, with the following doggerel verse:—

"This gate hangs well,
And hinders none;
Refresh and pay,
And travel on."

Although the Wanderer is nearly always taken for what she is—a private carriage on a large scale—still it is amusing sometimes to note what I am mistaken for, to wit:—

1. "General" in the Salvation Army.
2. Surgeon-attendant on a nervous old lady who is supposed to be inside.
3. A travelling artist.
4. A photographer.
5. A menagerie.
6. A Cheap-Jack.
7. A Bible carriage.
8. A madman.
9. An eccentric baronet.
10. A political agent.
11. Lord E.
12. Some other "nob."
13. And last, but not least, King of the Gipsies.

It must not be supposed that I mind a single bit what people think of me, so long as I have a quiet, comfortable meadow to stand in at night and a good stable for Corn-flower and Pea-blossom. But how would you like, reader, to be taken for a travelling show, and to make your way through a village followed by a crowd of admiring children, counting their pence, and wondering when you were going to open?

Polly's cage would occasionally be hanging from the verandah over the coupé, with Hurricane Bob lying on his rug, and I would hear such remarks as these from the juvenile crowd:—

"Oh! look at his long moustache."

"Oh! look at his hat, Mary."

"Susan, Susan, look at the Poll parrot."

"Look! it is holding a biscuit in its hand."

"Look at the bear."

"No, it's a dog."
"You're a hass! it's a bear."
"Lift me up to see, Tildie."
"Lift me up too."
Here again is my coachman being interviewed by some country bumpkins:—"Who be your master, matie?"
"A private gentleman."
"Is he a Liberal?"
"No."
"Is he a Tory?"
"Perhaps."
"Is he a Salvationist?"
"Not much."
"What does he do?"
"Nothing."
"What does he keep?"
"The Sabbath."
"Got anything to sell?"
"No! Do you take us for Cheap-Jacks?"
"Got anything to give away, then?" It will be observed that even a gentleman gipsy's life has its drawbacks, but not many. One, however, is a deficiency of privacy. For instance, though I have on board both a guitar and fiddle, I can neither play nor sing so much of an evening as I would like to do, because a little mob always gathers round to listen, and I might just as well be on the stage. But in quiet country places I have often, when I saw I was not unappreciated, played and sang just because they seemed to like it.
The faces I see on the road are often a study in themselves, and one might really make a kind of classification of those that are constantly recurring. I have only space to give a sample from memory.
1. This face to me is not a pleasing memory. It is that of the severe-looking female in a low pony carriage. She may or may not be an old maid. Very likely she is; and no wonder, for she is flat-faced and painfully plain. Beside her sits her companion, and behind her a man in a cheap livery; while she herself handles the ribbons, driving a rough, independent, self-willed pony. These people sternly refuse to look at us. They turn away their eyes from beholding vanity; or they take us for real gipsies—"worse than even actors." I can easily imagine some of the items of the home life of this party: the tidily kept garden; the old gardener, who also cleans the boots and waits at table; the stuffy little parlour, with the windows always down; the fat Pomeranian dog; the tabby cat; and the occasional "muffin shines," as Yankees call them, where bad tea is served—bad tea and ruined reputations. Avast! old lady; the sun shines more brightly when you are out of sight.
2. The joskin or country lout. He stops to stare. Probably he has a pitchfork

in his hand. On his face is a wondering, half-amused smile, but his eyes are so wide open that he looks scared. His mouth is open, too, and big enough apparently to hold a mangel-wurzel.

Go on, Garge; we won't harm thee, lad.

3. Cottage folks of all kinds and colours. Look at the weary face of that woman with the weary-looking baby on her arm. The husband is smoking a dirty pipe, but he smiles on us as we go whirling past; and his children, a-squat in the gutter, leave their mud pies and sing and shout and scream at us, waving their dusty hats and their little brown arms in the air.

4. Honest John Bull himself, sure enough, well-to-do-looking in face and dress. He smiles admiringly at us, and seems really to want us to know that he takes an interest in us and our mode of life.

5. The ubiquitous boarding-school girl of gentle seventeen. It may not be etiquette, she knows, to stare or look at passers-by, but for this once only she will have a glance. Lamps shimmering crimson through the big windows, and nicely draped curtains! how can she help it? We are glad she does not try to; her sweet young face refreshes us as do flowers in June, and we forget all about the severe-looking female, who turned away her eyes from beholding vanity.

Milestones and Finger-Posts.

England is the land of finger-posts and disreputable milestones. It is the land of lanes, and that is the reason finger-posts are so much needed.

In Scotland they keep up a decent set of milestones, but they do not affect finger-posts. If you want to know the road, climb a hill and look; or ask. In the wildest parts of the Highlands, about Dalwhinnie for instance, you have snow-posts. These look quite out of place in summer, but in winter you must steer straight from one to the other, else, as there is no vestige of a fence, you may tumble over the adjoining precipice.

Like the faces we meet on the roads, we have also types of milestones and finger-posts. Of the former we have—

1. The squat milestone, of stone (page 69).
2. The parallelogram milestone, of stone (page 115).
3. The triangular milestone, also of stone, with reading on two sides (page 124).
4. The round-headed, dilapidated milestone, that tells you nothing (page 141).
5. The wedge-shaped milestone, stone with an iron slab let in (page 159).
6. The reticent milestone, which, instead of names, only gives you letters (page 169).
7. The mushroom milestone, of iron. Forgive the Irish bull. This milestone grows at Nottingham (page 178). So also does—
8. The respectable iron milestone (page 208).
9. The aesthetic milestone, of iron, and found only in the border-land (page

219).

Of finger-posts I shall mention three types:—

1. The solid and respectable.
2. The limp and uncertain.
3. The aesthetic.

But what have we here? A milestone? Nay, but a murder-stone.

I stop the caravan and get down to look and to read the inscription, the gist of which is as follows:

"This stone was erected to mark the spot where Eliza Shepherd, aetat 17, was cruelly murdered in 1817."

I gaze around me. It is a lovely day, with large white cumulus clouds rolling lazily over a brilliant blue sky. It is a lonely but a lovely place, a fairy-like ferny hollow, close to the edge of a dark wood.

Yes, it is a lovely place now in the sunlight, but I cannot help thinking of that terrible night when poor young Eliza, returning from the shoemaker's shop, met that tramp who with his knife did the ugly deed. It is satisfactory to learn that he swung for it on the gallows-tree.

But here is a notice-board worth looking at. It is a warning to dog-owners. It reads thus:—

"Notis
Trespassers will be prosecuted
dowgs will be shote."

On a weird-looking tree behind it hangs a dead cur by the tail.

Here is a Highland post-office, simply a little red-painted dog-kennel on the top of a pole, standing all alone in the middle of a bleak moorland.

Tramps.

We meet these everywhere, but more especially on the great highway between Scotland and the South.

While cruising on the coast of Africa, in open boats, wherever we found cocoa-nut trees growing, there we found inhabitants; and so on the roads of England, wherever you find telegraph poles, you will find tramps.

They are of both sexes, and of all sorts and sizes; and, remember, I am not alluding to itinerant gipsies, or even to tinkers, but to the vast army of homeless nomads, who wander from place to place during all the sweet summer weather, and seem to like it.

Sometimes they sell trinkets, such as paper and pins, combs, or trashy jewellery, sometimes they get a day's work here and there, but mostly they "cadge," and their characters can be summed up in two words—"liars and vagabonds." There are honest men on the march among them, however, tradesmen out of work, and flitting south or north in the hopes of bettering their condition. But these latter seldom beg, and if they do, they talk intelligible English.

If a man comes to the back door of your caravan and addresses you thus:

"Chuck us a dollop o' stale tommy, guv'nor, will yer?" you may put him down as a professional tramp. But if you really are an honest tramp, reader—that is, a ragged pedestrian, a pedestrian minus purple and fine linen—then I readily admit that there is something to be said in favour of your peculiar kind of life after all.

To loll about on sunshiny days, to recline upon green mossy banks and dreamily chew the stalks of tender glasses, to saunter on and on and never know nor care what or where you are coming to, to gaze upon and enjoy the beautiful scenery, to listen to song of wild bird and drowsy hum of bee,—all this is pleasant enough, it must be confessed.

Then you can drink of the running stream, unless, as often happens, fortune throws the price of a pint of cold fourpenny in your way. And you have plenty of fresh air. "Too much," do you say? Yes, because it makes you hungry; but then, there are plenty of turnip fields. Besides, if you call at a cottage, and put on a pitiful face, you will nearly always find some one to "chuck you a dollop o' stale tommy."

Do you long for society? There is plenty on the road, plenty of people in the same boat.

And you are your own master; you are as free as the wind that bloweth where it listeth, unless indeed a policeman attempts to check your liberty. But he may not be able to prefer a charge against you; and if he ever goes so far as to lock you up on suspicion, it is only a temporary change in your modus vivendi; you are well-housed and fed for a week or two, then—out and away again.

When night comes on, and the evening star glints out of the himmel-blue, you can generally manage to creep into a shed or shieling of some sort; and if not, you have only to fall back upon the cosy hayrick.

Oh! I believe there are worse lives than yours; and if I were not a gipsy, I am not sure I would not turn a tramp myself.

The Man with the Iron Mask.

We came across him frequently away up in the north of England, and a mysterious-looking individual he is, nearly always old, say on the shady side of sixty.

There he sits now on a little three-legged stool by the wayside. In front of him is a kind of anvil, in his hand a hammer. To his right is a heap of stones mingled with gravel; from this he fills a mounted sieve, and rakes the stones therefrom with his hammer as he wants them.

The iron mask is to protect his face and eyes, and a curious spectacle he looks. He has probably been sitting there since morning, but as soon as the shades of evening fall, he will take up his stool and his hammer and wend his way homewards to his little cottage in the glen, and it is to be hoped his "old 'ooman" will have something nice ready for his supper.

The Scotch Collie Dog.

Where will you find a dog with a more honest and open countenance than Collie, or one more energetic and willing, or more devoted to his master's interest? Says Bobbie Burns in his "Twa Dogs:"

"The other was a ploughman's collie.
* * * * *
He was a gash (wise) and faithfu' tyke,
As ever lap a sheugh (ditch) or dyke.
His honest sonsy bawan't (white-striped) face,
Ay gat him friends in ilka place;
His breast was white, his towsie back
Weel clad wi' coat o' glossy black,
His gawcie tail, wi' upward curl,
Hung o'er his hurdils wi' a swirl."

You find the collie everywhere all over broad Scotland. The only place where I do not like to see him is on chain.

Yonder he is even now trotting merrily on in front of that farmer's gig, sometimes barking with half-hysterical joy, sometimes jumping up and kissing the old mare's soft brown nose, by way of encouraging her.

Yonder again, standing on the top of a stone fence herding cows, and suspiciously eyeing every stranger who passes. He is giving us a line of his mind even now. He says we are only gipsy-folk, and no doubt want to steal a cow and take her away in the caravan.

There runs a collie assisting a sheep-drover. There trots another at the heels of a flock of cattle.

Another is out in the field up there watching the people making hay, while still another is lying on his master's coat, while that master is at work. His master is only a ditcher. What does that matter? He is a king to Collie.

At Aberuthven was a retriever-collie who—his master, at whose farm I lay, told me—went every day down the long loaning to fetch the letters when the postman blew his horn. This dog's name is Fred, and it was Fred's own father who taught him this, and "in two lessons" Fred's father always went for the letters, and never failed except once to bring them. On this particular occasion, he was seen to disappear behind a bush with a letter in his mouth, and presently to come forth without it. No trace of it was to be found. But a week after another letter was received asking the farmer why he had not acknowledged the bride's cake. So the murder was out, for the dog's honesty had not been proof against a bit of cake, and he had swallowed it, envelope and all.

Gipsies' Dogs.

These are, as a rule, a mongrel lot, but very faithful, and contented with their roving life. They are as follows:—

1. The bulldog, used for guard and for fighting, with "a bit o' money on him" sometimes.

2. The retriever, a useful and determined guard dog and child's companion.
3. The big mongrel mastiff. The fatter and the uglier he is the better, and the greater the sensation he will create in country villages.
4. The whippet: a handy dog in many ways; and to him gipsies are indebted for many a good stew of hare or rabbit.
5. Lastly, the terribly fat, immensely big black Russian retriever. His tail is always cut off to make him resemble a bear, and give an air of greater éclat to the caravan that owns him.

A Midnight Attack on the "Wanderer."

We were lying in a lonely meadow, in a rough country away up on the borders of Yorkshire, and did not consider ourselves by any means in a very safe place. The Wanderer was pretty close to the roadside; and there were no houses about except a questionable-looking inn, that stood on the borders of a gloomy wood. The people here might or might not be villainous. At all events, it was not on their account we were uneasy. But a gang of the worst class of gipsies was to pass that night from a neighbouring fair, and there was a probability that they might attack the carriage.

Foley before lying down barricaded the back door with the large Rippingille stove, and I myself had seen to the chambers of my revolver, all six of them.

I had one lookout before lying down. It was a still and sultry summer's night, with clouds all over the stars, so that it was almost dark. In ten minutes more I was sound asleep.

It must have been long past midnight when I awoke with a start.

Hurricane Bob was growling low and ominously; I could distinctly hear footsteps, and thought I could distinguish voices confabbing in whispers near the van.

It was almost pitch dark now, and from the closeness of the night it was evident a thunderstorm would burst over us.

Silencing the dog, I quickly got on my clothes, just as the caravan began to shake and quiver, as if some one were breaking open the after-door.

My mind was made up at once. I determined to carry the war into the enemy's quarters, so, seizing my sword, I quietly opened the front door, and slid down to the ground off the coupé.

I got in beneath the caravan and crept aft. There they were, whoever they were; I could just perceive two pairs of legs close to the caravan, and these legs were arrayed in what seemed to me to be white duck trousers. "Now," said I to myself, "the shin is a most vulnerable part; I'll have a hack at these extremities with the back of the sword."

And so I did.

I hit out with all my might.

The effect was magical.

There was a load roar of pain, and away galloped the midnight marauders, in a wild and startled stampede.

And who were they after all? Why, only a couple of young steers, who had been chewing a bath towel—one at one end, the other at the other—that Foley had left hanging under the van.

Such then are some of the humours of an amateur gipsy's life.

SUNNY MEMORIES OF THE BORDER-LAND

"Pipe of Northumbria, sound;
War pipe of Alnwicke,
Wake the wild hills around;
Percy at Paynim war.
Fenwicke stand foremost;
Scots in array from far
Swell wide their war-host.
"Come clad in your steel jack,
Your war gear in order,
And down hew or drive back
The Scots o'er the border."
Old Ballad.

"I tell you what it is, my boy," said a well-known London editor to me one day, shortly before I started on my long tour in the Wanderer,—"I tell you what it is, you'll never do it."

He was standing a little way off my caravan as he spoke, so as to be able to take her all in, optically, and his head was cocked a-trifle to one side, consideringly. "Never do what?"

"Never reach Scotland."

"Why?"

"Why? First, because a two-ton caravan is too much for even two such horses as you have, considering the hills you will have to encounter; and, secondly," he added with a sly smile, "because Scotchman never 'gang back.'"

I seized that little world-wise editor just above the elbow. He looked beseechingly up at me.

"Let go?" he cried; "your fingers are made of iron fencing; my arm isn't."

"Can you for one moment imagine," I said, "what the condition of this England of yours would be were all the Scotchmen to be suddenly taken out of it; suddenly to disappear from great cities like Manchester and Liverpool, from posts of highest duty in London itself, from the Navy, from the Army, from the Volunteers? Is the bare idea not calculated to induce a more dreadful nightmare than even a lobster salad?"

"I think," said the editor, quietly, as I released him, "we might manage to meet the difficulty."

But despite the dark forebodings of my neighbours and the insinuations of this editor, here I am in bonnie Scotland.

"My foot in on my native heath,
And my name is—"

Well, the reader knows what my name is.

I have pleasant recollections of my last day or two's drive in Northumberland north, just before entering my native land.

Say from the Blue Bell Hotel at Belford. What a stir there was in that pretty little town, to be sure! We were well out of it, because I got the Wanderer brought to anchor in an immensely large stackyard. There was the sound of the circus's brass band coming from a field some distance off, the occasional whoop-la! of the merry-go-rounds and patent-swing folks, and the bang-banging of rifles at the itinerant shooting galleries; but that was all there was to disturb us.

I couldn't help thinking that I never saw brawnier, wirier men than those young farmers who met Earl P— at his political meeting.

I remember being somewhat annoyed at having to start in a procession of gipsy vans, but glad when we got up the hill, and when Pea-blossom and Corn-flower gave them all the slip.

Then the splendid country we passed through; the blue sea away on our right; away to the left the everlasting hills! The long low shores of the Holy Isle flanked by its square-towered castle. It is high water while we pass, and Lindisfarne is wholly an island.

"Stay, coachman, stay; let us think; let us dream; let us imagine ourselves back in the days of long, long ago. Yonder island, my Jehu John, which is now so peacefully slumbering 'neath the midday sun, half shrouded in the blue mist of distance, its lordly castle only a shape, its priory now hidden from our view—

"'The castle with its battled walls,
The ancient monastery's halls,
Yon solemn, huge, and dark-red pile,
Placed on the margin of the isle.'

"—Have a history, my gentle Jehu, far more worthy of being listened to than any romance that has ever been conceived or penned.

"Aidan the Christian lived and laboured yonder; from his home in that lone, surf-beaten island scintillated, as from a star, the primitive rays of our religion of love."

Jehu John (speaks): "Excuse me, sir, but that is all a kind o' Greek to me."

"Knowest thou not, my gentle John, that more than a thousand years ago that monastery was built there, that—

"'In Saxon strength that abbey frowned
With massive arches broad and round,
That rose alternate row and row
On pond'rous columns short and low,
Built ere the art was known,
By pointed aisle and shafted stalk
The arcades of an alleyed walk
To emulate in stone.
On those deep walls the heathen Dane
Had poured his impious rage in vain.'

"Hast never heard of Saint Cuthbert?"

"No, sir; can't say as ever I has."

"John! John! John! But that wondrous, that 'mutable and unreasonable saint' dwelt yonder, nor after death did he rest, John, but was seen by many in divers places and at divers times in this kingdom of Britain the Great! Have you never heard the legend that he sailed down the Tweed in a huge stone coffin?"

"Ha! ha! I can't quite swallow that, sir."

"That his figure may even until this day be seen, that—

"'On a rock by Lindisfarne
Saint Cuthbert sits and toils to frame
The sea-born beads that bear his name.
Such tales had Whitby's fishers told,
And said they might his shape behold,
And hear his anvil sound:
A deadened clang—a huge dim form
Seen but, and heard, when gathering storm
And night were closing round.'"

"It makes me a kind of eerie, sir, to hear you talk like that."

"I can't help it, John; the poetry of the Great Wizard of the North seems still to hang around these shores. I hear it in the leaves that whisper to the winds, in the wild scream of the sea-birds, and in the surf that comes murmuring across that stretch of sand, or goes hissing round the weed-clad rocks.

"But, John, you've heard of Grace Darling?"

"Ah! there I do feel at home."

"Then you know the story. At the Longstone Lighthouse out yonder she lived. You see the castle of Bamburgh, with its square tower, there. We noticed it all day yesterday while coming to Belford; first we took it for a lighthouse, then for a church, but finally a bright stream of sunshine fell on it from behind a cloud—on it, and on it alone, and suddenly we knew it. Well, in the churchyard there the lassie sleeps."

"Indeed, sir!"

"Shall we drop a tear to her memory, my gentle Jehu?"

"Don't think I could screw one out, sir."

"Then drive on, John."

I remember stopping at a queer old-fashioned Northumbrian inn for the midday halt. We just drew up at the other side of the road. It was a very lonely place. The inn, with its byres and stables, was perched on the top of a rocky hill, and men and horses had to climb like cats to get up to the doors. By the way, my horses do climb in a wonderful way. Whenever any one now says to me, "There is a terrible hill a few miles on," "Can a cat get up?" I inquire.

"Oh, yes, sir; a cat could go up," is the answer.

"Then," say I, "my horses will do it."

At this inn was a very, very old man, and a very, very old woman, and their son Brad. Brad was waiter, ostler, everything, tall, slow, and canny-looking. Brad, like most of the people hereabout, spoke as though he had swallowed a raw potato, and it had stuck in his throat.

Even the North Northumbrian girls talk as if they suffered from chronic tonsillitis, or their tongues were too broad at the base.

When the dinner had been discussed, the dishes washed, and I had had a rest, the horses staggered down the hill and were put in.

I said to Brad, "How much, my friend?"

"Whhateveh yew plhease, sirr; you'gh a ghentleman," replied Brad, trying apparently to swallow his tongue. I gave him two shillings.

No sooner had it been put in his trousers pocket than the coin started off on a voyage of discovery down his leg, and soon popped out on to the road. Brad evidently had sprung a leak somewhere, and for a time the money kept dropping from him. Whenever he moved he "layed" a coin, so to speak, and the last I saw of Brad he was leaning lazily against a fence counting his money.

I remember that near the borders we climbed a long, long hill, and were so happy when we got to the top of it—the horses panting and foaming, and we all tired and thirsty.

The view of the long stretch of blue hills behind as was very beautiful.

Here on the hilltop was an inn, with its gable and a row of stables facing the road, and here on a bit of grass we drew up, and determined to take the horses out for the midday halt. But we reckoned without our host. The place was called the Cat Inn.

The landlady was in the kitchen, making a huge pie.

No, we could have no stabling. Their own horses would be home in half an hour.

She followed me out.

"Half an hour's rest," I said, "out of the sun will do my poor nags some good."

"I tell ye, ye canna have it," she snapped.

"Then we can have a bucket or two of water, I suppose?"

"Never a drop. We've barely enough for ourselves."

I offered to pay for it I talked almost angrily.

"Never a drop. You're no so ceevil."

Talking of Northumbrian inns, I remember once having a good laugh.

A buxom young lassie, as fresh as a mountain-daisy, had served me, during a halt, with some ginger-ale.

After drinking and putting the glass down on the table, I was drying my long moustache with my handkerchief, and looking at the lassie thoughtfully—I trust not admiringly.

"Ah, sir," she said, nodding her head and smiling, "ye need na be wiping your mouth; you're no goin' to get a kiss from me."

But near Tweedmouth, in the fields of oats and wheat, we came upon whole gangs of girls cutting down thistles. Each was armed with a kind of reaping-hook at the end of a pole. Very picturesque they looked at a distance in their short dresses of green, grey, pink, or blue. But the remarkable thing about them was this. They all wore bonnets with an immense flap behind, and in front a wonderful contrivance called "an ugly"—a sunshade which quite protected even their noses. And this was not all, for they had the whole of the jaws, chin, and cheeks tied up with immense handkerchiefs, just as the jaws of the dead are sometimes bound up.

I could not make it out. Riding on with my tricycle some distance ahead of the Wanderer, I came upon a gang of them—twenty-one in all—having a noontide rest, sitting and reclining on the flowery sward.

I could not help stopping to look at them. From the little I could see of their faces some were really pretty. But all these "thistle lassies" had their "uglies" on and their jaws tied up.

I stopped and looked, and I could no more help making the following remark than a lark can help singing.

"By everything that's mysterious," I said, "why have you got your jaws tied up? You're not dead, and you can't all have the toothache."

I shall never forget as long as I live the chorus of laughing, the shrieks of laughter, that greeted this innocent little speech of mine. They did laugh, to be sure, and laughed and laughed, and punched each other with open palms, and laughed again, and some had to lie down and roll and laugh. Oh!

you just start a Northumbrian lassie laughing, and she will keep it up for a time, I can tell you.

But at last a young thing of maybe sweet seventeen let the handkerchief down-drop from her face, detached herself from the squad, and came towards me.

She put one little hand on the tricycle wheel, and looked into my face with a pair of eyes as blue and liquid as the sea out yonder.

"We tie our chins up," she said, "to keep the sun off."

"Oh-h-h!" I said; "and to save your beauty."

She nodded, and I rode on.

But in speaking of my adventure with the thistle lassies to a man in Berwick—"Yes," he said, "and those girls on a Sunday come out dressed like ladies in silks and satins."

I remember that our first blink o' bonnie Scotland was from the hill above Tweedmouth. And yonder below us lay Berwick, with its tall, tapering spires and vermilion-roofed houses. Away to the left, far as eye could reach, sleeping in the sunlight, was the broad and smiling valley of the Tweed. The sea to the right was bright blue in some places, and a slaty grey where cloud shadows fell. It was dotted with many a white sail, with here and there a steamboat, with a wreath of dark smoke, fathoms long, trailing behind it.

Berwick-on-Tweed, I have been told more than once, belongs neither to Scotland nor to England. It is neither fish, flesh, nor good red herring. It is a county by itself. My royal mistress ought therefore to be called Queen of Great Britain, Berwick, and Ireland. But I will have it thus: Berwick is part and parcel of Scotland. Tell me not of English laws being in force in the pretty town; I maintain that the silvery Tweed is the natural dividing line 'twixt England and the land of mountain and flood.

SCENES IN BERWICK

"Breathes there the man, with soul so dead,
Who never to himself hath said,
'This is my own, my native land;'
Whose heart has ne'er within him burned
As home his weary footsteps, turned
From wandering on a foreign strand?"

These lines naturally rang through my mind as I rode on my cycle over the old bridge of Tweed. The caravan was a long way behind, so after getting fairly into Berwick I turned and recrossed the bridge, and when I met the Wanderer I gave the tricycle up to Foley, my worthy valet and secretary, for I knew that he too wanted to be able to say in future that he had ridden into Scotland.

Yes, the above lines kept ringing through my mind, but those in the same stirring poem that follow I could not truthfully recite as yet—

"Oh! Caledonia, stern and wild,
Nurse meet for a poetic child;
Land of brown heath and shaggy wood,
Land of the mountain and the flood."

—Because round Berwick the scenery is not stern and wild, and though there may be roaring floods, the mountains hold pretty far aloof.

Through narrow archways, and up the long, steep streets of this border town, toiled the Wanderer. We called at the post-office and got letters, and went on again, seeking in vain for a place of rest. We were nearly out of the town, when, on stopping for a few minutes to breathe the horses, I was accosted by a gentleman, and told him my wants.

Ten minutes afterwards the great caravan lay comfortably in a pork-curer's yard, and the horses were knee-deep in straw in a neighbouring stable.

A German it is who owns the place. Taking an afternoon walk through his premises, I was quite astonished at the amount of cleanliness everywhere displayed. Those pigs are positively lapped in luxury; of all sorts and sizes are they, of all ages, of all colours, and of all breeds, from the long-snouted Berkshire to the pug-nosed Yorker, huddled together in every attitude of innocence. Here are two lying in each other's arms, so to speak, but head and tail. They are two strides long, and sound asleep, only dreaming, and grunting and kicking a little in their dreams. I wonder what pigs do dream about? Green fields, perhaps, hazel copses, and falling nuts and acorns. The owner of this property came in, late in the evening, and we had a pleasant chat for half an hour. About pigs? Yes, about pigs principally—pigs and politics.

Probably no town in the three kingdoms has a wilder, more chequered, or more romantic history than the once-circumvallated Berwick-on-Tweed. How far back that history dates is somewhat of a mystery, more in all likelihood than a thousand years, to the days of Kenneth the Second of Scotland. He it was, so it is written, who first made the Tweed the boundary between the two countries. Is it not, however, also said that the whole country north of Newcastle properly belongs to Caledonia? However this may be, Berwick was a bone of contention and a shuttlecock for many a century. Scores of fearful battles were fought in and around it; many a scene of carnage and massacre has its old bell-tower looked down upon; ay, and many a scene of pomp and pageantry as well.

"It is a town," says an old writer, "that has been the delight, nay, but also the ransom of kings—a true Helena, for which many bloody battles have been fought; it has been lost and regained many times within the compass of a century of years, held in the hands of one kingdom for a time, then tossed by the other—a ball that never found rest till the advent of the Union."

Very little, I found, remained of its ancient castle, only a crumbling corner or two, only a few morsels of mouldering ruin, which makes one sad to think of.

The atmosphere is not over pure, and there is an all-pervading odour of fried fresh herrings, which a starving man might possibly relish.

I saw much of Berwick, but that much I have no space here to describe.

Yet I would earnestly advise tourists to make this town their headquarters for a few weeks, and then to make excursions up the Tweed and into the romantic land of Scott and Hogg, the bard of Ettrick.

Indeed, the places of interest in this border country that lie on both sides of the Tweed are almost too numerous to be mentioned. Past the Ladies' Well you would go on your journey up stream, and there you would probably stop to drink, getting therefrom a cup that in reality cheers, but inebriates not. If an invalid, you might drink of this well for weeks, and perhaps continue your journey feeling in every vein and nerve the glad health-blood flowing free, feeling indeed that you had obtained a new lease of life. Onward you would go, pausing soon to look at the beautiful chain bridge, the tree-clad banks, and the merry fisher-boats.

Etal you would visit, and be pleased with its quiet beauty, its old castle on the banks of the smooth-flowing Till, and its cottages and gardens, its peace-loving inhabitants and happy children.

You would not miss Wooler, if only for the sake of the river and mountain scenery around it.

Nor Chillingham, with its parks of wild cattle, though you would take care to keep clear of the maned bulls.

If a Scot, while gazing on the battlefield of Flodden sad and melancholy thoughts would arise in your mind, and that mournful but charming song "The Flowers of the Forest" would run through your memory—

"I've seen Tweed's silver stream,
Glittering in the sunny beam,
Grow drumlie and dark as it rolled on its way.
O fickle fortune, why this cruel sporting?
O, why thus perplex us poor sons of a day?
Thy frowns cannot fear me,
Thy smiles cannot cheer me,
For the Flowers of the Forest are a' wede away."

(By the Flowers of the Forest he means the Scottish army at Flodden.)

The village of Norham would calm and delight an invalid, however nervous he might be, and the tree-foliage, the flowery sward, the grand old castle ruin once seen on a summer's day, or even in the quiet summer's gloaming, could never be forgotten.

Need I mention Floors Castle, Kelso Abbey, Melrose Abbey, or the abbeys of Jedburgh and romantic Dryburgh? Scott says—

"He who would see Melrose aright
Must see it by the pale moonlight."

The same may be said about Dryburgh too.

Just a word about Saint Abb's Head, then I'll put my horses to, and the Wanderer shall hurry on northwards ho!

Here were the nunnery and chapel of Saint Abb, the ruins of the former still to be seen on the top of precipitous cliffs that stand out into the sea. Go, visit Saint Abb's on a stormy day, when the wild waves are dashing on the rocks, and the sea-birds screaming around. A feeling of such awe will steal over you as probably you never felt before.

On the 17th of July, about 2:30 pm, the Wanderer rolled out of Berwick, and at four o'clock we crossed the undisputed line which divides Scotland from sister England.

There are two old cottages, one at each side of the road. This is Lamberton. Once there was a toll here, and here clandestine marriages used to be performed by priests, the last of whom died from an accident some time ago.

I was told I would see a sign pointing out the house for border marriages, but probably it has been removed. These border marriages were considered a saving in money and in time. The priests were not slow in looking out for custom, and would even suggest marriage to likely couples. One priest is said to have united no less than one thousand five hundred.

An old lady came out from the door of one of the cots. I asked her civilly, and I hope pleasantly, if she would marry either my coachman or my valet.

She said no, she kept hens, and they were care and trouble enough.

I found some ginger-ale in the cheffonier, and had it out, and we all drank—

"Here's a health, bonnie Scotland, to thee."

Then I got the guitar, and sang as the horses trotted merrily on, with music in their footsteps, music in every jingle of their harness, and poetry in their proudly tossing manes.

The scenery around us was pleasant enough, but strange. Of the land we could not see half a mile in any direction, for the scenery was a series of great round knolls, or small hills, cultivated to the top, but treeless and bare. It put me in mind of being in the doldrums in the tropics, every knoll or hill representing an immense smooth wave.

The sea, close down on our right beneath the green-topped beetling cliffs, was as blue as ever I had known it to be.

We stopped for a few minutes to gaze and admire.

There was a stiff breeze blowing, that made the Wanderer rock like a ship in a sea-way. There were the scream of gulls, the cawing of rooks, and the whistling of the wind through the ventilators, and the whispering of the waves on the beach beneath the cliffs, but no other sound to break the evening stillness.

Within two miles of Ayton the road sweeps inland, and away from the sea, and a beautiful country bursts all at once upon the view.

On this evening the sun's rays slanted downwards from behind great clouds, lighting up the trees and the hills, but causing the firs and spruces that were in shadow to appear almost black.

Ayton Castle was passed on the right, just before we crossed the bridge and rattled into the sweet wee town of Ayton itself. The castle is a modern house of somewhat fantastic appearance, but placed upon the braeland there, among the woods, it looks charming, and the braeland itself is a cloudland of green.

Ayton is placed in a lovely valley on the River Eye, which goes wimpling and winding round it. The town itself is pretty, rural, quaint, and quiet. I do wonder if it is a health resort or not, or whether turtle-doves go there to spend the honeymoon.

If they do not they ought to.

The landlord of the hotel where I put my horses, like myself, came from the far north; he soon found me a stand for the Wanderer, a quiet corner in a farmer's field, where we lay snug enough.

Towards sunset about ten waggon loads of happy children passed by. They had been at some fête or feast. How they did laugh and crow when they saw the great caravan, and how they did wave their green boughs and cheer! What else could I do but wave my hat in return? which had the effect of making them start to their feet and shout till the very welkin rang, and the woods of bonnie Ayton re-echoed the sound.

Reader, a word here parenthetically. I was not over-well when I started from home just one month ago. I got up from "the drudgery of the desk's dull wood" to start on my tour. Now I am hard in flesh, and I have the power to enjoy life as one ought to. Here is an extract from my diary of to-day written on the road:

"How brightly the sun is shining. What a delightful sensation of perfect freedom possesses me! I cannot be too thankful to God for this the most enjoyable of all travels or outings I have ever had during a somewhat chequered career. It would hardly be too much to say that at this moment I feel perfectly happy and content, and that is surely saying a deal in a world like this."

THE JOURNEY TO DUNBAR

"I lay upon the headland height and listened
To the incessant sobbing of the sea
In caverns under me,
And watched the waves that tossed and fled and glistened,
Until the rolling meadows of amethyst
Melted away in mist."
Longfellow.

July 18th.

We make an early start this morning. The horses are in, and we are out of the field before eight o'clock. We have a long journey before us—three-and-twenty miles to Dunbar—and do it we must.

It is raining in torrents; every hilltop is wrapped in mist as in a gauze veil. The country is fertile, but trees and hedges are dripping, and if the hills are high, we know it not, seeing only their foundations.

About four miles on, the road enters a beautiful wood of oak, through which the path goes winding. There is clovery sward on each side, and the trees almost meet overhead.

Some six miles from Co'burn's path we stop at a small wayside grocery to oil the wheel-caps, which have got hot. I purchase here the most delicious butter ever I tasted for ten pence a pound. The rain has ceased, and the breaking clouds give promise of a fine day.

I inquire of a crofter how far it is to Inverness.

"Inverness?" he ejaculates, with eyes as big as florins. "Man! it's a far cry to Inverness."

On again, passing for miles through a pretty country, but nowhere is there an extensive view, for the hills are close around us, and the road is a very winding one. It winds and it "wimples" through among green knolls and bosky glens; it dips into deep, deep dells, and rises over tree-clad steeps.

This may read romantic enough, but, truth to tell, we like neither the dips nor the rises.

But look at this charming wood close on our right, a great bank of sturdy old oaks and birches, and among them wild roses are blooming—for even here in Scotland the roses have not yet deserted us. Those birken trees, how they perfume the summer air around us! From among the brackens that grow beneath, so rank and green, rich crimson foxglove bells are peeping, and a thousand other flowers make this wild bank a thing of beauty. Surely by moonlight the fairies haunt it and hold their revels here.

We pass by many a quiet and rural hamlet, the cottages in which are of the most primitive style of architecture, but everywhere gay with gardens, flowers, and climbing plants. It does one good to behold them. Porches are greatly in vogue, very rustic ones, made of fir-trees with the bark left on, but none the less lovely on that account.

Here is the porch of a house in which surely superstition still lingers, for the porch, and even the windows, are surrounded with honeysuckle and rowan. (Rowan, or rantle tree,—the mountain ash.)

"Rantle tree and wood-bin
To haud the witches on come in."

(To keep the witches out.)

The mists have cleared away.

We soon come to a high hill overtopped by a wood. There are clearings here and there in this wood, and these are draped with purple heath, and just beneath that crimson patch yonder is a dark cave-like hole. That is the mouth of a loathsome railway tunnel. There may be a people-laden train in it now. From my heart I pity them. They are in the dark, we in the sunshine, with the cool breeze blowing in our faces, and as free as the birds. We are on the hill; they are in the hole.

As we near Co'burn's path the scenery gets more and more romantic. A peep at that wondrous tree-clad hill to the right is worth a king's ransom. And the best of it is that to-day we have all the road to ourselves.

I stopped by a brook a few minutes ago to cull some splendid wild flowers. A great water-rat (bank-vole) eyed me curiously for a few moments, then disappeared with a splash in the water as if he had been a miniature water-kelpie. High up among the woods I could hear the plaintive croodling of the cushie-doo, or wild pigeon, and Dear me, on a thorn-bush, the pitiful "Chick-chick-chick-chick-chee-e-e" of the yellow-hammer. But save these sweet sounds all was silent, and the road and country seemed deserted. Where are our tourists? where our health and pleasure-seekers? "Doing" Scotland somewhere on beaten tracks, following each other as do the wild geese.

We climb a hill; we descend into a deep and wooded ravine, dark even at midday, cross a most romantic bridge, and the horses claw the road as they stagger up again.

A fine old ruined castle among the pinewoods. It has a story, which here I may not tell.

If ever, reader, you come this way, visit Pease Dene and the bridge. What a minglement is here of the beautiful in art and the awesome in nature!

Are you fond of history? Well, here in this very spot, where the Wanderer rests for a little time, did Cromwell, with his terrible battle-cry, "The Lord of hosts," defeat the Scottish Covenanters. It was a fearful tulzie; I shudder when I look round and think of it.

"Drive on, John, drive on."

All round Co'burn's path is a wild land of romance. But here is the hamlet itself.

The inn—there is but one—stands boldly by the roadside; the little village itself hides upon a wooded braeland away behind.

"Is it a large village?" I inquired.

"No," was the canny Scotch reply, "not so vera large. It is just a middlin' bit o' a village."

So I found it when I rode round, a very middling bit of a village indeed.

The shore is about half a mile from the road. It is bounded by tall steep cliffs, and many of these are pierced by caves. The marks of chisels are visible on their walls, and in troublous times they were doubtless the hiding-places of unfortunate families, but more recently they were used by smugglers, concerning which the hills about here, could they but speak, would tell many a strange story.

Dined and baited at Co'burn's path, and started on again. And now the rain began to come down in earnest—Scotch rain, not Scotch mist, rain in continuous streams that fell on the road with a force that caused it to rebound again, and break into a mist which lay all along the ground a good foot deep.

Nothing could touch us in our well-built caravan, however; we could afford to look at the rain with a complacency somewhat embittered with pity for the horses.

The country through which we are now passing is beautiful, or would be on a fine day. It is a rolling land, and well-treed, but everything is a blur at present, and half hidden by the terrible rain.

When we reached Dunbar at last, we found the romantic and pretty town all astir. The yeomanry had been holding their annual races, and great was the excitement among both sexes, despite the downpour.

It was an hour or two before I could find a place to stand in. I succeeded at last in getting on to the top of the west cliff, but myself and valet had to work hard for twenty minutes before we got in here. We chartered a soldier, who helped us manfully to enlarge a gap, by taking down a stone wall and levelling the footpath.

At Dunbar, on this cliff-top, from which there was a splendid view of the ever-changing sea, I lay for several days, making excursions hither and thither, and enjoying the sea-bathing.

(For further notes about pleasant excursions, fishing streams, etc, see my "Rota Vitae; or, Cyclist's Guide to Health and Rational Enjoyment." Price 1 shilling. Published by Messrs Iliffe and Co, Fleet Street, London.)

The ancient town of Dunbar is too well-known to need description by me, although every one is entitled to talk about a place as he finds it. Dunbar, then, let me say parenthetically, is a town of plain substantial stone, with many charming villas around it. It has at least one very wide and spacious street, and it has the ruins of an ancient castle—no one seems to know how ancient; it has been the scene of many a bloody battle, and has a deal otherwise to boast about in a historical way.

I found the people exceedingly kind and hospitable, and frank and free as well.

English people ought to know that Dunbar is an excellent place for bathing, that it is an extremely healthy town, and could be made the headquarters for tourists wishing to visit the thousand and one places of interest and romance around it.

But it was the rock scenery that threw a glamour over me. It is indescribably wild and beautiful here. These rocks are always fantastic, but like the sea that lisps around their feet in fine weather, or dashes in curling wreaths of snow-white foam high over their summits, when a nor'-east storm is blowing, they are, or seem to be, ever-changing in appearance, never quite the same. Only, one rock on the horizon is ever the same, the Bass.

When the tide is back pools are left among the rocks; here bare-legged children dabble and play and catch the strange little fishes that have been left behind.

To see those children, by the way, hanging like bees—in bunches—on the dizzy cliff-tops and close to the edge, makes one's heart at times almost stand still with fear for their safety.

There is food here for the naturalist, enjoyment for the healthy, and health itself for the invalid. I shall be happy indeed if what I write about the place shall induce tourists to visit this fine town.

On the morning of the 23rd of July we left Dunbar, after a visit from the Provost and some members of the town council. Sturdy chiels, not one under six feet high, and broad and hard in proportion. An army of such men might have hurled Cromwell and all his hordes over the cliffs to feed the skate—that is, if there were giants in those days.

We got out and away from the grand old town just as the park of artillery opened fire from their great guns on their red-flagged targets far out to sea.

Fife-shire Militia these soldiers are, under command of Colonel the Hon. — Halket. Mostly miners, sturdy, strong fellows, and, like the gallant officer commanding them, soldierly in bearing.

I fear, however, that the good folks of Dunbar hardly appreciate the firing of big guns quite so close to their windows, especially when a salvo is attempted. This latter means shivered glass, frightened ladies, startled invalids, and maddened dogs and cats. The dogs I am told get into cupboards, and the cats bolt up the chimneys.

The first day of the firing an officer was sent to tell me that the Wanderer was not lying in quite a safe position, as shells sometimes burst shortly after leaving the gun's mouth. I took my chance, however, and all went well. Alas for poor Hurricane Bob, however! I have never seen a dog before in such an abject state of shivering terror. The shock to his system ended in sickness of a painful and distressing character, and it was one o'clock in the morning before he recovered.

One o'clock, and what a night of gloom it was! The sky over hills and over the ocean was completely obscured, with only here and there a lurid brown rift, showing where the feeble rays of moon and stars were trying to struggle through.

The wind was moaning among the black and beetling crags; far down beneath was the white froth of the breaking waves, while ever and anon from seaward came the bright sharp flash of the summer lightning. So vivid was it that at first I took it for a gun, and listened for the report.

It was a dreary night, a night to make one shiver as if under the shadow of some coming evil.

A DAY AT PRESSMANNAN

"Here springs the oak, the beauty of the grove,
Whose stately trunk fierce storms can scarcely move;
Here grows the cedar, here the swelling vine
Does round the elm its purple clusters twine;
Here painted flowers the smiling gardens bless,
Both with their fragrant scent and gaudy dress;
Here the white lily in full beauty grows;
Here the blue violet and the blushing rose."
Blackmore.

Had a gale of wind come on to blow during our stay at Dunbar, our position on the green cliff-top would undoubtedly have been a somewhat perilous one, for the wind takes a powerful hold of the Wanderer. Perhaps it was this fact which caused my illustrious valet and factotum to write some verses parodying the nursery rhyme of "Hush-a-bye baby, upon the tree top." I only remember the first of these:—

"Poor weary Wanderer on the cliff-top,
If the wind blows the carriage will rock,
If gale should come on over she'll fall
Down over the cliff, doctor and all."

Perhaps one of the most pleasant outings I had when at Dunbar was my visit to the beautiful loch of Pressmannan.

I give here a short sketch of it to show that a gentleman gipsy's life is not only confined to the places to which he can travel in his caravan. The Wanderer is quite a Pullman car, and cannot be turned on narrow roads, while its great height causes overhanging trees to form very serious obstacles indeed.

But I have my tricycle. I can go anywhere on her. Well, but if I want to take a companion with me on some short tour where the Wanderer cannot go, it is always easy to borrow a dogcart, pop Pea-blossom into the shafts, and scud away like the wind. This is what I did when I made up my mind to spend—

A Day at Pressmannan.

I would have preferred going alone on my cycle with a book and my fishing-rod, but Hurricane Bob unfortunately—unlike the infant Jumbo—is no cyclist, and a twenty-miles' run on a warm summer's day would have been too much for the noble fellow. Nor could he be left, in the caravan to be frightened out of his poor wits with thundering cannon and bursting shells. Hence Pea-blossom and a light elegant phaeton, with Bob at my feet on his rugs.

We left about ten am, just before the guns began to roar.

The day was warm and somewhat hazy, a kind of heat-mist.

Soon after rattling out of Dunbar we passed through a rural village. We bore away to the right, and now the scenery opened up and became very interesting indeed.

Away beneath us on our right—we were journeying north-west—was a broad sandy bay, on which the waves were breaking lazily in long rolling lines of foam. Far off and ahead of us the lofty and solid-looking Berwick Law could be seen, rising high over the wooded hills on the horizon with a beautiful forest land all between.

Down now through an avenue of lofty beeches and maples that makes this part of the road a sylvan tunnel. We pass the lodge-gates of Pitcox, and in there is a park of lordly deer.

On our left now are immensely large rolling fields of potatoes. These supply the southern markets, and the pomme de terre is even shipped, I believe, from this country to America. There is not a weed to be seen anywhere among the rows, all are clean and tidy and well earthed up.

No poetry about a potato field? Is that the remark you make, dear reader? You should see these even furrows of darkest green, going high up and low down among the hills; and is there any flower, I ask, moch prettier than that of the potato? But there we come to the cosy many-gabled farmhouse itself. How different it is from anything one sees in Yorks or Berkshire, for instance! A modern house of no mean pretensions, built high up on a knoll, built of solid stone, with bay windows, with gardens, lawns, and terraces, and nicely-wooded winding avenues. About a mile farther on, and near to the rural hamlet of Stenton, we stop to gaze at and make conjectures about a strange-looking monument about ten feet high, that stands within a rude enclosure, where dank green nettles grow.

What is it, I wonder? I peep inside the door, but can make nothing of it. Is it the tomb of a saint? a battlefield memorial? the old village well? or the top of the steeple blown down in a gale of wind?

We strike off the main road here and drive away up a narrow lane with a charming hedgerow at each side, in which the crimson sweetbriar-roses mingle prettily with the dark-green of privet, and the lighter green of the holly.

At the top of the hill the tourist may well pause, as we did, to look at the view beneath. It is a fertile country, only you cannot help admiring the woods that adorn that wide valley—woods in patches of every size and shape, woods in rows around the cornfields, woods in squares and ovals, woods upon hills and knolls, and single trees everywhere.

On again, and ere long we catch sight of a great braeland of trees—a perfect mountain of foliage—worth the journey to come and see. That hill rises up from the other side of the loch. We now open a gate, and find ourselves in a very large green square, with farm buildings at one side and a great stone well in the centre. Far beneath, and peeping through the trees, is the beautiful mansion-like model farmhouse. It is surrounded by gardens, in which flowers of every colour expand their petals to the sunshine. No one is at home about the farmyard. The servants are all away haymaking, so we quietly unlimber, stable, and feed Pea-blossom. Hurricane Bob, my Jehu, and myself then pass down the hill through a wood of noble trees, and at once find ourselves on the margin of a splendid sheet of water that winds for miles and miles among the woodlands and hills.

I seat myself in an easy-chair near the boathouse, a chair that surely some good fairy or the genii of this beautiful wildery has placed here for me. Then I become lapt in Elysium. Ten minutes ago I could not have believed that such scenery existed so near me.

What a lonesome delightful place to spend a long summer's day in! What a place for a picnic or for a lover's walk! Oh! to fancy it with a broad moon shining down from the sky and reflected in the water!

The road goes through among the trees, not far from the water's edge, winding as the lake winds. The water to-day is like a sheet of glass, only every now and then and every here and there a leaping fish makes rings in it; swallows are skimming about everywhere, and seagulls go wheeling round or settle and float on the surface. We see many a covey of wild ducks too, but no creature—not even the hares and rabbits among the brackens—appear afraid of us.

Nowhere are the trees of great height, but there is hardly one you can give a name to which you will not find here by the banks of this lovely lonesome lake, to say nothing of the gorgeous and glowing undergrowth of wild shrubs and wild flowers.

Weary at last, because hungry, we returned to the green square where we had left our carriage, and, first giving Pea-blossom water, proceeded to have our own luncheon.

We had enough for the three of us, with plenty to spare for the feathered army of fowls that surrounded us. They were daring; they were greedy; they were insolent; and stole the food from our very fingers.

Ambition in this world, however, sometimes over-reaches itself. One half-bred chick at last stole a whole polonie, which was to have formed part of Bob's dinner. Bob knew it, and looked woefully after the thieving chick; the brave little bird was hurrying off to find a quiet place in which to make its dinner.

It had reckoned rather rashly, though.

A cochin hen met the chick. "What daring audacity!" cried the hen. "Set you up with a whole polonie, indeed!"

A dig on the back sent the chick screaming away without the sausage, and the big hen secured it.

"I'll go quietly away and eat it," she said to herself, "behind the water-butt."

But the other fowls spied her.

"Why, she's got a whole polonie!" cried one.

"The impudence of the brazen thing!" cried another.

"A whole polonie! a whole polonie!" was now the chorus, and the chase became general. Bound and round the great stone well flew the cochin, but she was finally caught and thrashed and deprived of that polonie. But which hen was to have it? Oh! every hen, and all the four cocks wanted it.

A more amusing scene I never witnessed at a farmyard. It was like an exciting game of football on the old Rugby system, and at one time, while the game was still going on, I counted three pairs of hens and one pair of Dorking cocks engaged in deadly combat, and all about that polonie. But sly old Bob watched his chance. He was not going to lose his dinner if he could help it. He went round and lay flat down behind the well, and waited. Presently the battle raged in that direction, when suddenly, with one glorious spring, Bob flung himself into the midst of the conflict. The fowls scattered and fluttered and fled, and flew in all directions, and next minute the great Newfoundland, wagging his saucy tail and laughing with his eyes, was enjoying his polonie as he lay at my feet.

Returning homewards, instead of passing the Pitcox lodge-gate, we boldly enter it; I cannot help feeling that I am guilty of trespass. However, we immediately find ourselves in a great rolling park, with delightful sylvan scenery on every side, with a river—the winding Papana—meandering through the midst of the glen far down beneath and to the right.

After a drive of about a mile we descend by a winding road into this glen, and cross the river by a fine bridge. Then going on and on, we enter the archway, and presently are in front of the mansion house of Biel itself. It is a grand old place, a house of solid masonry, a house of square and octangular towers, long and low and strong.

It is the seat of a branch of the Hamilton ilk. Miss Hamilton was not then at

home.
"No, the lady is not at home at present, sir," a baker who was driving a cart informed me, "but it would have been all one, sir. Every one is welcome to look at the place and grounds, and she would have been glad to see you."
We really had stopped at the back of the house, which is built facing the glen, but I soon found my way to the front.
I cannot describe the beauty of those terraced gardens, that one after another led down to the green glen beneath, where the river was winding as if loth to leave so sweet a place. They were ablaze with flowers, the grass in the dingle below was very green, the waters sparkled in the sunlight, and beyond the river the braeland was a rolling cloudland of green trees.
We drove out by an avenue—two miles long—bordered by young firs and cypresses.
Altogether, the estate is a kind of earthly paradise.
And think of it being constantly open to tourist or visitor!
"What a kind lady that Miss Hamilton must be, sir!" said my coachman.
"Yes, John," I replied. "This is somewhat different from our treatment at Newstead Abbey."
I referred to the fact that on my arrival at the gates of the park around that historical mansion where the great Byron lived, I could find no admission. In vain I pleaded with the lodge-keeper for liberty only to walk up the avenue and see the outside of the house.
No, she was immovable, and finally shut the gates with an awful clang in my face.
I have since learned that many Americans have been treated in the same way.
The heat of July the 23rd was very great and oppressive, and a haze almost hid the beautiful scenery 'twixt Dunbar and Haddington from our view.
Arrived at the latter quaint old town, however, we were soon at home, for, through the kindness of the editor of the Courier, the Wanderer found a resting-place in the beautiful haugh close by the riverside, and under the very shadow of the romantic old cathedral and church adjoining.
The cathedral was rendered a ruin by the soldiery of Cromwell, and very charming it looks as I saw it to-night under the rays of the moon.
The people of Haddington are genuinely and genially hospitable, and had I stayed here a month I believe I would still have been a welcome guest.
It is said that the coach-builders here are the best in Scotland. At all events I must do them the credit of saying they repaired a bent axle of my caravan, and enabled me on the afternoon of the 24th to proceed on my way in comfort and safety.
Not, however, before I had made a pilgrimage to the grave of poor Mrs Carlyle. The graveyard all around the church and cathedral is spacious and well-kept, but her grave is inside the ruin.

It was very silent among these tall red gloomy columns; the very river itself glides silently by, and nothing is to be heard except the cooing of the pigeons high over head. The floor is the green sward, and here are many graves.

It was beside Mrs Carlyle's, however, that I sat down, and the reader may imagine what my thoughts were better than I can describe them.

An old flat stone or slab covers the grave, into which has been let a piece of marble bearing the following inscription beneath other names:

"Here likewise now rests
Jane Welsh Carlyle,
Spouse of Thomas Carlyle, Chelsea, London.
She was born at Haddington, 14th July, 1800,
The only child of the above John Welsh,
And of Grace Welsh, Caplegill,
Dumfriesshire, his wife.
In her bright existence she
Had more sorrows than are common, but also a soft
Invincibility and clearness of discernment, and a noble
Loyalty of heart which are rare. For 40 years she was
The true and ever-loving helpmate of her husband,
And by act and word unwearily forwarded him as none
Else could, in all of worthy, that he did or attempted.
She died at London on the 21st April, 1866,
Suddenly snatched away from him, and
The light of his life, as if gone out."

I believe the above to be a pretty correct version of this strange inscription, though the last line seems to read hard.

There is a quaint old three-arched bridge spanning the river near the cathedral, and in it, if the tourist looks up on the side next the ruin, he will notice a large hook. On this hook culprits used to be hanged. They got no six-foot drop in those days, but were simply run up as sailors run up the jib-sail, the slack of the rope was belayed to something, and they were left to kick until still and quiet in death.

A visit to a celebrated pigeonry was a pleasant change from the churchyard damp and the gloom of that ruined cathedral. Mr Coalston is a famous breeder of pigeons of many different breeds. The houses are very large, and are built to lean against a tall brick wall. The proprietor seemed pleased to show me his lovely favourites, and put them up in great flocks in their aviaries or flights.

So successful has this gentleman been in his breeding that the walls are entirely covered with prize cards.

He loves his pigeons; and here in the garden near them he has built himself an arbour and smoking-room, from the windows of which he has them all in view.

We started about two pm. I would willingly have gone sooner, but the Wanderer was surrounded on the square by a crowd of the most pleasant and kindly people I ever met in my life. Of course many of these wanted to come in, so for nearly an hour I held a kind of levée. Nor did my visitors come empty-handed; they brought bouquets of flowers and baskets of strawberries and gooseberries, to say nothing of vegetables and eggs. Even my gentle Jehu John was not forgotten, and when at length we rolled away on our road to Musselburgh, John had a bouquet in his bosom as large as the crown of his hat.

God bless old Haddington, and all the kindly people in it!

EDINBURGH

"Edina! Scotia's darling seat!
All hail thy palaces and towers,
Where once beneath a monarch's feet
Sat legislation's sov'reign powers.
From marking wildly-scattered flowers,
As on the banks of Ayr I strayed,
And singing, lone, the lingering hours
I shelter in thy honour'd shade."
Burns.

So sang our immortal Burns. And here lies the Wanderer snugly at anchor within the grounds of that great seminary, the High School of Edinburgh. This by the courtesy of the mathematical teacher and kindness of the old janitor, Mr Rollo. She is safe for the midday halt, and I can go shopping and visiting with an easy mind. Sight-seeing? No. Because I have learnt Edinburgh, "my own romantic town," by heart long ago. Besides, it is raining to-day, an uncomfortable drizzle, a soaking insinuating Scotch mist. But the cathedral of Saint Giles I must visit, and am conducted there by W. Chambers, Esq, of Chambers's Journal. I think he takes a pride in showing me the restorations his father effected before death called him away. And I marvel not at it.

The day before yesterday, being then lying in Musselburgh, in the tan-yard of that most genial of gentlemen, Mr Millar, I took my servants to the capital of Scotland by way of giving them a treat. They were delighted beyond measure, and I did not neglect them in the matter of food and fluid. Remember, though, that they are English, and therefore not much used to climbing heights. I took them first, by way of preparation, to the top of

Scott's monument. What a sight, by the way, were the Princes Street gardens as seen from here! A long walk in the broiling sunshine followed, and then we "did" (what a hateful verb!) the castle.

"The pond'rous wall and massy bar,
Grim-rising o'er the rugged rock,
Have oft withstood assailing war,
And oft repelled th' invader's shock."

Another long walk followed, and thus early I fancied I could detect symptoms of fag and lag in my gentle Jehu.

But I took them down to ancient Holyrood, and we saw everything there, from the picture gallery to Rizzio's blood-stain on the floor.

Another long walk. I showed them old Edinburgh, some of the scenes in which shocked their nerves considerably. Then on and up the Calton Hill, signs of fag and lag now painfully apparent. And when I proposed a run up to the top of Nelson's monument, my Jehu fairly struck, and laughingly reminded me that there could be even too much of a good thing. So we went and dined instead.

I was subjected to a piece of red-tapeism at the post-office here which I cannot refrain from chronicling as a warning to future Wanderers.

I had hitherto been travelling incog. Letters from home had been sent in registered packets, addressed to "The Saloon Caravan Wanderer," to be left at the post-offices till I called for them; but those sent to Edinburgh were promptly sent back to Twyford, because, according to these clever officials, the name was fictitious. It was really no more so than the name of a yacht is, the Wanderer being my land-yacht.

When a clerk showed me a letter from some bigwig anent the matter, I indignantly dashed my pen through the word "fictitious." You should have seen that clerk's face then. I believe his hair stood on end, and his eyes stuck out on stalks.

"Man!" he cried, "you've done a bonnie thing noo. I'll say no more to you. You must go round and speak to that gentleman."

As that gentleman was at one end of the counter and this gentleman at the other, this gentleman refused to budge, albeit he had done "a bonnie thing." For, I reasoned, this gentleman represents the British public, that gentleman is but a servant of the said British public.

So it ended. But was it not hard to be refused my letters—not to be able to learn for another week whether my aged father was alive, whether my little Inie's cough was better, or Kenneth had cut that other tooth?

If further proof were needed that Midlothian is a smart country, it was forthcoming at Corstorphine, a pretty village some miles from Edina. I had unlimbered on the side of the road, not in any one's way. Soon after there was a rat-tat-tat-tat at my back door—no modest single knock, mind you.

A policeman—tall, wiry, solemn, determined.

"Ye maun moove on. Ye canna be allooed to obstruct the thoro'fare."

I told the fellow, as civilly as I could, to go about his business, that my horses should feed and my own dinner be cooked and eaten ere I "mooved on."

He departed, saying, "Ye maun stand the consekences."

I did stand the "consekences," and dined very comfortably indeed, then jogged leisurely on. This was the first and last time ever a policeman put an uninvited foot on my steps, and I do but mention it to show intending caravanists that a gipsy's life has its drawbacks in the county of Midlothian.

It is about six miles from Musselburgh to Edinburgh, through Portobello, and one might say with truth that the whole road is little else than one long street. We had stayed over the Sunday in that spacious old tan-yard. We were not only very comfortable, but quiet in the extreme. Close to the beach where we lay, great waves tumbled in from the eastern ocean on sands which I dare not call golden. We were in the very centre of the fisher population, and a strange, strange race of beings they are. Of course I cultivated their acquaintance, and by doing so in a kindly, friendly way, learned much of their "tricks and their manners" that was highly interesting. The street adjoining my tan-yard was quaint in the extreme. Clean? Not very outside, but indoors the houses are tidy and wholesome. They are not tall houses, and all are of much the same appearance outdoors or in. But washing and all scullery work is done in the street. Looking up Fishergate, you perceive two long rows of tubs, buckets, and baskets, with boxes, and creels, and cats and dogs galore. Being naturally fond of fish, cats here must have a high old time of it.

The older dames are—now for a few adjectives to qualify these ladies; they are short, squat, square, apparently as broad as they are long; they are droll, fresh, fat, and funny, and have right good hearts of their own. The most marvellous thing is their great partiality for skirts. As a rule I believe they wear most of their wardrobes on their bodies; but ten to fifteen skirts in summer and twenty in winter are not uncommonly worn.

The children on week days look healthy and happy; a dead puppy or a cod's head makes a delightful doll to nurse in the gutter, and any amount of fun can be got out of "partans' taes and tangles." (Crabs' toes and seaweed canes.)

But these children are always clean and tidy on the Sabbath day.

At the village of Kirkliston, some miles from Corstorphine, with its intelligent policemen, I stopped for the night in a little meadow. It was a pleasant surprise to find in the clergyman here a man from my own University.

Kirkliston was all en gala next day; flags and bands, and games and shows, and the greatest of doings. But after an early morning ride to those wonderful works where the Forth is being bridged, we went on our way, after receiving gifts of fruit and peas from the kindly people about.

By the way, Kirkliston boasts of one of the biggest distilleries in Scotland. But it quite knocks all the romance out of Highland whisky to be told it is made from American maize instead of from malt. Ugh!

Splendid road through a delightful country all the way to Linlithgow. Pretty peeps everywhere, and blue and beautiful the far-off Pentlands looked.

At Linlithgow even my coachman and valet were made to feel that they really were in Scotland now, among a race of people whose very religion causes them to be kindly to the stranger.

Through Polmont and on through a charming country to Falkirk, celebrated for its great cattle tryst.

July 29th.—At Linlithgow I visited every place of note—its palace and its palace prison, and its quaint and ancient church. Those gloomy prison vaults made my frame shiver, and filled my mind with awe. "Who enters here leaves hope behind" might well have been written on the lintels of those gruesome cells.

There are the remains of a curious old well in the palace courtyard. A facsimile of it, when at its best, is built in a square in the town. Standing near it to-day was a white-haired, most kindly visaged clergyman (The Rev. Dr Duncan Ogilvie), with whom I entered into conversation. I found he came originally from my own shire of Banff, and that he was now minister of a church in Falkirk.

He gave me much information, and it is greatly owing to his kindness that I am now, as I write, so comfortably situated at Falkirk.

A pleasant old stone-built town it is, with homely, hearty, hospitable people. Many a toil-worn denizen of cities might do worse than make it his home in the summer months. There is plenty to see in a quiet way, health in every breeze that blows, and a mine of historical wealth to be had for merely the digging. The town is celebrated for its great cattle fair, or tryst.

Away from Falkirk, after holding a levée as usual, during which a great many pleasant and pretty people stepped into the Wanderer.

The country altogether from Edinburgh to Glasgow is so delightful that I wonder so few tourists pass along the road.

As soon as we leave the last long straggling village near Falkirk, with its lovely villas surrounded by gardens and trees, and get into the open country, the scenery becomes very pretty and interesting, but on this bright hot day there is a hazy mist lying like a veil all over the landscape, which may or may not be smoke from the great foundries; but despite this, the hills and vales and fertile tree-clad plains are very beautiful to behold.

Stone fences (dykes) by the wayside now divide the honour of accompanying us on our journey with tall hedges snowed over with flowering brambles, or mingled with the pink and crimson of trailing roses. (A dyke in Scotland means a stone or turf fence.)

What beauty, it might be asked, could a lover of nature descry in an old stone fence? Well, look at these dykes we are passing. The mortar between the stones is very old, and in every interstice cling in bunches the bee-haunted bluebells. The top is covered with green turf, and here grow patches of the yellow-flowering fairy-bedstraw and purple "nodding thistles," while every here and there is quite a sheet of the hardy mauve-petalled rest-harrow.

Four miles from Falkirk we enter the picturesque and widely scattered village of Bonny Bridge. This little hamlet, which is, or ought to be, a health resort, goes sweeping down a lovely glen, and across the bridge it goes straggling up the hill; the views—go where you like—being enchanting. Then the villas are scattered about everywhere, in the fields and in the woods. No gimcrack work about these villas, they are built of solid ornamentally-chiselled stone, built to weather the storms of centuries.

By-and-bye we rattle up into the village of Dennyloanhead. Very long it is, very old and quaint, and situated on a hill overlooking a wide and fertile valley. The houses are low and squat, very different from anything one ever sees in England.

Through the valley yonder the canal goes wimpling about, and in and out, on its lazy way to Glasgow, and cool, sweet, and clear the water looks. The farther end of the valley itself is spanned by a lofty eight-arched bridge, over which the trains go noisily rolling. There is probably not a more romantic valley than this in all the diversified and beautiful route from Edinburgh to Glasgow. Tourists should take this hint, and health-seekers too.

Passing through this valley over the canal, under the arches and over a stream, the road winds up a steep hill, and before very long we reach the hamlet of Cumbernauld.

An unpretentious little place it is, on a rocky hilltop and close to a charming glen, but all round here the country is richly historical.

We stable the horses at the comfortable Spurr Hotel and bivouac by the roadside. A little tent is made under the hedge, and here the Rippingille cooking-range is placed and cooking proceeded with.

Merry laughing children flock round, and kindly-eyed matrons knitting, and Hurricane Bob lies down to watch lest any one shall open the oven door and run away with the frizzling duck. Meanwhile the sun shines brightly from a blue, blue sky, the woods and hedges and wild flowers do one good to behold, and, stretched on the green sward with a pleasant book and white sun umbrella, I read and doze and dream till Foley says,—

"Dinner's all on the table, sir."

No want of variety in our wanderings to-day. Change of scenery at every turn, and change of faces also.

On our way from Cumbernauld we meet dozens and scores of caravans of all descriptions, for in two days' time there is to be a great fair at Falkirk, and these good people are on their way thither.

"Thank goodness," I say to my coachman, "they are not coming in our direction."

"You're right, sir," says John.

For, reader, however pleasant it may be to wave a friendly hand to, or exchange a kindly word or smile with, these "honest" gipsies, it is not so nice to form part in a Romany Rye procession.

Here they come, and there they go, all sorts and shapes and sizes, from the little barrel-shaped canvas-covered Scotch affair, to the square yellow-painted lordly English van. Caravans filled with real darkies, basket caravans, shooting-gallery caravans, music caravans, merry-go-round caravans, short caravans, long caravans, tall caravans, some decorated with paint and gold, some as dingy as smoke itself, and some mere carts covered with greasy sacking filled with bairns; a chaotic minglement of naked arms and legs, and dirty grimy faces; but all happy, all smiling, and all perspiring.

Some of these caravans have doors in the sides, some doors at front and back; but invariably there are either merry saucy children or half-dressed females leaning out and enjoying the fresh air, and—I hope—the scenery.

The heat to-day is very great. We are all limp and weary except Polly, the parrot, who is in her glory, dancing, singing, and shrieking like a maniac.

But matters mend towards evening, and when we pause to rest the horses, I dismount and am penning these lines by the side of a hedge. A rippling stream goes murmuring past at no great distance. I could laze and dream here for hours, but prudence urges me on, for we are now, virtually speaking, in an unknown country; our road-book ended at Edinburgh, so we know not what is before us.

"On the whole, John," I say, as I reseat myself among the rugs, "how do you like to be a gipsy?"

"I'm as happy, sir," replies my gentle Jehu, "as a black man in a barrel of treacle."

GLASGOW AND GRIEF

"O rain! you will but take your flight,
Though you should come again to-morrow,
And bring with you both pain and sorrow;
Though stomach should ache and knees should swell,
I'll nothing speak of you but well;
But only now, for this one day,
Do go, dear rain! do go away."
Coleridge.

In Scotland there are far fewer cosy wee inns with stabling attached to them than there are in England; there is therefore greater difficulty in finding a comfortable place in which to bivouac of a night. In towns there are, of course, hotels in abundance; but if we elected to make use of these, then farewell peace and quiet, and farewell all the romance and charm of a gipsy life.

It was disheartening on arriving at the village of Muirhead to find only a little lassie in charge of the one inn of the place, and to be told there was no stabling to be bad. And this village was our last hope 'twixt here and Glasgow. But luckily—there always has been a sweet little cherub sitting up aloft somewhere who turned the tide in times of trouble—luckily a cyclist arrived at the hostelry door. He was naturally polite to me, a brother cyclist.

"Let us ride over to Chryston," he said; "I believe I can get you a place there."

A spin on the tricycle always freshens me up after a long day's drive, and, though I was sorry to leave the poor horses a whole hour on the road, I mounted, and off we tooled. Arrived at the farm where I now lie, we found that Mr B— was not at home, he had gone miles away with the cart. But nothing is impossible to the cyclist, and in twenty minutes we had overtaken him, and obtained leave to stable at the farm and draw into his field.

A quiet and delightful meadow it is, quite at the back of the little village of Chryston, and on the brow of a hill overlooking a great range of valley with mountains beyond.

The sky to-night is glorious to behold. In the east a full round moon is struggling through a sea of cumulus clouds. Over yonder the glare of a great furnace lights up a quarter of the sky, the flashing gleams on the clouds reminding one of tropical wild-fire. But the sky is all clear overhead, and in the northern horizon over the mountains is the Aurora Borealis. Strange that after so hot a day we should see those northern lights.

But here comes Hurricane Bob.

Bob says, as plainly as you please, "Come, master, and give me my dinner."

Whether it be on account of the intense heat, or that Hurricane Bob is, like a good Mohammedan, keeping the feast of the Ramadan, I know not, but one thing is certain—he eats nothing 'twixt sunrise and sunset.

Glasgow: Glasgow and grief. I now feel the full force of the cruelty that kept my letters back. My cousins, Dr McLennan and his wife, came by train to Chryston this Saturday forenoon, and together we all rode (seven miles) into Glasgow in the Wanderer. We were very, very happy, but on our arrival at my cousins' house—which I might well call home—behold! the copy of a telegram containing news I ought to have had a week before!

My father was dying!

Then I said he must now be gone. How dreadful the thought, and I not to know. He waiting and watching for me, and I never to come!

Next morning I hurried off to Aberdeen. The train goes no farther on Sunday, but I was in time to catch the mail gig that starts from near the very door of my father's house, and returns in the evening.

The mail man knew me well, but during all that weary sixteen-mile drive I never had courage to ask him how the old man my father was. I dreaded the reply.

Arrived at my destination, I sprang from the car and rushed to the house, to find my dear father—better. And some days afterwards—thank God for all His mercies—I bade him good-bye as he sat by the fire.

No quieter meadow was ever I in than that at Chryston, so I determined to spend a whole week here and write up the arrears of my literary work, which had drifted sadly to leeward. Except the clergyman of the place, and a few of the neighbouring gentry, hardly any one ever came near the Wanderer.

If an author could not work in a place like this, inspired by lovely scenery and sunny weather, inhaling health at every breath, I should pity and despise him.

I never tired of the view from the Wanderer's windows, that wondrous valley, with its fertile farms and its smiling villas, and the great Campsie range of hills beyond. Sometimes those hills were covered with a blue haze, which made them seem very far away; but on other days, days of warmth and sunshine, they stood out clear and close to us; we could see the green on their sides and the brown heath above it, and to the left the top of distant Ben Ledi was often visible.

Thunderstorm at Chryston.

It had been a sultry, cloudy day, but the banks of cumulus looked very unsettled, rolling and tossing about for no apparent reason, for the wind was almost nil.

Early in the afternoon we, from our elevated position, could see the storm brewing—gathering and thickening and darkening all over Glasgow, and to both the north and south-west of as, where the sky presented a marvellous sight.

The thunder had been muttering for hours before, but towards four pm the black clouds gathered thick and fast, and trooped speedily along over the Campsie Hills. When right opposite to us, all of a sudden the squall came down. The trees bent before its fury, the caravan rocked wildly, and we had barely time to place a pole under the lee-side before the tempest burst upon us in all its fury.

Everything around us now was all a smother of mist. It reminded me of a white squall in the Indian Ocean. The rain came down in torrents, mingled with hail. It rattled loudly on the roof and hard and harsh against the panes, but not so loud as the pealing thunder.

The lightning was bright, vivid, incessant. The mirrors, the crystal lamps, the coloured glasses seemed to scatter the flashes in all directions; the whole inside of the Wanderer was like a transformation scene at a pantomime.

It was beautiful but dangerous.

I opened the door to look out, and noticed the row of ash-trees near by, sturdy though they were, bending like fishing-rods before the strength of the blast, while the field was covered with twiglets and small branches.

But the squall soon blew over, and the clouds rolled by, the thunder ceased or went growling away beyond the hills, and presently the sun shone out and began to dry the fields.

By the twelfth day of August—sacred to the Scottish sportsman—I had made up my literary leeway and got well to windward of editors and printers. I was once more happy.

That Terrible Twelfth of August.

We were to start on the twelfth of August for the north, en route for the distant capital of the Scottish Highlands—Inverness.

What is more, we were going to make a day of it, for my brave little Highland cousin Bella (Mrs McLennan) and her not less spirited friend Mrs

C were to go a-gipsying and journey with me from Chryston to Stirling.

It was all nicely arranged days beforehand. We promised ourselves sunshine and music and general joy, with much conversation about the dear old days of long ago. And we were to have a dinner al fresco on the green sward after the manner of your true Romany Rye.

Alas for our hopes of happiness! The rain began at early morn. And such rain! I never wish to see the like again. The sky reminded me of some of Doré's pictures of the Flood.

During one vivid blink of sunshine the downpour of rain looked like glass rods, so thick and strong was it.

In less than two hours the beautiful meadow that erst was so hard and firm was a veritable Slough of Despond. This was misfortune Number 1. Misfortune Number 2 lay in the fact that the 'busman did not meet the train the ladies were coming by, so for two long Scotch miles they had to paddle on as best they could through pelting rain and blackest mud.

Nor had the ladies come empty-handed, for between them they carried a large parrot-cage, a parcel, and a pie. (Polly had been spending a week in Glasgow, and was now returning.)

It was a pie of huge dimensions, of varied contents, and of curious workmanship—nay, but curious workwomanship—for had not my cousin designed it, and built it, and furnished it with her own fair fingers? It was a genuine, palpable, edible proof of feminine forethought.

Not, however, all the rain that ever fell, or all the wind that ever blew, could damp the courage of my cousin. Against all odds they came up smiling, the Highland lass and her English friend—the thistle and the rose.

But the rain got worse: it came down in bucketfuls, in torrents, in whole water. It was a spate.

Then came misfortune Number 3, for the wheels of the Wanderer began to sink deep in the miry meadow. We must draw on to the road forthwith, so Corn-flower and Pea-blossom were got out and put-to.

But woe is me! they could not start or move her. They plunged and pawed, and pawed and plunged in vain—the Wanderer refused to budge.

"I've a horse," said Mr R—, quietly, "that I think could move a church, sir."

"Happy thought!" I said; "let us put him on as a tracer."

The horse was brought out. I have seldom seen a bigger. He loomed in the rain like a mountain, and appeared to be about nineteen hands high, more or less.

The traces were attached to buckles in our long breeching. Then we attempted to start.

It might now have been all right had the trio pulled together, but this was no part of Pea-blossom's or Corn-flower's intention.

They seemed to address that tall horse thus: "Now, old hoss, we've had a good try and failed, see what you can do."

So instead of pulling they hung back.

I am bound to say, however, that the tall horse did his very best. First he gave one wild pull, then a second, then a third and a wilder one, and at that moment everything gave way, and the horse coolly walked off with the trace chains.

It was very provoking, all hopes of enjoyment fled. Hardly could the strawberries and cream that Mrs R brought console us. Here we were stuck in a meadow on the glorious twelfth, of all days, in a slough of despair, in a deluge of rain, and with our harness smashed.

No use lamenting, however. I sent my servant off to Glasgow to get repairs done at once, and obtain hydraulic assistance for the semi-wrecked Wanderer.

About noon there came round a kindly farmer Jackson.

"Men can do it," he said, after eyeing us for a bit. "There's nothing like men."

I had sent the ladies into the farmhouse for warmth, and was in the saloon by myself, when suddenly the caravan gave herself a shake and began to move forward.

In some surprise I opened the door and looked out. Why, surely all the manhood of Chryston was around us, clustering round the wheels, lining the sides, pushing behind and pulling the pole. With a hip! ho! and away we go!

"Hurrah, lads, hurrah!"

"Bravo, boys, bravo!"

In less time than it takes me to tell it, the great caravan was hoisted through that meadow and run high and dry into the farmer's courtyard.

To offer these men money would have been to insult them—they were Scotch. Nor can a kindness like this be measured by coin. I offered them liquid refreshment, however, but out of all who helped me I do not think that half-a-dozen partook.

All honour to the manly feelings of the good folks of Chryston.

But our day's enjoyment was marred and we were left lamenting.

August 13th. We are off.

We are gone, over bank, bush, and scaur. And happy we feel, on this bright, bracing morning, to be once more on the road again with our backs to old England, our faces to the north.

Click, click—click, click! Why, there positively does seem music in the very horses' feet. They seem happy as well as ourselves. Happy and fresh for, says my gentle Jehu, "They are pulling, sir, fit to drag the very arms out of ye."

"Never mind, John," I reply, "the Highland hills are ahead of us, and the heather hills, my Jehu. Knowest thou this song, John?"

"'O! glorious is the sea, wi' its heaving tide,

And bonnie are the plains in their simmer pride;
But the sea wi' its tide, and the plains wi' their rills,
Are no half so dear as my ain heather hills.
I may heedless look on the silvery sea,
I may tentless muse on the flowery lee,
But my heart wi' a nameless rapture thrills
When I gaze on the cliffs o' my ain heather hills.
Then hurrah, hurrah, for the heather hills,
Where the bonnie thistle waves to the sweet bluebells,
And the wild mountain floods heave their crests to the clouds,
Then foam down the steeps o' my ain heather hills.'"

No wonder the rattling chorus brought half-dressed innocent cottage children to their doors to wave naked arms and shout as we passed, or that their mothers smiled to us, and fathers doffed their bonnets, and wished us "good speed."

But summer has gone from nature if not from our hearts. All in a week the change has come, and many-tinted autumn was ushered in with wild and stormy winds, with rain and floods and rattling thunder.

Not as a lamb has autumn entered, but as a lion roaring; as a king or a hero in a pantomime, with blue and red fire and grand effects of all kinds.

There is a strong breeze blowing, but it is an invigorating one, and now, at eight o'clock on this morning, the sun is shining brightly enough, whatever it may do later on.

What a grand day for the moors! It will quite make up for the loss of yesterday, when doubtless there were more drams than dead grouse about.

In Glasgow, days ago, I noticed that the poulterers' windows were decorated with blooming heather in anticipation of the twelfth.

I saw yesterday afternoon some "lads in kilts"—Saxons, by the shape of their legs. But I do not hold with Professor Blackie, that if you see a gentleman in Highland garb "he must either be an Englishman or a fool."

For I know that our merriest of professors, best of Greek scholars, and most enthusiastic of Scotchmen, would himself wear the kilt if there was the slightest possibility of keeping his stockings up!

ON THE HIGH ROAD TO THE HIGHLANDS

"... Here the bleak mount,
The bare bleak mountain speckled thin with sheep;
Grey clouds, that shadowing spot the sunny fields;
And river, now with bushy rocks o'erbrowed,
Now winding bright and full, with naked banks;
And seats and lawns, the abbey and the wood;
And cots and hamlets, and faint city spire."
Coleridge.

At Cumbernauld, the people were pleased to see us once more, and quite a large crowd surrounded the Wanderer. On leaving the village we were boarded by a young clergyman and his wife, such pleasant enthusiastic sort of people that it does one good to look at and converse with.

Passed strings of caravans at Dennyloanhead, and exchanged smiles and good-morrows with them. Then on to the Stirling road, through an altogether charming country.

Through Windsor Newton, and the romantic village of Saint Ninian's, near which is Bannockburn.

Then away and away to Stirling, and through it, intending to bivouac for the night at Bridge of Allan, but, Scot that I am, I could not pass that monument on Abbey Craig, to Scotland's great deliverer; so here I lie on the grounds of a railway company, under the very shadow of this lovely wooded craig, and on the site of a memorable battle.

How beautiful the evening is! The sun, as the song says, "has gone down o'er the lofty Ben Lomond," but it has left no "red clouds to preside o'er the scene."

A purple haze is over all yonder range of lofty mountains, great banks of cloud are rising behind them. Up in the blue, a pale scimitar of a moon is shining, and peace, peace, peace, is over all the wild scene.

By-the-bye, at Saint Ninian's to-day, we stabled at the "Scots wha hae," and my horses had to walk through the house, in at the hall door and out at the back. (Travellers will do well to ask prices here before accepting accommodation.) But nothing now would surprise or startle those animals. I often wonder what they think of it all.

We were early on the road this morning of August 14th, feeling, and probably looking, as fresh as daisies. Too early to meet anything or anyone except farmers' carts, with horses only half awake, and men nodding among the straw.

Bridge of Allan is a sweet wee town, by the banks of the river, embosomed in trees, quite a model modern watering-place.

We travel on through splendid avenues of trees, that meet overhead, making the road a leafy tunnel, but the morning sun is shimmering through the green canopy, and his beams falling upon our path make it a study in black and white.

The road is a rolling one, reminding us forcibly of Northumbrian banks and Durham braes.

The trains here seem strangely erratic, we meet them at every corner. They come popping out from and go popping into the most unlikely places, out from a wood, out of the face of a rock, or up out of the earth in a bare green meadow, disappearing almost instantly with an eldritch shriek into some other hole or glen or wood.

Through the city of Dunblane, with its Ruined cathedral, by narrow roads across country fifteen miles, till we reach Blackford, and as there are to be games here to-morrow, we get run into a fine open meadow behind Edmund's Hotel, and bivouac for the night.

Both my coachman and my valet were Englishmen, and it would be something new for them, at all events.

The meadow into which I drove was very quiet and retired. The games were to be held in an adjoining rolling field, and from the roof of the Wanderer a very good view could be had of all the goings-on.

On looking at my notes, written on the evening before the Highland gathering, I find that it was my doggie friend Hurricane Bob who first suggested my stopping for the games.

"Did ever you see such a glorious meadow in your life?" he seemed to say, as he threw himself on his broad back and began tumbling on the sward. "Did you ever see greener grass," he continued, "or more lovely white clover? You must stay here, master."

"Well, I think I will stay, Bob," I replied.

"What say you, Pea-blossom?" I continued, addressing my saucy bay mare.

"Stay?" replied Pea-blossom, tossing her head. "Certainly stay. You stopped a whole week at Chryston, and I thought I was going to be a lady for life."

"And what say you, Corn-flower?" I continued, addressing my horse, who, by the way, is not quite so refined in his ideas as Pea-blossom.

"Which I'd stop anyw'eres," said Corn-flower, taking an immense mouthful of clover, "where there be such feeding as this."

Well, when both one's horses, besides his Newfoundland dog and his servants, want to stay at a place for the night, compliance in the master becomes a kind of a virtue.

The Evening before the Games.

"Now rose
Sweet evening, solemn hour; the sun, declined,
Hung golden o'er this nether firmament,
Whose broad cerulean mirror, calmly bright,
Gave back his beamy image to the sky
With splendour undiminished."
Mallet.

The village is all a-quiver to-night with the excitement of expectancy, and many an anxious eye is turned skywards.

"If the breeze holds from this direction," says the landlord of the hotel, "it will be fine for certain."

Poor fellow! little could he dream while he spoke of the dreadful accident that would befall him but a few hours after he thus talked so hopefully.

At sunset to-night a balloon-like cloud settles down on the peak of distant Ben Voirloch, and as this soon becomes tinged with red, the lofty hill has all the appearance of a burning mountain. But all the northwestern sky is now such a sight to see that only the genius of a Burns could describe it in words, while no brush of painter could do justice to it, now that the immortal Turner is no longer on earth.

There are leaden-grey clouds banked along near the horizon; behind these and afar off are cloud-streaks of gold, which—now that the sun is down—change slowly to crimson, then to grey and to bronze.

An hour after sunset these cloud-streaks are of a strange pale yellow colour, only one shade deeper than the sky-tint itself. Even while I am still gazing on it this last turns to a pale sea-green of indescribable beauty, and high up yonder rides a half-moon.

Deeper and deeper grows the yellow of the cloud-streaks till they assume a fiery orange colour; above this is the green of the empty sky, while higher still, betwixt this and the blue vault of heaven, in which the moon is sailing, is a misty blush of crimson.

But now all the distant mountain-tops get enveloped in clouds of leaden-grey, the night-air becomes chill; I close my notes and retire to my caravan, and soon I hope to be sleeping as soundly as my honest dog yonder.

Travelling about, as I constantly do, in all sorts of queer places and among all kinds of scenes, both in towns and in the country, it may not seem surprising that I am often the right man in the right place when an accident occurs. I am certain I have saved many lives by being on the spot when a medical man was wanted instantly.

I did retire to my caravan; but, instead of going to bed, all inviting though it looked, I began to read, and after an hour spent thus the beauty of the night lured me out again. "Happy thought!" I said to myself; "it must be nearly eleven o'clock; I shall go and see what sort of people are emptied out of the inns."

But at the very moment I stood near the door of the hotel already mentioned, the innkeeper had been hurled from the topmost banisters of the stairs by a drunken farmer who had fallen from above on him.

The shrieks of women folks brought me to the spot.

"Oh! he is killed, he is killed!" they were screaming.

And there he lay on his back on the cold stones with which his head had come into fearful contact. On his back he was, still as death, to all appearance dead. With half-open eyes and dilated pupils, and pulseless. His injuries to the skull were terrible. Two medical men besides myself despaired of his life. But above him, a few steps up the stairs, and lying across them half asleep and unhurt, lay the doer of the deed. Oh! what a sermon against the insinuating horribleness of intoxicating drink did the whole scene present!

The Morning of the Games.

It is going to be a beautiful day, that is evident. White fleecy clouds are constantly driving over the sun on the wings of a south-east wind.

Bands of music have been coming from every direction all the morning. They bring volunteers, and they bring their clansmen and the heroes who will soon take part in the coming struggle.

Now Highland gatherings and games, such as I am describing, are very ancient institutions indeed in Scotland I have no reference book near me from which to discover how old they are. But in "the '45" last century, as most of my readers are probably aware, a great gathering of the clans took place among the Highland hills, presumably to celebrate games, but in reality to draw the claymore of revolt and to fight for Royal Charlie. They will know also how sadly this rebellion ended on the blood-red field of Culloden Moor.

During the summer and autumn seasons nearly every country district in the north has its great Highland gathering; but the two chief ones are Braemar and Inverness. The latter is called the northern meeting, and has a park retained all the year round for it. At Braemar, the Queen and Royal family hardly ever fail to put in an appearance.

The clans, arrayed in all the pomp and panoply of their war-dress, in "the garb of old Gaul," each wearing its own tartan, each headed by its own chieftain, come from almost every part of the north-eastern Highlands to Braemar with banners floating and bagpipes playing, a spirit-stirring sight to see.

The ground on which the games take place is entirely encircled by a rope fence, and near are the white tents of the officers in charge, the various refreshment-rooms, and the grand stand itself. The whole scene is enlivening in the extreme; the dense crowd of well-dressed people around the ropes, the stand filled tier on tier with royalty, youth, and beauty, the white canvas, the gaily-fluttering flags, the mixture of tartans, the picturesque dresses, the green grass, the cloud-like trees, and last, but not least, the wild and rugged mountains themselves—the effect of the whole is charming, and would need the pen of a Walter Scott to do justice to it.

But to return to the games about to begin before me. Crowds are already beginning to assemble and surround the ropes, and independent of the grand stand, there are on this ground several round green hills, which give lounging-room to hundreds, who thus, reclining at their ease, can view the sports going on beneath them.

I am lying at full length on the top of my caravan, a most delightful position, from which I can see everything. Far down the field a brass band is discoursing a fantasia on old Scottish airs. But the effect is somewhat marred, for this reason—on the grass behind the grand stand, with truly Scottish independence of feeling, half-a-dozen pipers are strutting about in full Highland dress, and with gay ribbons fluttering from their chanters, while their independence is more especially displayed in the fact that every piper is playing the tune that pleases himself best, so that upon the whole it must be confessed that at present the music is of a somewhat mixed character.

From the top of my caravan I call to my gentle Jehu John, alias my coachman, who comes from the shire of bonnie Berks.

"John," I shout, "isn't that heavenly music? Don't you like it, John? Doesn't it stir your blood?"

Now John would not offend my national feelings for all the world; so he replies,—

"It stirs the blood right enough, sir, but I can't say as 'ow I likes it quite, sir. Dessay it's an acquired taste, like olives is. Puts me in mind of a swarm o' bees that's got settled on a telegraph pole."

But the games are now beginning. Brawny Scots, tall, wiry Highlanders, are already trying the weights of the great caber, the stones, and the hammers. So I get down off my caravan, and, making my way to the field, seat myself on a green knoll from which I can see and enjoy everything.

Throwing the Heavy Hammer.—This is nearly always the first game. The competitors, stripped to the waist, toe the line one after the other, and try their strength and skill, the judges after each throw being ready with the tape. Though an ordinary heavy hammer will suit any one for amateur practice, the real thing is a large ball fastened to the end of a long handle of hard, tough wood.

It is balanced aloft and swung about several times before it quits the hands of Hercules, and comet-like flies through the air with all the velocity and force that can be communicated to it.

Donald Dinnie, though he wants but two years of being fifty, is still the champion athlete and wrestler of the world. There is a good story told of Donald when exhibiting his prowess for the first time in America. The crowd it seems gave him a too limited ring. They did not know Donald then.

"Gang back a wee bit!" cried Donald.

The ring was widened.

"Gang back a wee yet?" he roared.

The crowd spread out. But when a third time Donald cried "Gang back!" they laughed in derision.

Then Donald's Scotch blood got up. He swung the great hammer—it left his hands, and flew right over the heads of the onlookers, alighting in the field beyond.

No one in San Francisco would compete with Donald, so he got the records of other athletes, and at a public exhibition beat them all.

Throwing the light hammer is another game of the same kind.

Putting the Stone.—The stone, as an Irishman would say, is a heavy round iron ball. You plant the left foot firmly in advance of the right, then balancing the great stone or ball on the palm of the right hand on a level with the head for a few moments, you send it flying from you as far as possible. There is not only great strength required, but a good deal of "can," or skill, which practice alone can give.

Tossing the Caber.—The caber is a small tree, perhaps a larch with the branches all off. You plant your foot against the thin end of it, while a man raises it right up—heavy end uppermost—and supports it in the air until you have bent down and raised it on your palms. The immense weight of it makes you stagger about to keep your balance, and you must toss it so that when the heavy end touches the ground, it shall fall right over and lie in a line towards you. This game requires great skill and strength, and it is seldom indeed that more than one man succeeds in tossing the caber fair and square.

There are heavy and light hammers, there are heavy and light putting-stones, but there is but one caber (at principal games), and at this game the mighty Donald Dinnie has no rival.

The jumping and vaulting approach more to the English style of games, and need not be here described; and the same may be said about the racing, with probably one exception—the sack race. The competitors have to don the sacks, which are then tied firmly round the neck, then at the given signal away they go, hopping, jumping, or running with little short steps. It is very amusing, owing to the many tumbles the runners get, and the nimble way they sometimes recover the equilibrium, though very often no sooner are they up than they are down again.

There usually follows this a mad kind of steeplechase three times round the course, which is everywhere impeded with obstructions, the favourite ones being soda-barrels with both ends knocked out. Through these the competitors have to crawl, if they be not long-legged and agile enough to vault right over them.

The dancing and the bagpipe-playing attract great attention, and with these the games usually conclude. At our sports to-day both are first-class.

The dancing commences with a sailor's hornpipe in character, and right merrily several of the competitors foot it on the floor of wood that has been laid down on the grass for the purpose. Next comes the Highland fling, danced in Highland dress, to the wild "skirl" of the great Highland bagpipe. Then the reel of Tulloch to the same kind of music.

Here there are of course four Highlanders engaged at one time.

I hope, for the sake of dear auld Scotland, none of my readers will judge the music of the Highland bagpipes from the performances of the wretched specimens of ragged humanity sometimes seen in our streets. But on a lovely day like this, amidst scenery so sublime, it is really a pleasure to lie on the grass and listen to the stirring war march, the hearty strathspey or reel, the winning pibroch, or the sad wail of a lament for the dead.

Few who travel by train past the village or town of Auchterarder have the faintest notion what the place is like. "It is set on a hill," that is all a train traveller can say, and it looks romantic enough.

But the country all round here, as seen by road, is more than romantic, it is wildly beautiful.

Here are some notes I took in my caravan just before coming to this town. My reason for giving them now will presently be seen.

"Just before coming to Auchterarder we cross over a hill, from which the view is singularly strange and lovely. Down beneath us is a wide strath or glen, rising on the other side with gentle slope far upwards to the horizon, with a bluff, bare, craggy mountain in the distance. But it is the arrangement and shape of the innumerable dark spruce and pinewoods that strike the beholder as more than curious. They look like regiments and armies in battle array—massed in corps d'armée down in the hollow, and arranged in battalions higher up; while along the ridge of yonder high hill they look like soldiers on march; on a rock they appear like a battery in position, and here, there, and everywhere between, e'en long lines of skirmishers, taking advantage of every shelter."

It was not until Monday morning that I found out from the kindly

Aberuthven farmer, in whose yard I had bivouacked over the Sunday, that I had really been describing in my notes a plan of the great battle of Waterloo. The woods have positively been planted to represent the armies in action.

Had not this farmer, whom we met at the village, invited us to his place, our bivouac over the Sunday would have been on the roadside, for at Aberuthven there was no accommodation for either horses or caravan.

But the hospitality and kindnesses I meet with everywhere are universal.

The morning of the 17th of August was grey and cloudy, but far from cold. Bidding kindly Farmer M— and his family good-bye, we went trotting off, and in a short time had crossed the beautiful Earn, and then began one of the longest and stiffest ascents we had ever experienced.

A stiff pull for miles with perspiring horses; but once up on the braeland above this wild and wonderful valley the view was indescribably fine. The vale is bounded by hills on every side, with the lofty Ben Voirloch far in the rear.

The Earn, broad, clear, and deep, goes winding through the level and fertile bottom of the valley, through fields where red and white cattle are grazing, through fields of dark-green turnips, and fields yellow with ripening barley. And yonder, as I live, is a railway train, but so far away, and so far beneath us, that it looks like a mere mechanical toy.

High up here summer still lingers. We are among hedgerows once more and wild roses; the banks beneath this are a sight. We have thistles of every shade of crimson, and the sward is covered with beds of bluebells and great patches of golden bird's-foot trefoil; and look yonder is an old friend, the purple-blue geranium once more.

From the fifth milestone, the view that suddenly bursts upon our sight could hardly be surpassed for beauty in all broad Scotland. A mighty plain lies stretched out beneath us, bounded afar off by a chain of mountains, that are black in the foreground and light blue in the distance, while great cloud-banks throw their shadows over all.

But soon we are in a deep dark forest. And here I find the first blooming heath and heather, and with it we make the Wanderer look quite gay.

How sweetly sound is the sleep of the amateur gipsy! At Bankfoot, where we have been lying all night, is a cricket-ground. I was half awakened this morning (August 18th) at 5:30 by the linen manufactory hooter—and I hate a hooter. The sound made me think I was in Wales. I simply said to myself, "Oh! I am in South Wales somewhere. I wonder what I am doing in South Wales. I daresay it is all right." Then I sank to sleep again, and did not wake till nearly seven.

The village should be a health resort.

Started by eight. A lovely morning, a mackerel sky, with patches of blue. Heather hills all around, some covered with dark waving pine forests.

But what shall I say about the scenery 'twixt Bankfoot and Dunkeld? It is everywhere so grandly beautiful that to attempt to describe it is like an insult to its majesty and romance.

Now suppose the reader were set down in the midst of one of the finest landscape gardens, in the sweetest month of summer, and asked to describe in a few words what he saw around him, would he not find it difficult even to make a commencement? That is precisely how I am now situated.

But to run through this part of the country without a word would be mean and cowardly in an author.

Here are the grandest hills close aboard of us that we have yet seen—among them Birnam; the most splendid woods and trees, forest and streams, lakes and torrents, houses and mansions, ferns and flowers and heather wild. Look where I will it is all a labyrinth, all one maze of wildest beauty, while the sweet sunshine and the gentle breeze sighing thro' the overhanging boughs, combined with the historical reminiscences inseparable from the scenery, make my bewilderment pleasant and complete.

Yes! I confess to being of a poetic turn of mind, so make allowance, mon ami, but—go and see Dunkeld and its surroundings for yourself—

"Here Poesy might woke her heaven-taught lyre,
And look through nature with creative fire
The meeting cliffs each deep-sunk glen divides;
The woods, wild scattered, clothe their ample sides.
Th' outstretching lake, embosomed 'mong the hills,
The eye with wonder and amazement fills.
The Tay meandering sweet in infant pride,
The Palace rising by its verdant side,
The lawns wood-fringed in nature's native taste,
The hillocks dropt in nature's careless haste;
The arches striding o'er the newborn stream,
The village glittering in the noontide beam."

The above passage, from the poet Barns, refers to the village and scenery of Kumon, but it equally well describes the surroundings of Dunkeld.

Pitlochrie is our anchorage to-night.

The little town, when I first approached it, seemed, though picturesque and lovely in the extreme, almost too civilised for my gipsy ideas of comfort; the people had too much of the summer-lodging caste about them; there were loudly dressed females and male mashers, so I felt inclined to fly through it and away as I had done through Perth.

But the offer of a quiet level meadow at the other end of this village of villas, surrounded by hills pine-clad to their summits, and hills covered with heather, the maiden-blush of the heather just appearing on it, tempted me, and here I lie.

Met many delightful people, and still more delightful, happy children.

The wandering tourist would do well to make his headquarters here for at least a week. There is so much to be seen all around. It is indeed the centre of the land of romance and beauty.

Started next day through the Pass of Killiecrankie. Who has not heard of the wild wooded grandeur of this wonderful pass, or of the battle where the might of Claverhouse was hurled to the ground, and the hero himself slain?

It was a sad climb for our horses, but the pass is fearfully, awesomely grand. One cannot but shudder as he stands on the brink of the wooded chasm, over which the mounted troopers were hurled by the fierce-fighting Highlanders.

Just after leaving the pass, on the right is a meadow, in the centre of which is a stone, supposed by most tourists to mark the spot where the great Claverhouse fell. It is not so, but a preaching stone, where outdoor service was held in days of yore.

Behold up yonder, high above it on the hillside, the granite gables of "Ard House" peeping out above the trees. Near here was Claverhouse slain, shot while his horse was stooping to drink some water.

Made our midday halt in front of Bridge of Tilt Hotel. Were visited by many good people. Brakes laden with tourists pass and repass here all day long, for the scenery around here is far famed; splendid forests and wild rugged mountains, lochs and waterfalls—everything Highland.

A wretched kilted piper strutted round the Wanderer after dinner, playing pibrochs. I like the bagpipes and I love the Highland garb, but when the former is wheezy and shrieking, when the latter is muddy and ragged, and the musician himself pimply-faced and asthmatical, it takes away all the romance.

I saw this miserable piper afterwards dancing and shrieking. He was doing this because an ostler belaboured his bare legs with a gig whip.

I was glad to hear the real Highland bagpipes soon after. The wild music came floating on the autumn air from somewhere in the pine forest, and I could not help thinking of McGregor Simpson's grand old song, the March of the Cameron Men—

"I hear the pibroch sounding, sounding,
Deep o'er the mountains and glen,
While light springing footsteps are trampling the heath -
'Tis the march of the Cameron men."

The day is fiercely hot, but a breeze is blowing and the roads are good.

On leaving Blair Athol the way continues good for a time; we catch a glimpse of the Duke's whitewashed castle on the right, among the trees and wood.

But we soon leave trees behind us, though on the left we still have the river. It is swirling musically round its bed of boulders now; in winter I can fancy how it will foam, and rage, and rush along with an impetuosity that no power could resist!

We are now leaving civilisation behind us—villas, trees, cultivated fields, and even houses—worth the name—will for a time be conspicuous only by their absence.

Some miles on, the road begins to get bad and rough and hilly, rougher by far than the roads in the Wolds of York or among the banks of Northumberland. It gets worse and worse, so rough now that it looks as if a drag-harrow had been taken over it.

We are soon among the Grampians, but the horses are wet and tired. Even Pea-blossom, hardy though she be, is dripping as if she had swum across a river, while poor Corn-flower is a mass of foam, and panting like a steam engine.

We were told we ought to go past the Highland hamlet of Struan. We find now, on enquiring at a wayside sheiling, that Struan is out of our way, and that it consists of but one small inn and a hut or two, where accommodation could hardly be found for man or beast.

So we go on over the mountains.

About a mile above Struan, we stop to let the horses breathe, and to gaze around us on the wild and desolate scene. Nothing visible but mountains and moorland, heath, heather, and rocks, the only trees being stunted silver birches.

Close beside the narrow road, so close indeed that a swerve to one side, of a foot or two, would hurl the Wanderer over the rock, is the roaring river Garry. Its bed is a chaos of boulders, with only here and there a deep brown pool, where great bubbles float and patches of frothy foam, and where now and then a great fish leaps up. The stream is a madly rushing torrent, leaping and bounding from crag to crag, and from precipice to precipice, with a noise like distant thunder.

We see an occasional small covey of whirring grouse. We see one wriggling snake, and a lizard on a heather stem, and we hear at a distance the melancholy scream of the mountain whaup or curlew,—a prolonged series of shrill whistling sounds, ending in a broken shriek—but there are no other signs of life visible or audible.

Yes, though, for here comes a carriage, and we have to go closer still—most dangerously close—to the cliff edge, to give it room to pass.

The horses are still panting, and presently up comes a Glasgow merchant and his little boy in Highland dress.

He tells us he is a Glasgow merchant. Anybody would tell anyone anything in this desolate place; it is a pleasure to hear even your own voice, and you are glad of any excuse to talk.

He says,—

"We are hurrying off to catch the train at Blair Athol."

But he does not appear to be in much of a hurry, for he stays and talks, and I invite him and his child up into the saloon, where we exchange Highland experiences for quite a long time.

Then he says,—

"Well, I must positively be off, because, you know, I am hurrying to catch a train."

I laugh.

So does the Glasgow merchant.

Then we shake hands and part.

SNOW-POSTS

"The rugged mountain's scanty cloak
Was dwarfish shrubs of birch and oak,
And patches bright of bracken green,
And heather red that waved so high,
It held the copse in rivalry;
But where the lake slept deep and still,
Dank osiers fringed the swamp and hill."
Scott.

"Now wound the path its dizzy ledge
Around a precipice's edge."
Idem.

Farther and farther on we walk or trot, and wilder and still more wild grows the scenery around us.

Not a tree of any kind is now visible, nor hedge nor fence bounds the narrow road; we are still close to the Garry. Beyond it are heath-clad banks, rising up into a braeland, a hill, or mountain, while the river is far down at the bottom of a cutting, which its own waters have worn in their rush of ages.

The road gets narrower now.

It cannot be more than nine feet at its widest. But the hills and the mountains are very beautiful; those nearest us are crimsoned over with blooming heather; afar off they are half hidden in the purple mist of distance.

All my old favourite flowers have disappeared. I cannot see even a Scottish bluebell, nor a red, nodding foxglove, only on mossy banks the pink and odorous wild thyme-blooms grow among the rocks, tiny lichens paint the boulders, and wherever the water, from some rill which has trickled down the mountain side, stops, and spreads out and forms a patch of green bog land, there grow the wild sweet-scented myrtle, and many sweetly pretty ferns. (The sweet gall, or candleberry myrtle.)

In some places the hills are so covered with huge boulders as to suggest the idea that Titans of old must have fought their battles here,—those rocks their weapons of warfare.

We must now be far over a thousand feet above the sea-level, and for the first time we catch sight of snow-posts, sometimes singly, sometimes in pairs.

The English tourist would in all probability imagine that these were dilapidated telegraph poles. They serve a far different purpose, for were it not for them in winter, when the ground is covered with snow, and the hollows, and even the ravines, are filled up,—were it not for these guiding posts, the traveller, whether on foot or horseback, might get off the path, and never be heard of or seen any more, until the summer's sun melted the snow and revealed his corpse.

Toiling on and on through these mountain fastnesses, we cannot help wondering somewhat anxiously where we can rest to-night Dalwhinnie, that sweetest spot in this highland wilderness, is still seventeen miles away. We cannot reach there to-night. A fall moon will rise and shine shortly after sunset—this is true, but to attempt so long a journey with tired horses, with so great a weight behind them, and in so rugged a country, would be to court an accident, if not destruction.

There is, about four miles ahead of us, a shooting lodge at Dalnacardoch. Yes, but they who live there may not consider hospitality and religion to be nearly akin. We'll try.

"Pull up, Corn-flower."

"Pull up, Pea-blossom."

Pea-blossom is tired herself. If you but shake the whip over her she angrily nibbles at Corn-flower's nose.

"He," she says as plain as horse can speak, "is in the fault. I am pulling all I can, but he is not doing half the work."

Dalnacardoch at long last.

Dalnacardoch! Why, the name is big enough for a good-sized town, or a village at the very least, but here is but a single house. In the good old coaching days it had been a coaching inn.

I go to the door and knock.

The butler appears.

"Who lives here?"

"A Mr Whitely, sir, from Yorkshire has the shooting."

"Ha," I think, "from Yorkshire? Then am I sure of a welcome."

Nor was I mistaken. On a green flat grass plot, near to this Highland shooting-box lies the Wanderer; the horses are in a comfortable stable, knee-deep in straw, with corn and hay to eat in abundance, and I am happy and duly thankful.

It is now past nine o'clock; I have dined, and Hurricane Bob and I go out for a stroll in the sweet moonlight, which is flooding mountain, moor, and dell.

The day has been fiercely hot, but the night is still and starry, and before morning there will be ice on every pool.

How black and bare the hills are, and how lonesome and wild! but what must they be in winter, when the storm winds sweep over them, and when neither fur nor feather can find food and shelter anywhere near them?

"Bob, my boy, we will go to bed."

The stillness of the night is sublime, unbroken save by the distant murmur of the Garry, a sound so soothing that I verily believe it would have lulled even Maecenas himself to sleep.

On August 20th, as fresh as larks, cold though it had been all night, we started on our route for Dalwhinnie. What an appetite the Highland air gives one! I felt somewhat ashamed of myself this morning, as rasher after rasher of bacon, and egg after egg, disappeared as if by legerdemain; and after all, the probability is that a biscuit and cheese at eleven o'clock may be deemed a necessity of existence.

It is a bright sunny morning, but the road is rough and stony; on some parts the débris has been washed from the mountain sides, and left to lie across the road, in others some faint attempts at repairs have been undertaken. The plan is primitive in the extreme. A hole is dug in the hillside, and the earth and shingle spaded on to the road.

Plenty of sheep are grazing on the boulder-covered mountains, plenty of snakes and lizards basking in the morning sunshine. Some of the snakes are very large and singularly beautiful, and glitter in the sunlight as if they had been dipped in glycerine.

This is a land of purple heath, but not of shaggy wood. It would be impossible for any one to hang himself here, unless he requisitioned one of the snow-posts. It is the land of the curlew, the grouse, and the blackcock,—the land mayhap of the eagle, though as yet we have not seen the bird of Jove. The road now gets narrower and still more narrow, while we ride close to the cliffs, with—far below us—the turbulent Garry. Were we to meet a carriage now, passing it would be impossible, and there is no room to draw off.

Never before perhaps did a two-ton caravan attempt to cross the Grampians. There are heath-clad braelands rising around us at all sides. Some of the banks near Dalnaspiddal are a sight to behold. The heather that clothes them is of all shades, from pink to the deepest, richest red. So too are the heaths. These last rest in great sheets, folded over the edge of cliffs, clinging to rocks, or lying in splendid patches on the bare yellow earth. Here, too, are ferns of many kinds, the dark-green of dwarf-broom, and the crimson of foxglove bells.

When we stop for a few minutes, in order that I may gather wild flowers, the silence is very striking, only the distant treble of the bleating lamb far up the mountain side, and the answering cry of the dam.

Here we drive now, close under the shadow of a mountain cliff about two thousand feet high; and from the top cascades of white water are flowing.

My coachman marvels. Where on earth, he asks, do these streams come from? He knows not that still higher hills lie behind these.

Owing to our great height above the sea-level, the horses pant much in climbing. But the wind has got up, and blows keen and cold among these bleak mountains.

Shortly after leaving Dalnaspiddal, the road begins to ascend a mountain side, amidst a scene of such wild and desolate grandeur, as no pen or pencil could do justice to.

It was a fearful climb, with Bob running behind, for even his weight, 120 pounds, lightens the carriage appreciably; with the roller down behind an after wheel, and my valet and I pushing behind with all our might, the horses at long last managed to clamber to the highest point. I threw myself on a bank, pumped and almost dead. So were the horses, especially poor Corn-flower, who shook and trembled like an aspen leaf. On looking back it seemed marvellous how we had surmounted the steep ascent. To have failed would have meant ruin. The huge caravan would have effectually blocked the road, and only gangs of men—where in this dreary, houseless wilderness would they have come from?—could have taken us out of the difficulty.

Dalwhinnie Hotel is indeed an oasis in the wilderness. It is a hospice, and in railway snow-blocks has more than once saved valuable lives. Both master and mistress are kindness personified.

Here, near the hotel, is a broad but shallow river; there is a clump of trees near it too. Fact! I do not mean to say that an athlete could not vault over most of them, but they are trees nevertheless. The house lies in what might be called a wide moorland, 1,200 feet above the sea-level, with mountains on all sides, many of them covered with snow all the year round.

I started next day for Kingussie, six hundred feet below the level of Dalwhinnie, where we encamped for the night behind the chief hotel.

My dear cousin, Mrs McDonald, of Dalwhinnie, had come with me as far as this town, accompanied by some of her sweet wee children, and what a happy party we were, to be sure! We sang songs and told fairy tales, and made love—I and the children—all the way.

Honest John, my cousin's husband, came in the dogcart, and showed me all the beauties of this charming village, which is situated among some of the finest and wildest scenery in the Scottish Highlands. Beauties of nature, I mean, but we met some pretty people too. Among the latter is old Mrs Cameron, who keeps a highland dram-shop at the other end of the village, and talked to John as she would to a child. She is far over seventy, but so pleasant, and so stout, and so nice.

I promised to stop at her door next day as I drove past, and though we started before the hills had thrown off their nightcaps, our old lady was up and about. She entered and admired the caravan, then went straight away and brought out her bottle. Oh! dear reader, she would take no denial.

The lady loved to talk, and did not mind chaff. I tried to make it a match between herself and my young valet. But—

"'Deed, indeed, no, sir," she replied, "it is your coachman I'm for, and when he comes back I'll be all ready to marry him."

So we drove away laughing.

Though frosty dews fell last night, the morning is delightful. So also is the scenery on all sides. Hills there are in abundance to climb and descend, but we surmount every difficulty, and reach the romantic village of Carrbridge long before dusk.

Here we are to spend the Sunday, and the caravan is trotted on to a high bit of tableland, which is in reality a stackyard, but overlooks the whole village.

Narrow Escape of "Wanderer."

This happened to-day, and our adventure very nearly led to a dark ending of our expedition. On our road to Carrbridge, and just at the top of a hill, with a ravine close to our near wheel, the horse in a dogcart, which we met, refused to pass, shied, and backed right against our pole end.

For a moment or two we seemed all locked together. The danger was extreme; our horses plunged, and tried to haul us over, and for a few brief seconds it seemed that the Wanderer, the dogcart, plunging horses, and all, would be hurled off the road and over the brae. Had this happened, our destruction would have been swift and certain; so steep and deep was it that the Wanderer must have turned over several times before reaching the bottom.

Monday, August 24th.—I am this morning en route for Inverness, five-and-twenty miles, which we may, or may not, accomplish. We have now to cross the very loftiest spurs of the Grampian range.

We are now 800 feet above the level of the sea. We have to rise to 1,300, and then descend to Inverness. Were it all one rise, and all one descent, it would simplify matters considerably, but it is hill and dale, and just at the moment when you are congratulating yourself on being as high as you have to go, behold, the road takes a dip into a glen, and all the climbing has to be repeated on the other side.

My last Sunday among the mountains! Yes! And a quiet and peaceful one it was; and right pleasant are the memories I bear away with me from Carrbridge; of the sweet little village itself, and the pleasant natural people whom I met; of the old romantic bridge; of the hills, clad in dark waving pine-trees; of the great deer forests; of moorlands clad in purple heather; of the far-off range of lofty mountains—among them, Cairngorm—their sides covered with snow, a veritable Sierra Nevada; of the still night and the glorious moonlight, and of the murmuring river that sang me to sleep, with a lullaby sweeter even than the sound of waves breaking on a pebbly beach.

We are off at 8:15 am, and the climb begins. After a mile of hard toil, we find ourselves in the centre of a heather-clad moor. Before and around us hills o'er hills successive rise, and mountain over mountain. Their heads are buried in the clouds. This gives to the scene a kind of gloomy grandeur.

A deep ravine, a stream in the midst, roaring over its pebbly bed.

A dark forest beyond.

Six miles more to climb ere we reach our highest altitude.

Three miles of scenery bleaker and wilder than any we have yet come to.

A dark and gloomy peat moss, with the roots of ancient forest trees appearing here and there.

It gets colder and colder, and I am fain to wrap myself in my Highland plaid.

We meet some horses and carts; the horses start or shy, and remembering our adventure of yesterday we feel nervous till they pass.

On and on, and up and up. We are among the clouds, and the air is cold and damp.

We now near the gloomy mountains and deep ravines of Slochmuichk.

We stop and have a peep ahead. Must the Wanderer, indeed, climb that terrible hill? Down beneath that narrow mountain path the ravine is 500 feet deep at the least. There is a sharp corner to turn, too, up yonder, and what is beyond?

WILD FLOWERS

"Ye wildlings of Nature, I doat upon you,
For ye waft me to summers of old,
When the earth teemed around me with fairy delight.
And when daisies and buttercups gladdened my sight,
Like treasures of silver and gold."
Campbell.

"Fair, my own darling, are the flowers in spring...
Rathe primrose, violet, and eglantine,
Anemone and golden celandine.
Not less delicious all the birds that sing
Carols of joy upon the amorous wing,
Earine, in these sweet hours of thine."
Mortimer Collinz (to his wife).

From the day we started from the tree-clad plains of bird-haunted Berks till that on which, after crossing the wild Grampian range, we rolled into the capital of the Scottish Highlands, the Wanderer was gay interiorly with wild and garden flowers.

Did we purchase these flowers? Never once, for, strange as it may seem, I do not think that I ever left a town or village or humblest hamlet without having a bouquet or two presented to me.

Nor were the persons who brought those flowers always such as one would feel inclined to associate with the poetry that floated around their floral gifts.

A rosebud or a lily, in the fair fingers of a beautiful girl, is idyllic; it is in keeping with nature. But what say you to a bunch of sweet-scented carnations, pinks, and lilac pea-blooms trailing over the toil-tinted fingers of some rustic dame of forty?

Would you not accept the latter almost as readily as the former? Yes, you would, especially if she said,—

"Have a few flowers, sir? I know you are fond of them."

Especially if you knew that a great kindly lump of a heart was beating under a probably not over-fashionable corset, and a real living soul peeping out through a pair of merry laughing eyes.

But rough-looking men, ay, even miners, also brought me flowers.

And children never failed me. Their wee bits of bouquets were oft-times sadly untidy, but their wee bits of hearts were warm, so I never refused them.

Some bairnies were too shy to come right round to the back door of the Wanderer with their floral offerings; they would watch a chance when they imagined I was not looking, lay them on the coupé, and run.

Which of the wild flowers, I now wonder, did I love the best? I can hardly say. Perhaps the wild roses that trailed for ever over the hedgerows. But have they not their rivals in the climbing honeysuckle and in the bright-eyed creeping convolvulus? Yes, and in a hundred other sweet gems.

Not a flower can I think of, indeed, that does not recall to my mind some pleasant scene.

"Even now what affections the violet awakes;
What loved little islands, twice seen in their lakes,
Can the wild water-lily restore;
What landscapes I read in the primrose's looks,
And what pictures of pebbles and minnowy brooks,
In the vetches that tangle the shore."

If any proof were needed that I had derived the most intense pleasure from the constant companionship of the wild flowers in my caravan rambles, it is surely to be found in the fact that I am writing this chapter, on a bitter winter's morning in the month of March, sitting in my garden wigwam. When I essayed to commence work to-day I found my writing fluid was frozen, and I could not coax even a dip from the bottle until I had set it over the stove.

And yet it is a morning in March.

Last year at this time the sun was warm, the air was balmy, the crocuses, primroses, snowdrops, and even the tulips were in bloom, and the brown earth was soft and dry. Now it is as hard as adamant. But there is beauty even in this wintry scene. If I take a walk into the garden I find that the hoarfrost brightens everything, and that the tiniest object, even a blade of grass or a withered leaf, is worthy of being admired.

That tall row of spectre-like poplar trees—whether it be winter or summer—is a study in itself. But last night those trees were pointing at the stars with dark skeleton fingers. Those fingers are pointing now at the blue,

blue sky, but they seem changed to whitest coral. Those elm trees along the side of yonder field are clothed with a winter foliage of hoarfrost. Seems as though in a single night they had come again into full leaf, and those leaves had been changed by enchantment into snow. As the sunlight streams athwart them they are beautiful beyond compare.

My wild-birds are here in the garden and on the lawns in dozens, huddled in under the dwarf spruces, firs, and laurels, and even cock-robin looks all of a heap.

Hey presto! I have but to shut my eyes and think back, and the scene is changed. I see before me—

A Hedgerow in July.

Where am I? Away up north on a Yorkshire wold. The horses are out and grazing on the clovery sward by the roadside.

How silent it is!

As I lie here on my rugs on the coupé, I can hear a mole rustling through the grass at the hedge-foot. But the hedgerow itself, and all about it, how refreshing to look upon!

Surely no billhook or axe of woodsman has ever come near it since first it began to grow. Its very irregularity gives it additional charm. The hedge itself is really of blackthorn, but its white or pink-ticked blossoms have faded and given place to haws. Here and there, as far as you can see, up through it grow wild dwarf oak bushes, their foliage crimson or carmine tipped, dwarf plane-trees, with broad sienna leaves, that glitter in the sunshine as if they had been varnished; and elder-trees with big white stars of blossom, and rougher leaves of darkest green. Young elms, too, are yonder, and infant ash trees with stems as black as ink and strangely tinted leaves.

(Plane-trees, so-called, but in reality the Sycamore: the Acer pseudo-platanus of naturalists.)

"The sycamore, capricious in attire,
Now green, now tawny, and ere autumn yet
Has changed the woods, in scarlet honours bright."

Here and there wild roses, pale pink or deepest crimson, blush out; here and there are patches of honeysuckle, and here and there waves of the white flowery bryony roll foaming over the green.

In some places the light and tender-leaved woody nightshade, whose berries in bunches of crimson and green are so pretty in autumn, impart a spring-like appearance to this hedgerow.

Nor does the beauty of my hedgerow end here for all along beneath grow rare and lovely grasses, interspersed with star-eyed silenes and gorgeous spikes of the purple stachys, while the adjoining sward is carpeted over with beds of brilliant clover, red and white, with golden bird's-foot trefoil, and patches of pale blue speedwells.

Bees are very busy all over this glory of colour, humming as they fly from flower to flower, but becoming abruptly silent as soon as their feet touch the silken blossoms. And birds there are too, though now they have for the most part ceased to sing, except the robin and a yellow-hammer, and these birds will continue lilting long after even the autumn tints are on the trees.

Hedgerows in General.

These were almost ever with us—one long-drawn delight. For five hundred miles, indeed, they accompanied the Wanderer on her journey. When, at any time, they left us for a space, and stone fences or wooden palings took their place, we were never happy until they again appeared.

From memory I jot down the names of a few of the plants and flowers that mingled with them, or trailed over or through them, constituting their chief charm and beauty.

First on the list, naturally enough, come the rose gems, including the sweetbriar or eglantine, with its deep pink flowers and sweetly-scented leaves; the field-rose, the Rosa arvensis, with pale pink blossoms, and the charming Rosa canina, or dog-rose, with petals of a darker red.

As I have already said, these roses grew everywhere among the hedges, in garlands, in wreaths, and in canopies, and always looked their best where the blackthorns had not been disfigured by touch of billhook or pruning shears.

In the earlier spring the hedges had a beauty of their own, being snowed over with clustering blossoms.

The bryony and the honeysuckle I have already mentioned. The green and crimson berries on the former, when the summer begins to wane, are rivalled only by those of the charming woody nightshade.

Regarding the honeysuckle, a naturalist in a London magazine wrote the other day as follows:—

"In the ordinary way, the branches grow out from the parent stem and twine round the first support they meet front right to left;"—the italics are mine—"but should they fail to find that support, two branches will mutually support each other, one twining from left to right, the other from right to left."

Now the fact is that the honeysuckle twines from left to right, and if two or three branches are together, as we often find them, it is the weaker who twine round the stronger,—still from left to right.

The wild convolvulus, with its great white bell-like blossoms, that so often stars the hedgerows with a singular beauty, twines always to meet the sun.

The Vicia cracca, or purple climbing vetch, is an object of rare loveliness in July and August. It is a species of clustering-blossomed tare or sweet-pea, with neat, wee green leaves, and flowers of a bluish purple. It is not content with creeping up through the hedge, but it must go crawling along over the top to woo the sunshine.

Later on in summer and early autumn blooms the well-known bramble—the black-fruited rubus.

No poet, as far as I am aware, has yet celebrated the purple trailing vetch in song, but the bramble has not been forgotten.

Hear Elliott's exquisite lines:—

"Though woodbines flaunt and roses glow
O'er all the fragrant bowers,
Thou needst not be ashamed to show
Thy satin-threaded flowers.
For dull the eye, the heart is dull,
That cannot feel how fair,
Amid all beauty, beautiful,
Thy tender blossoms are.
* * * * *.
"While silent showers are falling slow,
And 'mid the general hush,
A sweet air lifts the little bough,
Low whispering through the bush.
The primrose to the grave has gone;
The hawthorn flower is dead;
The violet by the moss'd grey stone
Hath laid her weary head;
But thou, wild bramble, back dost bring,
In all their beauteous power,
The fresh green days of life's fair spring,
And boyhood's blossoming hour."

Nestling down by the hedgerow foot, among tall reeds and grey or brown seedling grasses, is many and many a charming wild flower, such as the stachys, the crimson ragged-robbin, with flowers like coral, and the snow-white silene.

Woodland and Copse.

Far away in bonnie Scotland, where the woods are mostly composed of dark, waving, brown-stemmed pine-trees, feathery larches—crimson-tasselled in early spring—or gloomy spruces, there is often an absence of any undergrowth, unless it be heather. But English copses are often one wild tanglement of trailing flowering shrubs, with banks of bracken or ferns.

I have often stopped to admire the marvellous beauty of these copse-lands; their wealth of silent loveliness has more than once brought the tears to my eyes.

So now I refrain from describing them, because any attempt to do so would end in failure. But, reader, have you seen an English woodland carpeted with deep-blue hyacinths, with snowy anemones, or with the sweet wee white pink-streaked sorrel, with its bashful leaves of bending green? Have you seen the golden-tasselled broom waving in the soft spring wind? Or, later on in the season, the tall and stately foxgloves blooming red amidst the greenery of a fern bank? If not, a treat, both rich and rare, may still be yours.

Is it not said that the wild anemone or wind-flower grew from the tears shed by Venus over the grave of Adonis?

"But gentle flowers are born, and bloom around,
From every drop that falls upon the ground:
Where streams his blood, there blushing springs the rose,
And where a tear has dropped a wind-flower blows."

I think it must be the wood-anemone that is referred to as the snowdrop in that bonnie old Scottish song, My Nannie's awa':—

"The snowdrop and primrose our woodlands adorn,
And violets blaw in the dews o' the morn,
They pain my sad bosom, sae sweetly they blaw,
They mind me on Nannie—and Nannie's awa'."

Fields and Moorland.

Turning to these, what oceans of beauty I saw everywhere around me during all the months of my travel!

In May, many of the uplands were covered with the yellow-blooming furze or whins. The black forest, for instance, 'twixt Guildford and Frimley, was a sight worth travelling long miles to look upon; while nothing could excel the fragrance of the perfume shed everywhere around.

The furze lies low to the ground where it has plenty of sunlight, but straggles upwards to seek the light when it grows in the woodlands.

Sweet-scented thistles of every shade—I had almost added "and every shape"—grew plentifully in corners of fields we passed, mostly prickly, but some harmless; lilac, pale pink, dark crimson, and purple; field thistles, milk thistles, melancholy thistles, and nodding thistles.

This latter species I found growing in glorious profusiòn on the links of Musselburgh, and I quite adorned my caravan with them.

Wherever thistles grow in fields, the tansy is not far off; a showy, yellow, too-hardy flower, without, in my opinion, a vestige of romance about it. Perhaps the sheep think differently, for long after Scottish fields and "baulks" are picked bare, they can always find a pluck of sweet green grass by taking their tongues round a tansy stem.

The yellow meadow vetchling is a beautiful, bright-yellow, pea-like flower, that dearly loves a snug corner under a hedge or bush of furze.

The pink-blossomed geranium-like mallow we all know. It is none the less lovely, however, because common; and here is a hint worth knowing—it looks well in a vase, and will bloom for weeks in water.

But a far more lovely flower, that I first foregathered with, I think, in

Yorkshire, is the wild blue geranium, or meadow crane's-bill. Words alone could not describe its beauty, it must be seen. It mostly grows by the wayside.

Need I even name the corn-marigold, or the blush of the corn-poppies among green growing wheat, or the exquisitely lovely sainfoin, that sheds its crimson beauty over many a southern field; or the blue and charming corn-flower, that delights to bloom amid the ripening grain?

Oh! dear farmer, call it not a weed, hint not at its being a hurt-sickle—rather admire and love it.

Nay, but the farmer will not, he has no romance about him, and will quote me lines like these:—

"Bluebottle, thee my numbers fain would raise,
And thy complexion challenge all my praise,
Thy countenance like summer skies is fair;
But ah! how different thy vile manners are.
A treacherous guest, destruction thou dost bring
To th' inhospitable field where thou dost spring,
Thou blunt'st the very reaper's sickle, and so
In life and death becom'st the farmer's foe."

But cowslips, and buttercups—

"The winking Mary-buds begin
To ope their golden eyes."
Shakespeare.

—And the chaste and pretty ox-eye daisy, even a farmer will not object to my adoring, for the very names of these bring to his mind sleek-sided cattle wading in spring time knee-deep in fields of green sweet grass.

And what shall I say of gowan or mountain-daisy? Oh! what should I say, but repeat the lines of our own immortal bard:—

"Wee, modest, crimson-tipped flower,
Thou's met me in an evil hour,
For I maun crush among the stoure
  Thy slender stem:
To save thee now is past my power,
  Thou bonnie gem?"

The spotted orchis is a sweet-scented Highland moorland gem, but right glad I was to find it meeting me on the banks of Northumberland. Far over the borders grew the pretty Scottish bluebell, and on rough patches of ground the trailing lilac rest-harrow.

Singly, a sprig of bluebells may not look to much advantage, but growing in great beds and patches, and hanging in heaps to old rained walls, or turf-capped dykes, they are very effective indeed.

I had meant to speak in this chapter of many other flowers that grow by the wayside—of the dove's foot cranebill, of the purple loose-strife, of the sky-blue chicory and the pink-eyed pimpernel, of the golden bird's-foot trefoil, of purple bugles, of yellow celandine, and of clover red and white. I had even meant to throw in a bird or two—the lark, for instance, that seems to fan the clouds with its quivering wing, the fluting blackbird of woodland and copse, the shrill-voiced mocking mavis, that makes the echoes ring from tree to tree; the cushat, that croodles so mournfully in the thickets of spruce; the wild-screaming curlew, and mayhap the great eagle itself.

But I fear that I have already wearied the reader, and so must refrain.

Stay though, one word about our Highland heather—one word and I have done. I have found both this and heath growing in England, but never in the same savage luxuriance as on the wilds of the Grampian range. Here you can wander in it waist-deep, if you are not afraid of snakes, and this Erica cineria you will find of every shade, from white—rare—to pink and darkest crimson:—

"Those wastes of heath
That stretch for leagues to lure the bee,
Where the wild bird, on pinions strong,
Wheels round, and pours his piping song,
And timid creatures wander free."

I trust I may be forgiven for making all these poetical quotations, but as I commenced with one from the poet Campbell, so must I end with one from the selfsame bard. It is of the purple heath and heather he is thinking when he writes:—

"I love you for lulling me back into dreams
Of the blue Highland mountains, and echoing streams,
And of birchen glades breathing their balm.
While the deer is seen glancing in sunshine remote,
And the deep-mellow gush of the wood-pigeon's note,
Makes music that sweetens the calm."

A CHAPTER ABOUT CHILDREN

"On these laughing rosy faces
There are no deep lines of sin;
None of passion's dreary traces,
That betray the wounds within."
Tupper.

As much even as the wild flowers themselves were the children a feature in the seemingly interminable panorama, that flitted past me in my long tour in the Wanderer. The wild flowers were everywhere; by wayside, on hillside, by streamlet, in copse, hiding in fairy nooks among the brackens in the woodlands, carpeting mossy banks in the pine forests, floating on the lakes, nodding to the running brooklets, creeping over ruined walls and fences, and starring the hedgerows,—wild flowers, wild flowers everywhere.

Wild flowers everywhere, and children everywhere.

Country children: minding cows or sheep or pigs; trotting Blondin-like along the parapets of high bridges; riding or swinging on gateways; stringing daisies on flowery meads; paddling in stream or in burn; fishing by lonely tarns; swinging in the tree-tops; or boring head first through hedges of blackthorn and furze.

Village children: sitting in dozens on door-steps; a-squat on the footpath, nursing babies as big as themselves; at play on the walks or in the street midst; toddling solemnly off to school, with well-washed faces, and book-laden; or rushing merrily home again, with faces all begrimed with mud and tears.

Seaside children: out in boats, rocked in the cradle of the deep; bathing in dozens, swimming, sprawling, splashing, whooping; squatting among the seaweed; dabbling in pools, or clinging to the cliffs with all the tenacity of crabs.

Children everywhere, all along. Curly-pated children, bare-legged children, well-dressed children, and children in rags, but all shouting, screaming, laughing, smiling, or singing, and all as happy, seemingly, as the summer's day was long.

"Harmless, happy little treasures,
Full of truth, and trust, and mirth;
Richest wealth and purest pleasures
In this mean and guilty earth.

"But yours is the sunny dimple,
Radiant with untutored smiles;
Yours the heart, sincere and simple,
Innocent of selfish wiles.

"Yours the natural curling tresses,
Prattling tongues and shyness coy;
Tottering steps and kind caresses,
Pure with health, and warm with joy."

Look at that little innocent yonder in that cottage doorway. There is a well-kept garden in front of the house, but not a flower in it more sweet than she. Round-faced, curly-tressed, dimpled chin and cheeks and knee. It is early morning, she has rushed to the door in her little night-dress; one stocking is on, the other she waves wildly aloft as she cheers the Wanderer.

Here at a village door is a group—a bouquet you may say—worth looking it. Three such pretty children, seated in a doorway, on the steps. They are dressed in blue, with white socks and fairy-like caps, and the oldest is holding a bald-headed crowing baby in her lap.

Here is another tableau: three pretty little well-dressed maidens, hand-in-hand, dancing and whirling in Indian circle round a hole which has been dug in the green sward; a fourth seated close by the hole, flicking the dust up in clouds with a green bough, and giving each a full share of it. Never mind the lace-edged dresses, heed not the snow-white pinafores, round and round and round they go, and how they laugh and shout, and enjoy it!

And here is a bouquet from Musselburgh, though perhaps it has a somewhat fishy flavour. A group of chubby children on the beach, among the somewhat black sand; one has a large crab-shell with a string to it—this is his cart, and it is laden with cockle-shells and star-fish; another boy has a dead eel on a string; a baby is lying on its face digging holes in the sand with a razor shell, and a little girl is nursing a cod's head for a doll, and has dressed it up with seaweed. They have bare heads and feet, and smudgy faces, but dear me! they do look happy!

Five little kilted boys, squatting on the grass; between them is a round kettle pot half-filled with porridge, and each holds in his hand a "cogie" of milk. But they start to their feet as the Wanderer rolls past, wave aloft their horn spoons, and shout till we are out of sight.

Here is a little cherub of some seven summers old. He very likely belongs to that pretty cottage whose redbrick gable peeps out through a cloudland of trees yonder. He has a barrow, and it is nearly full, for the boy has been scavenging on the road, gathering material to make the mushrooms grow in his father's garden. Right in the centre of this he has dug a nest, and in this nest is seated his baby brother. He is telling him a story, and the baby brother is crowing and kicking, and looking all over so delighted and joyful in his questionable nest, that one almost envies him. That youngster may emigrate some day, and he may become President of America yet. When I think of that I cannot help feeling a kind of respect for him.

The most smudgy-faced children I noticed on my tour were, I think, some of those in the outlying villages of the North Riding of Yorks. Of course, they always came trooping out to view the caravan, from cottage doors, from garden gates, from schools, and from playgrounds, the foremost calling aloud to those behind to come quick, to run, for a show was coming. If we happened to stop, they would gather around us and stare with saucer eyes and open mouths astonished, expectant. If we drove on quickly, they speedily set up an impromptu "Hip, hip, hoor—ay—ay!" and waved their arms or ragged caps in the air.

Talk about the great unwashed! These were the little unwashed, and a far larger section of the public than their bigger brethren.

Do not blame the poor things because their faces are not over cleanly. It may not even be the fault of their parents. Early of a morning we often met children going toddling off to school, with books and slates, and, mind you, with faces that positively glistened and reflected the sunbeams, the result of recent ablutions, and a plentiful use of soap. We met school children again coming from school of an evening, but sadly different in facial aspect, for lo! and alas! grief soon begins of a morning with a child, and tears begin to flow, so cheeks get wet, and are wiped, and dust begrimes them, and long ere evening the average boy's face is woefully be-smudged.

I found a little Scotch boy once standing with his face against a hayrick weeping bitterly. I daresay he had been chastised for some fault and had come here to indulge in the luxury of a good cry. But would he own it? No, he was too Scotch for that.

"What are ye greetin' (weeping) about, my wee laddie?" I said, pulling him round.

"I'm no greetin'," he replied through his tears.

"It looks unco' like it," I ventured to remark.

"I tell you, si-si-sir," he sobbed, "I'm no gaga—greetin'. I'm only just letting—

"'The tears doon fa',
For Jock o' Hadedean.'"

I gave him a penny on the spot, and that changed his tune.

Children by the "Sad Sea-Wave."

There is nothing sad about the sea from a child's point of view. On many a long voyage I have known children be the light and the life of a ship fore and aft.

Coming from the Cape once I remember we had just one child passenger, a fair-haired, blue-eyed, curly-polled little rascal whom the sailors had baptised Tommy Tadpole. He was a saloon passenger, but was quite as often forward among the men on deck or down below. Not more than seven years of age, I often wondered he did not have his neck broken, for even in half a gale of wind he would be rushing about like a mad thing, or up and down the steep iron ladder that led to the engine room. He had a mother on board, and a nurse as well, but he was too slippery for either, and for the matter of that everyone on board was Tommy's nurse or playmate.

Catch-me-who-catch-can was the boy's favourite game, and at this he would keep three sailors busy for half-an-hour, and still manage to elude their grasp. How he doubled and bolted and dived, to be sure, round the binnacle, round the capstan, over the winch, under the spare anchor, down one ladder and up another—it was marvellous! One day I remember he was fairly caught; he got up into the main-rigging, and actually through the lubber hole into the main-top. Ah! but Tommy couldn't get back, and there he sat for some time, for all the world like that sweet little cherub who sits up aloft to look after the life of poor Jack, till a sturdy seaman ran up, and Tommy rode down on his shoulder.

And the waves were never high enough, nor the wind stormy enough, to frighten Tommy Tadpole.

But country children on a visit to the seashore find fun and joy and something to laugh at in every breaker or tumbling wave.

A storm was raging at Brighton the day after my arrival there in the Wanderer. Great seas were thundering in upon the shingly beach and leaping madly over pier and wall.

"Look, look!" cried my little daughter Inez delightedly, "how the waves are smoking!"

"Surely," she added, "great whales must be in the water to make it wobble so."

But it was great fun to her to watch them "wobbling," all the same.

She crowed with joy at the scene.

"Oh! they do make me laugh so," she cried, clapping her tiny hands, "they are such fun!" Yes, and for weeks afterwards, whenever she thought of that storm-tossed ocean she would laugh.

But really you can find everlasting amusement at the seaside in summer or in autumn—supposing you are a child, I mean. Shingle is not very nice to dig among, perhaps, with a wooden spade, but then you find such quantities of pretty stones and shells among it, and morsels of coloured glass worn round by the action of the waves. You cannot build a very satisfactory house or fortification with the smaller kinds of shingle, but you can throw spadefuls of it in all directions—over your companions or over your nurse, and if a shower of it does fall on that old gentleman's long hat, what matters it whether he be angry or not? it was fun to hear it rattle, and you would do it again and again if you only dared.

If you are permitted to take off shoes and stockings and tuck up your dress, what a glorious treat to wade on the soft sand, and feel the merry wee waves playing soft and warm about your legs! If you cannot have shoes and stockings off, then you can chase each receding wave, and let the advancing ones chase you. This will make you laugh, and if one should overtake you and go swilling round your ankles, why, what matters it? to listen to the water jerking in your boots at every step is in itself good fun.

There is endless amusement to be got out of seaweed, too, and if you have a big dog the fun will be fast and furious.

Perhaps he is a large Newfoundland, like our Hurricane Bob. By the seaside Bob is always on the best of terms with himself and every other living creature. You can bury him in the sand all but the nose; you can clothe him from head to tail with broad bands of wet seaweed, he enjoys it all, takes everything in good part. He will go splashing and dashing into the sea after a stick or a stone, and if you were to fall plump into the sea yourself he would jump after you, carry you out, and lay you on the beach in the most businesslike fashion imaginable; then shake himself, the water that flies from his great jacket of jet making rainbows all round him in the sunshine.

No; there is no sadness about the sea-wave in the happy, merry days of childhood.

Littlehampton is altogether a children's watering-place. There they were by the dozen and score, sailing yachts in little pools, flying kites and building castles, playing at horses, riding on donkeys, gathering shells and seaweed, dancing, singing, laughing, screaming, racing, chasing, paddling and puddling, and all as happy as happy could be.

I was always pleased enough to have interesting children come and see me; whether they brought little bouquets of flowers with them—which they often did—or not, they always brought sunshine.

Let me give just one or two specimens of my juvenile visitors. I could, give a hundred.

Sweet Maudie Brewer.

I could not help qualifying her name with a pretty adjective from the first moment I saw her. Not that Maudie is a very beautiful child, but so winning and engaging, and exceedingly old-fashioned. I made her acquaintance at the inn where my horses were stabled. She is an orphan—virtually, at all events—but the landlord of the hotel is exceedingly good to her, and very proud also of his wee six-year-old Maudie.

It is as a conversationalist that Maudie shines. She has no shyness, but talks like an old, old world-wise mite of a woman.

"Now," she said, after we had talked on a variety of topics, "come into the parlour and I shall play and sing to you?"

As she took me by the hand I had to go, but had I known the little treat I was to have I should have gone more willingly. For not only can Maudie sing well, but she plays airs and waltzes in a way that quite surprised me; and I found myself standing by the piano turning over the leaves for this child of six summers as seriously as if she had been seventeen. That was Maudie Brewer.

Wee Dickie Ellis.

Dickie is another old-fashioned child, a handsome, healthful country boy, who lives in Yorkshire. Very chatty and very free was Dickie, but by no means impertinent. Age about seven. But his age does not cost Dickie a thought, for when I asked him how old he was, he said it was either six or sixteen, but he wasn't sure which. He admired the caravan, and admired Hurricane Bob, but it was my talking cockatoo that specially took his fancy.

He had not been gone half-an-hour till I found him on the steps again.

"I've just coome," he said, "to have another look at t'ould Poll parrot."

Polly took to him, danced to him and sang to him, and finally make a great grab at his nose.

Dickie was back in an hour.

"Coome again," he explained, "to have a look at t'ould Poll parrot."

I thought I was rid of him now for the day; but after sunset, lo! Dickie appeared once more.

"I'm gangin' to bed noo," he said, "and I want to say 'good-night' to t'ould Poll parrot."

And next morning, before I started, up came Dickie sure enough.

"Just coome," he sadly remarked, "to have t'last look at t'ould Poll parrot."

The Miner's Sprite.

The Wanderer was lying in a quiet meadow in a mining district. It was a lovely summer's evening; tall trees and a church tower not far off stood out dark against a crimson sky, for the sun had but just gone down. I was seated reading on the back steps, and all alone.

"Peas, sir," said a voice close to me; "peas, sir."

"I don't buy peas," I replied, looking up in some surprise, for I'd heard no footstep.

"Peas, sir," persisted the child—"I mean, if oo peas, sir, I've come to see your talavan."

What a sprite she looked! What a gnome! Her little face and hands and bare legs and feet were black with coal dust, only her lips were pink. When she smiled she showed two rows of little pearly teeth, and her eyes were very large and lustrous. I took all this in at a glance, and could not help noticing the smallness of her feet and hands and ears.

"Take my hand and help me up the stails. Be twick." I did as I was told, and everything inside was duly criticised and admired. She sat on a footstool, and told me a deal about herself. She spent all the day in the mine, she said, playing and singing, and everybody loved her, and was so "dood" to her.

She lived with her pa and ma in a cottage she pointed to.

"But," she added, "my pa isn't my real faddel (father), and ma isn't my real muddel (mother)." Here was a mystery.

"And where is your real father and mother?"

"Oh!" she replied, "I never had a real faddel and muddel."

As she was going away she said,—

"You may tiss me, and tome and see me."

I could not see my way to kiss so black a face, but I promised to go and see her at her "faddel's" cottage. I did so in an hour, but only to find the mystery that hung around my little gnome deepened.

My little gnome was a gnome no more, but a fairy, washed and clean and neatly dressed, and with a wealth of sunny hair floating over her shoulders. The miner himself was clean, too, and the cottage was the pink of tidiness and order. There were even flowers in vases, and a canary in a gilded cage hanging in the window.

Though I stayed and talked for quite a long time, I did not succeed in solving the mystery.

"She ain't ours, sir, little Looie ain't," said the sturdy miner. "Come to us in a queer way, but lo! sir, how we does love her, to be sure!"

FROM INVERNESS TO LONDON

"While he hath a child to love him
No man can be poor indeed;
While he trusts a Friend above him
None can sorrow, fear, or need."
Tupper.

I would willingly draw a veil over the incidents that occurred, and the accidents that happened, to the Wanderer from the time she left Inverness by train, till the day I find myself once more out on the breezy common of Streatham, with the horses' heads bearing southward away!

But I am telling a plain unvarnished tale, not merely for the amusement of those who may do me the honour to read it, but for the guidance of those who may at some future date take it into their heads to enjoy a gipsy outing.

When I arrived in Glasgow the summer had so far gone, that it became a question with me whether I should finish my northern tour there and journey back to the south of England by a different route, or push on and cross the Grampians at all hazards, take the whole expedition, men, horses, and caravan, back by train to London, and tour thence down through the southern counties. The New Forest had always a charm for me, as all forests have, and I longed to take the Wanderer through it.

So I chose the latter plan, and for sake of the experience I gained—dark as it was—I do not now regret it.

I ought to say that the officials of all ranks belonging to the railway (North-Eastern route) were exceedingly kind and considerate, and did all for my comfort and the safety of the Wanderer that could be done. I shall never forget the pains Mr Marsters, of Glasgow, took about the matter, nor that of Mr McLean and others in Inverness.

The wheels were taken off the Wanderer as well as the wheel carriages, and she was then shipped on to a trolly and duly secured. The one great mistake made was not having springs under her.

Men and horses went on before, and the caravan followed by goods. In due time I myself arrived in town, and by the aid of a coachmaker and a gang of hands the great caravan was unloaded, and carefully bolted once more on her fore and aft carriages. Her beautiful polished mahogany sides and gilding were black with grime and smoke, but a wash all over put them to rights.

I then unlocked the back door to see how matters stood there. Something lay behind the door, but by dint of steady pushing it opened at last.

Then the scene presented to my view beggars description. A more complete wreck of the interior of a saloon it is impossible to conceive.

The doors of every cupboard and locker had been forced open with the awful shaking, and their contents lay on the deck mixed up in one chaotic heap—china, delft, and broken glass, my papers, manuscripts, and letters, my choicest photographs and best bound books, butter, bread, the cruets, eggs, and portions of my wardrobe, while the whole was freely besprinkled with paraffin, and derisively, as it were, bestrewn with blooming heather and hothouse flowers! Among the litter lay my little ammunition magazine and scattered matches—safety matches I need not say, else the probability is there would have been a bonfire on the line, and no more Wanderer to-day.

It seemed to me to be the work of fiends. It was enough to make an angel weep. The very rods on which ran the crimson silken hangings of the skylight windows were wrenched out and added to the pile.

It struck me at first, and the same thought occurred to the goods manager, that burglars had been at work and sacked the Wanderer.

But no, for nothing was missing.

Moral to all whom it concerns: Never put your caravan on a railway track.

It took me days of hard work to restore the status quo ante.

And all the while it was raining, and the streets covered with mud. The noise, and din, and dirt around me, were maddening. How I hated London then! Its streets, its shops, its rattling cabs, its umbrellaed crowds, the very language of its people. And how I wished myself back again on the wolds of Yorkshire, among the Northumbrian hills or the Grampian range—anywhere—anywhere out of the world of London, and feel the fresh, pure breezes of heaven blowing in my face, see birds, and trees, and flowers, and listen to the delightful sounds of rural life, instead of to cockney-murdered English.

Caravans like the Wanderer have no business to be in cities. They ought to give cities a wide, wide berth, and it will be my aim to do so in future.

The journey through London was accomplished in safety, though we found ourselves more than once in a block. When we had crossed over Chelsea Bridge, however, my spirits, which till now had been far below freezing point, began to rise, and once upon the common, with dwarf furze blooming here and there, and crimson morsels of ling (Erica communis), a balmy soft wind blowing, and the sun shining in a sky of blue, I forgot my troubles, and found myself singing once more, a free and independent gipsy.

But now to hark back a little. Who should meet me in London, all unexpectedly as it were, but "mamma"? I mean my children's mother, and with her came my little daughter Inez! Long flaxen hair hath she, and big grey wondering eyes, but she is wise in her day and generation.

And Inez had determined in her own mind that she would accompany me on my tour through England—south, and be the little mistress of the land-yacht Wanderer.

So mamma left us at Park Lane, and went away home to her other wee "toddlers." She took with her Polly, the cockatoo. It was a fair exchange: I had Inez and she had Polly; besides, one parrot is quite enough in a caravan, though for the matter of that Inie can do the talking of two.

A few silent tears were dropped after the parting—tears which she tried to hide from me.

But London sights and wonders are to a child pre-eminently calculated to banish grief and care, especially when supplemented by an unlimited allowance of ripe plums and chocolate creams.

Inez dried her eyes and smiled, and never cried again.

But if her cares were ended mine were only commencing, and would not terminate for weeks to come. Henceforward a child's silvery treble was to ring through my "hallan," (Scottice, cottage or place of abode) and little footsteps would patter on my stairs.

I was to bear the onus of a great responsibility. I was to be both "ma" and "pa" to her, nurse and lady's maid all in one. Might not, I asked myself, any one or more of a thousand accidents befall her? Might she not, for instance, catch her death of cold, get lost in a crowd, get run over in some street, fall ill of pear and plum fever, or off the steps of the caravan?

I must keep my eye on her by night and by day. I made special arrangements for her comfort at night. The valet's after-cabin was requisitioned for extra space, and he relegated to sleep on shore, so that we and Bob had all the Wanderer to ourselves.

I am writing these lines at Brighton, after having been a week on the road, and I must record that Inie and I get on well together. She is delighted with her gipsy tour, and with all the wonders she daily sees, and the ever-varying panorama that flits dreamlike before her, as we trot along on our journey. She nestles among rags on the broad coupé, or sits on my knee beside the driver, talking, laughing, or singing all day long. We never want apples and pears in the caravan—though they are given to us, not bought—and it is Inie's pleasure sometimes to stop the Wanderer when she sees a crowd of schoolchildren, pitch these apples out, and laugh and crow to witness the grand scramble.

But some sights and scenes that present themselves to us on the road are so beautiful, or so funny, or so queer withal, that merely to laugh or crow would not sufficiently relieve the child's feelings. On such occasions, and they are neither few nor far between, she must needs clap her tiny hands and kick with delight, and "hoo-oo-ray-ay!" till I fear people must take her for a little mad thing, or a Romany Rye run wild.

Such are the joys of gipsy life from a child's point of view.

She eats well, too, on the road; and that makes me happy, for I must not let her get thin, you know. Probably she does get a good deal of her own way.

"You mustn't spoil her," ma said before she left. I'll try not to forget that next time Inie wants another pineapple, or more than four ices at a sitting.

My great difficulty, however, is with her hair of a morning. She can do a good deal for herself in the way of dressing, but her hair—that the wind toys so with and drives distracted—sometimes is brushed out and left to float, but is more often plaited, and that is my work.

Well, when a boy, I was a wondrous artist in rushes. Always at home in woodland, on moor, or on marsh—I could have made you anything out of them, a hat or a rattle, a basket or creel, or even a fool's cap, had you chosen to wear one. And my adroitness in rush-work now stands me in good stead in plaiting my wee witch's hair.

Hurricane Bob is extremely fond of his little mistress. I'm sure he feels that he, too, has—when on guard—an extra responsibility, and if he hears a footstep near the caravan at night, he shakes the Wanderer fore and aft with his fierce barking, and would shake the owner of the footstep too if he only had the chance.

Our first bivouac after leaving London was in a kindly farmer's stackyard, near Croydon. His name is M—, and the unostentatious hospitality of himself, his wife, and daughter I am never likely to forget.

I will give but one example of it.

"You can stay here as long as you please," he said, in reply to a query of mine. "I'll be glad to have you. For the bit of hay and straw your horses have you may pay if you please, and as little as you please, but for stable room—no."

He would not insult my pride by preventing me from remunerating him for the fodder, nor must I touch his pride by offering to pay for stable room.

It was nearly seven o'clock, but a lovely evening, when I reached the gate of this farmer's fine old house. Almost the first words he said to me as he came out to meet me on the lawn were these: "Ha! and so the Wanderer has come at last! I'm as pleased as anything to see you."

He had been reading my adventures in the Leisure Hour.

We remained at anchor all next day, and Inez and I went to the Crystal Palace, and probably no two children ever enjoyed themselves more.

Next day was Saturday, and we started from the farm about eleven, but owing to a mishap it was two pm before we got clear of the town of Croydon itself.

The mishap occurred through my own absent-mindedness. I left the Wanderer in one of the numerous new streets in the outskirts, not far off the Brighton Road, and walked with Inez about a mile up into the town to do some shopping.

On returning, a heavy shower, a pelting shower in fact, came on, and so engrossed was I in protecting my little charge with the umbrella, that when I at last looked up, lo! we were lost! The best or the worst of it was that I did not know east from west, had never been in Croydon before, and had neglected to take the name of the street in which I had left the Wanderer.

It was a sad fix, and it took me two good hours to find my house upon wheels.

On through Red Hill, and right away for Horley; but though the horses were tired and it rained incessantly, it could not damp our spirits. At the Chequers Inn we found a pleasant landlord and landlady, and a delightfully quiet meadow in which we spent the Sabbath.

The Chequers Inn is very old-fashioned indeed, and seems to have been built and added to through many generations, the ancient parts never being taken down.

Sunday was a delightful day, so still, so quiet, so beautiful. To live, to exist on such a day as this amid such scenery is to be happy.

September 7th.—We are on the road by nine. It is but five-and-twenty miles to Brighton. If we can do seven-and-twenty among Highland hills, we can surely do the same in tame domestic England.

But the roads are soft and sorely trying, and at Hand Cross we are completely storm-stayed by the terrible downpours of rain. I do not think the oldest inhabitant could have been far wrong when he averred it was the heaviest he ever could remember.

During a kind of break in the deluge we started, and in the evening reached the cross roads at Aldbourne, and here we got snugly at anchor after an eighteen-mile journey.

My little maiden went to sleep on the sofa hours before we got in, and there she was sound and fast. I could not even wake her for supper, though on my little table were viands that might make the teeth of a monk of the olden times water with joyful anticipation.

So I supped alone with Bob.

I spent a gloomy eerisome evening. It was so gloomy! And out of doors when I dared to look the darkness was profound. The incessant rattling of the raindrops on the roof was a sound not calculated to raise one's spirits. I began to take a dreary view of life in general, indeed I began to feel superstitions. I—

"Papa, dear."

Ha! Inez was awake, and smiling all over. Well, we would have a little pleasant prattle together, and then to bed. The rattling of the raindrops would help to woo us to sleep, and if the wind blew the Wanderer would rock. We would dream we were at sea, and sleep all the sounder for it.

"Good-night, dearie."

"Good-night, darling papie."

STORM STAYED AT BRIGHTON

"Dim coasts and cloud-like hills and shoreless ocean,
It seemed like omnipresence! God methought
Had built Himself a temple; the whole world
Seem'd imaged in its vast circumference."
Coleridge.

"Rides and rambles, sports and farming,
Home the heart for ever warming;
Books and friends and ease;
Life must after all be charming,
Full of joys like these."
Tupper.

I love Brighton, and if there were any probability of my ever "settling down," as it is called, anywhere in this world before the final settling down, I would just as soon it should be in Brighton as in any place I know.

It is now the 13th of September, and the Wanderer has been storm-stayed here for days by equinoctial gales. She occupies a good situation, however, in a spacious walled enclosure, and although she has been rocking about like a gun-brig in Biscay Bay, she has not blown over.

As, owing to the high winds and stormy waves, digging on the sands, gathering shells, and other outdoor amusements have been denied us, we have tried to make up for it by visiting the theatre and spending long hours in the Aquarium.

The Aquarium is a dear delightful place. We have been much interested in the performances of the Infant Jumbo, the dwarf elephant, and no wonder. He kneels, and stands, and walks, plays a mouth organ, makes his way across a row of ninepins, and across a bar, balancing himself with a pole like a veritable Blondin. He plays a street-organ and beats a drum at the same time; and last, and most wonderful of all, he rides a huge tricycle, which he works with his legs, steering himself with his trunk. This infant is not much bigger than a donkey, but has the sense and judgment of ten thousand donkeys. I should dearly like to go on a cycling tour with him to John o' Groat's. I believe we would astonish the natives.

How the wind has been blowing to be sure, and how wild and spiteful the waves have been; how they have leapt and dashed and foamed, wrecking everything within reach, and tearing up even the asphalt on the promenade!

Sunday was a pleasant day, though wind and sea were still high, and on Monday we made an early start.

It is a muggy, rainy morning, with a strong head wind. The sea is grey and misty and all flecked with foam, and the country through which we drive is possessed of little interest. Before starting, however, we must needs pay a farewell visit to the shore, and enjoy five minutes' digging in the sand. Then we said,—

"Good-bye, old sea; we will be sure to come back again when summer days are fine. Good-bye! Ta, ta!"

Shoreham is a quaint and curious, but very far from cleanly little town.

We heard here, by chance, that the storm waves had quite destroyed a portion of the lower road to Worthing, and so we had to choose the upper and longer route, which we reached in time for dinner with the kindly landlord of the Steyne Hotel. If children are a blessing, verily Mr C— is blessed indeed; he hath his quiver full, and no man deserves it more.

Worthing, I may as well mention parenthetically, is one of the most delightful watering-places on the south coast, and I verily believe that the sun shines here when it does not shine anywhere else in England.

Two dear children (Winnie and Ernie C—) came with us for three miles, bringing a basket to hold the blackberries they should gather on their way back.

Winnie was enchanted with this short experience of gipsy life, and wanted to know when I would return and take her to Brighton. Ernie did not say much; he was quietly happy.

It broke up a fine afternoon, and now and then the sun shone out, making the drive to Littlehampton, through the beautiful tree scenery, quite a delightful one.

Reached Littlehampton-on-Sea by five o'clock, and, seeing no other place handy, I undid the gate of the cricket-field and drove right in. I then obtained the address of the manager or secretary, and sent my valet to obtain leave. I have found this plan answer my purposes more than once. It is the quickest and the best. It was suggested to me long, long ago on reading that page of "Midshipman Easy" where that young gentleman proposes throwing the prisoners overboard and trying them by court-martial afterwards.

So when Mr Blank came "to see about it" he found the fait accompli, looked somewhat funny, but forgave me.

Littlehampton-on-Sea is a quiet and pleasant watering-place, bracing, too, and good for nervous people. I am surprised it is not more popular. It has the safest sea-bathing beach in the world, and is quite a heaven on earth for young children.

We had a run and a romp on the splendid sands here last night, and I do not know which of the two was the maddest or the merriest, Hurricane Bob or his wee mistress. We are down here again this morning for half-an-hour's digging and a good run before starting.

Now last night the waves were rippling close up to the bathing-machines, and Bob had a delicious dip. When we left the Wanderer this morning he was daft with delight; he expected to bathe and splash again. But the tide is out, and the sea a mile away; only the soft, wet, rippled sands are here, and I have never in my life seen a dog look so puzzled or nonplussed as Bob does at this moment.

He is walking about on the sand looking for the sea.

"What can have happened?" he seems to be thinking. "The sea was here last night, right enough. Or can I have been dreaming? Where on earth has it gone to?"

In the same grounds where the Wanderer lay last night, but far away at the other end of the field, is another caravan—a very pretty and clean-looking one. I was told that it had been here a long time, that the man lived in it with his young wife, supporting her and himself by playing the dulcimer on the street. A quiet and highly respectable gipsy indeed.

Delayed by visitors till eleven, when we made a start westward once again.

'Tis a glorious morning. The sky is brightly blue, flecked with white wee clouds, a haze on the horizon, with rock-and-tower clouds rising like snowbanks above it.

The road to Arundel is a winding one, but there are plenty of finger-posts in various stages of dilapidation. A well-treed country, too, and highly cultivated. Every three or four minutes we pass a farm-steading or a cottage near the road, the gardens of the latter being all ablaze with bright geraniums, hydrangeas, dahlias, and sunflowers, and all kinds of berried, creeping, and climbing plants.

How different, though, the hedgerows look now from what they did when I started on my rambles in early summer, for now sombre browns, blues, and yellows have taken the place of spring's tender greens, and red berries hang in clusters where erst was the hawthorn's bloom.

The blossom has left the bramble-bushes, except here and there the pink of a solitary flower, but berries black and crimson cluster on them; only here and there among the ferns and brackens, now changing to brown, is the flush of nodding thistle, or some solitary orange flowers, and even as the wind sweeps through the trees a shower of leaves of every hue falls around us.

A steep hill leads us down to the valley in which Arundel is situated, and the peep from this braeland is very pretty and romantic.

The town sweeps up the opposite hill among delightful woodlands, the Duke of Norfolk's castle, with its flagstaff over the ruined keep, being quite a feature of the landscape.

We turn to the left in the town, glad we have not to climb that terrible hill; and, after getting clear of the town, bear away through a fine beech wood. The trees are already assuming their autumnal garb of dusky brown and yellow, and sombre shades of every hue, only the general sadness is relieved by the appearance here and there of a still verdant wide-spreading ash.

On and on. Up hill and down dell. Hardly a field is to be seen, such a wildery of woodlands is there on every side. The brackens here are very tall, and, with the exception of a few dwarf oak, elm, or elder-bushes, constitute the only undergrowth.

We are out in the open again, on a breezy upland; on each side the road is bounded by a great bank of gorse. When in bloom in May, how lovely it must look! We can see fields now, pale yellow or ploughed, suggestive of coming winter. And farm-steadings too, and far to the left a well-wooded fertile country, stretching for miles and miles.

Near to Bell's Hut Inn we stop to water, and put the nosebags on. There is a brush-cart at the door, and waggons laden with wood, and the tap-room is crowded with rough but honest-looking country folks, enjoying their midday repast of bread and beer.

The day is so fine, the sun is so bright, and the sward so green, that we all squat, gipsy-fashion, on the grass, to discuss a modest lunch. Fowls crowd round us and we feed them. But one steals Foley's cheese from off his plate, and hen steals it from hen, till the big Dorking cock gets it, and eats it too. Corn-flower scatters his oats about, and a feathered multitude surround him to pick them up. Pea-blossom brings her nosebag down with a vicious thud every now and then, and causes much confusion among the fowls.

Bob is continually snapping at the wasps.

Bread-and-cheese and ginger-ale are not bad fare on a lovely day like this, when one has an appetite.

Gipsies always have appetites.

A drunken drover starts off from the inn door without paying for his dinner. The landlady's daughter gives chase. I offer to lend her Bob. She says she is good enough for two men like that. And so she proves.

We are very happy.

One's spirits while on the road to a great extent rise and fall with the barometer.

Chichester seems a delightful old place. But we drove rapidly through it, only stopping to admire the cross and the cathedral. The former put me in mind of that in Castle-gate of Aberdeen.

Between Littlehampton and the small town of Botley, which the reader may notice on the map of Hampshire, we made one night's halt, and started early next morning.

The view from the road which leads round the bay at Porchester is, even with the tide back, picturesque. Yonder is the romantic old castle of Porchester on the right middle distance, with its battlements and ivied towers; and far away on the horizon is Portsmouth, with its masts, and chimneys, and great gasworks, all asleep in the haze of this somewhat sombre and gloomy day.

Porchester—the town itself—could supply many a sketch for the artist fond of quaintness in buildings, in roofs, picturesque children, and old-fashioned public-houses. Who, I wonder, drinks all the "fine old beer," the "sparkling ales," and the "London stout," in this town of Porchester? Every third house seems an inn.

Through Fareham, where we stopped to admire a beautiful outdoor aviary, and where a major of marines and his wife possessed themselves of my little maiden, and gave her cake and flowers enough to set up and beautify the Wanderer for a week at least.

Botley is one of the quietest, quaintest, and most unsophisticated wee villages ever the Wanderer rolled into. It is rural in the extreme, but like those of all rural villages, its inhabitants, if unsophisticated, are as kind-hearted as any I have ever met.

Botley can boast of nearly half-a-score of public-houses, but it has only one hotel, the Dolphin, and one butcher's shop.

That milkman who let us into his field was right glad to see the caravan, which he had read a good deal about, and seemed proud to have us there, and just as pleased was the honest landlord of the Dolphin to have our horses. In the good old-fashioned way he invited my little daughter and me into the cosy parlour behind the bar, where we spent a few musical hours most enjoyably.

It seems though that Botley has not always borne the reputation of being a quiet place. For example, long ago, though the recollection of the affair is still green in the memory of the oldest inhabitants, there used to be held at Botley what were called "beef-fairs." For months beforehand "twopences" were saved, to raise a fund for fair-day. When this latter came round, the agreement among these innocents was that having once taken the cup of beer in his hand every man must drain it to the bottom, to prove he was a man.

In his bacchanalian song "Willie brew'd a peck o' maut," Burns says:—

"The first that rises to gang awa'
A cuckold cowardly loon is he.
The first that in the neuk does fa'
We'll mak' him king amang the three."

But at the beef-fair of Botley matters were reversed, and the first that "in the neuk did fa'" was fined two shillings, and failing payment he was condemned to be hanged.

On a certain fair-day a certain "innocent" fell in the nook but refused to pay. Honour was honour among these fair folks, so first they stood the culprit on his head, and endeavoured to shake the money out of him. Disappointed and unsuccessful, they really did hang him, not by the neck but by the waist, to a beam.

Unfortunately for the poor fellow, the band came past, and away rushed his confrères to listen.

It did not matter much to the condemned joskin that he was trundled about the town for two hours after they had returned, and finally deposited under the settle of an inn. For he was dead!

One other example of the congeniality of the Botley folks of long ago. My attention was attracted to a large iron-lettered slab that hangs on the wall of the coffee-room of the Dolphin. The following is the inscription thereon:—

This Stone is Erected To Perpetuate a
Most Cruel Murder Committed on the Body
of Thos. Webb a Poor Inhabitant of Swanmore
on the 11th of Feb. 1800 by John Diggins
a Private Soldier in the Talbot Fencibles
Whose Remains are Gibbeted on the Adjoining Common.

And there doubtless John Diggins' body swung, and there his bones bleached and rattled till they fell asunder.

But the strange part of the story now has to be told; they had hanged the wrong man!

It is an ugly story altogether. Thus: two men (Fencibles) were drinking at a public-house, and going homewards late made a vow to murder the first man they met. Cruelly did they keep this vow, for an old man they encountered was at once put to the bayonet. Before going away from the body, however, the soldier who had done the deed managed to exchange bayonets with Diggins. The blood-stained instrument was therefore found in his scabbard, and he was tried and hanged. The real murderer confessed his crime twenty-one years afterwards, when on his deathbed.

So much for the Botley of long ago.

The iron slab, by the way, was found in the cellar of the Dolphin, and the flag of the Talbot Fencibles, strange to say, was found in the roof.

We took Southampton as our midday halt, driving all round the South Park before we entered—such a charming park—and stopped to dine among the guns away down beside the pier.

Then on for a few miles, bivouacking for the night in an inn yard, in order that we might return to Southampton and see the play.

Next day we reached Lyndhurst, and came safely to anchor in a meadow behind the old Crown Hotel, and this field we made our headquarters for several days.

It had always been my ambition to see something of the New Forest, and here I was in the centre of it. I had so often read about this wondrous Forest; I had thought about it, dreamt about it, and more than once it had found its way into the tales I wrote. And now I found the real to exceed the imaginary.

One great beauty about the New Forest is that it is open. There is nothing here of the sombre gloom of the Scottish pine wood. There are great green glades in it, and wide wild patches of heatherland. Even at the places where the trees are thickest the giant oaks thrust their arms out on every side as if to keep the other trees off.

"Stand back," they seem to say. "We will not be crowded. We must not keep away the sunshine from the grass and the brackens beneath us, for all that has life loves the light. Stand back."

What charmed me most in this Forest? I can hardly tell. Perhaps its gnarled and ancient oaks, that carried my thoughts back to the almost forgotten past; perhaps its treescapes in general, now with the tints of autumn burnishing their foliage; perhaps its glades, carpeted with soft green moss and grass, and surrounded with brackens branched and lofty, under which surely fairies still do dwell.

They say that the modern man is but a savage reformed by artificial means, and if left to himself would relapse to his pristine state. Well, if ever I should relapse thus, I'd live in the New Forest. Referring to the forest, Galpin says—"Within equal limits, perhaps, few parts of England afford a greater variety of beautiful landscapes than this New Forest. Its woody scenes, its extended lawns, and vast sweeps of wild country, unlimited by artificial boundaries, together with its river views and distant coasts, are all in a great degree magnificent. (There have been many portions of the Forest enclosed since these lines were written, but their gates are never closed against the stranger or sight-seer.) Still, it must be remembered that its chief characteristic, and what it rests on for distinction, is not sublimity but sylvan beauty."

And this last line of Galpin's naturally enough leads my thoughts away northward to the wild Highlands of Scotland, where sublimity is in advance of sylvan beauty, and brings the words of Wilson to my mind:—

"What lonely magnificence stretches around,
Each sight how sublime, how awful each sound,

All hushed and serene as a region of dreams,
The mountains repose 'mid the roar of the streams."

I have mentioned the wide-spreading oak-trees. Is it not possible that the mountain firs of our Scottish Highlands would spread also had they room? I mean if they were not planted so thickly, and had not to expend their growth in towering skywards in search of sunlight, their stems all brown and bare beneath, till looking into a pine wood is like looking into some vast cave, its dark roof supported by pillars.

Not very far from Carrbridge, in the Grampians, is one of the strangest and weirdest bits of pine forest it is possible to imagine. Here the trees have plenty of room to spread; they evidently owe their existence to birds that have brought the seeds from afar. Be that as it may, they are not very tall, but gnarled and branched in the most fantastic fashion, while in the open spaces between them grow heather and brackens of such height and magnificence that among them an army could hide. If fairies still dwell anywhere in this land of ours, surely it is in this weirdlike ferny forest of Alpine pine-trees.

I very greatly enjoyed my long drive through Sherwood Forest, on the Duke of Portland's estate. There, I think, many of the oaks are even more aged than those in the New Forest here, though, perhaps, I am mistaken. Spenser's lines would better therefore describe the former—

"Great oaks, dry and dead,
Still clad with relics of their trophies old,
Lifting to heaven their aged hoary heads,
Whose feet on earth have got but feeble hold,
And half disbowelled stand above the ground,
With wreathed roots and naked arms,
And trunks all rotten and unsound."

In one of our rambles through the New Forest—driven we were in a dogcart over the green sward, through the ferns and through the furze, over glades and natural lawns, into tree caves, and round and about the gigantic monarchs of the woods—we were taken by our guide to see the king and queen oaks, a morsel of the bark of each of which now lies in the caravan. I would not like even to guess how old these oaks were—probably a thousand years and more. Yet had you and I, reader, a chance of living as long as these majestic trees may still exist, it would not be profitable for an assurance company to grant us an annuity.

But before seeing the king and queen I pointed out to our guide one particular oak.

"What a splendid old oak!" I remarked.

"Old," was the reply—"why, sir, that's only a hinfant hoak. He ain't mebbe more'n three or four 'undred year old."

And this was an infant!

I was silent for a spell after that. I was thinking.

'Twixt three and four hundred years of age! My mind was carried away back to the days of Henry the Eighth. He would be on the throne about that time, if I remember my school history aright, marrying and giving in marriage, cutting off heads right and left, and making himself generally jolly; and Cardinal Wolsey was up and about, and poor Buckingham was murdered under guise of an execution; and on the whole they were very busy and very bloody times, when this "hinfant hoak" first popped out of its acorn.

Lyndhurst may well be called the capital of this romantic forest.

It is quite a charming little town, chiefly built on the slope of a hill, with many beautiful villas and houses surrounding it.

It is well removed from the din and roar of the railway, and from shouts of station porters. It is a quiet place. No, I must qualify that statement; it would be quiet except for those everlasting bells. They clang-clang-clang every quarter of an hour all day long and all night, and all the year round. Poe speaks about:—

"The people, ah! the people,
They that live up in the steeple,
  They are ghouls!"

Are the good folks of Lyndhurst ghouls? Anyhow, the whole of the inhabitants of the sweet little town may be said to live up in the steeple. Their nerves and ears are encased in felt perhaps, but may heaven help any nervous invalid who happens to make the neighbourhood of that church steeple his or her habitat. The bells, however, did not bother me much, for a gipsy can always sleep.

If he can stand the bells the visitor will be happy at Lyndhurst. There are capital shops, several excellent inns, lots of well-furnished apartments, and a most comfortable family hotel, the Crown, and everywhere you will meet civility,—at all events I did; and what is more I mean to go back to Lyndhurst, and do a deal more of the Forest.

The visitor should go to Mr Short's, and secure bits of Forest scenery and his guide-book—author Mr Phillips. This gentleman is most enthusiastic in his descriptions of the Forest and everything in and about it.

I cannot refrain from making one or two extracts. Phillips gives a nice description of the beautiful church of Lyndhurst—the church with the bells, and is loud in his praises of Sir F. Leighton's splendid wall painting, which all who visit the Forest must go and gaze on and study for themselves. Phillips is quoting Eustace Jones in his "picture parables" when he says:—

"All the shade is so graduated from either end to the glory in the centre, that the picture will not let you rest till you have gazed on Him, the Bridegroom—the King in His beauty. There is no light in the centre of the palace where the Bridegroom is; yet it is dazzling bright and shining, because He is the light thereof for ever and ever. All the light comes from Him, glowing out from His garments in some strange way, that makes it seem to come and go, as when you look full in the sun's face at midday, and see him burn—till he leaves his image in your eyes, glowing now large, and now small, yet dazzling alway. The face I cannot describe. There is joy in it for those who have kept their lamps still burning; there is sadness in it for those from whom it turns away—ineffable pity. But is hope quite past, even for these? His glance is averted from them, but does the hand that holds out the lily sceptre only mean to taunt their stainfulness by the sight of purity which may never more be theirs? Is He mocking at their calamity? Surely, if so, the Iron Sceptre would be less cruel than the White Lily. It cannot be, for there is nothing like it in His face.

"It may be a reflection awakened of His pity: it may be for relief from the brightness, that makes one turn from Him to look at those sorrowful faces on His left hand. It is all His palace. It is as light here as on His right hand. But there is this difference—the same sun shines winter on the Foolish virgins and summer on the Wise. It is so cold. It would not be, but that the wings of the angel who sorrowfully warns them back, shut out His light, leaving them only a strange garish brightness, wherein the waning moonlight, straggling through a troubled sky, chills and deadens the glory that yet would fall if it might. Not one of these looks at Him. They cannot. Their eyes, used to the darkness, cannot bear His light. One, who has ventured nearest and looked, has covered her face with her mantle and bowed herself that she may not see His radiance even through the angel's wing. The farthest off, who has strained her eyeballs to see the Bridegroom, must needs cover her dazzled eyes and turn away, for she cannot bear the sight. One lies, like Lazarus, at the gate, if perchance some crumbs from the banquet may be thrown to her;—but she has looked at Him for a moment, and cowers down, awestricken with the glory, lest she see Him and her heart be scorched like her eyes. Two have not yet dared to raise their eyes to look. They have come very near, but the angel, with eyes so full and compassionate (tears must be in them), prays them not. A broken vine trails across their way, to remind them of the True Vine, whose broken branches they are. But the branch still holds by a tiny splinter to the Vine, and even to these, now turned away with empty lamps, lightless, into the cold night where the moon is fast being obscured by stormy clouds, the angel at the outer porch still displays a scroll: 'Ora!'—'Pray.' This cannot be to mock their agony! Pray yet, if perchance the door may still open to their knocking, though their lamps were lighted late. The Bridegroom has risen up; but the door is not yet shut. The eleventh hour is nearly gone, but He is long-suffering still. Will they return with but a glimmer of light before it is for ever too late? Who can tell? It is dark without, and late, and there is no hope in their faces, and the angels have hushed their golden music, that it may not jar upon the sadness of those who leave His gate in tears.

"But on His right they all look at Him—every eye. They must, lest they see the sorrow of their sisters; and His very brightness interposes a blinding screen of glory to hide the sadness and the awful chill that is outside and beyond. And looking on Him, their faces are lightened, and beam radiant. They have brought their little lamps to Him, burning. Oh! how tiny the flames look, and how brown is their light against His glory, for they are all shone down and dazzled out before Him, like earthly lights before the sun—candles fading blear-eyed before the noon. One of the figures, eager, with the smallest lamp of them all, has pressed by all the rest, and caught the Bridegroom's hand, that she who was last might be first; whilst another, in the very background, is content to bear aloft her largest lamp, with three wicks bravely burning, calmly confident and trustful; for they who are first shall be last. One, half-averted, nurses and tends the flame of her lamp still—it has had but a little oil in it, and that scarce eked out till now. Close to the Bridegroom, an angel holds out a child's hand, with a little feeble light, so that even if it does not last on, it shall only go out in His very presence. But the little one is safe, for of such is His kingdom, and in heaven her Angel has always beheld the Father's face. These are all in the sunshine of His favour, and glow with the light that streams from Him. Yet the angel at the porch still says even to these, 'Vigila!'—'Watch ye!' and still pours oil into the fading lamp at the gate."

Barley, Holmsley, and Sway are within easy reach of Lyndhurst, even to the pedestrian lady.

Queen's Bower Wood—

"Beautiful, beautiful Queen of the Forest,
How art thou hidden so wondrously deep!"

—Is one of the most charming of forest woods, its handsome aged oak picturesquely overhanging the clear and bubbling stream, so soon to mix its waters with the all-absorbing sea. The stream here, as in so many other parts of the Forest, is covered in summer time with white water-lilies.

We visited Lymington in the Wanderer, and although the rained poured down in torrents all day, from under the broad canopy of the coupé we viewed the scenery safely and were delighted therewith.

Of course the Wanderer visited Minstead and Stony Cross.

What a magnificent view is to be got of the Forest from the breezy furze-clad common near the inn at Bramble Hill!

Hurricane Bob led the way with a rush down the grassy slope to Rufus's Stone, and Inie and myself came scampering on after, all three of us as full of life as mavises in May time.

The scenery about this sacred spot is pretty enough, but we did not greatly admire the stone itself. Nor did Hurricane Bob, though he paid his respects to it after his own canine fashion.

It somewhat detracts from the romance of the place that close adjoining you can have three shies at a cocoa-nut for a penny. I spent a shilling unsuccessfully; Inie knocked one down at the first shot, and Bob, not to be behindhand, watched his chance and stole one, for which may goodness forgive him.

I wish I could spare space to say something about the birds and beasts and creeping things of the Forest, and about its wild flowers, but this chapter the reader will doubtless think too long already.

I must mention Forest flies and snakes, however. Of the latter we saw none in the wilds, but the well-known snake-catcher of the New Forest, who supplies the Zoological Gardens, paid us a visit at the caravan, and brought with him some splendid specimens. Many of these were very tame, and drank milk from a saucer held to them by my wee girl.

The adders he catches with a very long pair of surgical forceps presented to him by Dr Blaker, of Lyndhurst, whose kindness and hospitality, by-the-bye, to us, will ever dwell in my memory.

We heard great accounts of the Forest flies. They say—though I cannot verify it by my own experience—that long before the transatlantic steamers reach New York, the mosquitoes, satiated with Yankee gore, smell the blood of an Englishman, and come miles to sea to meet him.

And so we were told that the Forest flies would hardly care to bite a Forest horse, but at once attacked a strange one and sent him wild.

Hearing us talk so much about this wondrous Forest fly, it was not unnatural that it should haunt wee Inie's dreams and assume therein gigantic proportions. One day, when ranging through a thicket—this was before ever we had become acquainted with the fly—we came upon a capital specimen of the tawny owl, winking and blinking on a bough. Inez saw it first.

"Oh, papa," she cried aghast, "there's a Forest Fly!"

This put me in mind of the anecdote of the woman who was going out to India with her husband, a soldier in the gallant 42nd.

"You must take care of the mosquitoes," said another soldier's wife, who had been out.

"What's a mosquito, 'oman?"

"Oh!" was the reply, "a creature with a long snout hangin' doon in front, that it sucks your blood wi'."

On landing in India almost the first animal she saw was an elephant.

"May the Lord preserve us!" cried the soldier's wife, "is that a mosquito?"

But we had to leave the dear old Forest at last, and turn our horses' heads to the north once more. "It is," says Phillips, "in such sequestered spots as these, removed from the everlasting whirl and turmoil of this high-pressure age, that we may obtain some glimpses of a life strangely contrasting in its peaceful retirement with our own; and one cannot envy the feelings of him who may spend but a few hours here without many happy and pleasant reflections."

"The past is but a gorgeous dream,
And time glides by us like a stream
While musing on thy story;
And sorrow prompts a deep alas!
That like a pageant thus should pass
To wreck all human glory."

We met many pleasant people at Lyndhurst and round it, and made many pleasant tours, Lymington being our limit.

Then we bade farewell to the friends we had made, and turned our horses' heads homewards through Hants.

When I left my little village it was the sweet spring time, and as the Wanderer stood in the orchard, apple-blossoms fell all about and over her like showers of driven snow. When she stood there again it was the brown withered leaves that rustled around her, and the wind had a wintry sough in it. But I had health and strength in every limb, and in my heart sunny memories—that will never leave it—of the pleasantest voyage ever I have made in my life.

CARAVANNING FOR HEALTH

"Life is not to live, but to be well."

This chapter, and indeed the whole of this appendix, may be considered nothing more or less than an apology for my favourite way of spending my summer outing.

Now there are no doubt thousands who would gladly follow my example, and become for a portion of the year lady or gentlemen gipsies, did not circumstances over which they have no control raise insuperable barriers between them and a realisation of their wishes. For these I can only express my sorrow. On the other hand, I know there are many people who have both leisure and means at command, people who are perhaps bored with all ordinary ways of travelling for pleasure; people, mayhap, who suffer from debility of nerves, from indigestion, and from that disease of modern times we call ennui, which so often precedes a thorough break-up and a speedy march to the grave. It is for the benefit of these I write my appendix; it is to them I most cordially dedicate it.

There may be some who, having read thus far, may say to themselves:—

"I feel tired and bored with the worry of the ordinary everyday method of travelling, rushing along in stuffy railway carriages, residing in crowded hotels, dwelling in hackneyed seaside towns, following in the wake of other travellers to Scotland or the Continent, over-eating and over-drinking; I feel tired of ball, concert, theatre, and at homes, tired of scandal, tired of the tinselled show and the businesslike insincerity of society, and I really think I am not half well. And if ennui, as doctors say, does lead the way to the grave, I do begin to think I'm going there fast enough. I wonder if I am truly getting ill, or old, or something; and if a complete change would do me good?" I would make answer thus:—You may be getting ill, or you may be getting old, or both at once, for remember age is not to be reckoned by years, and nothing ages one sooner than boredom and ennui. But if there be any doubts in your mind as regards the state of your health, and seeing that ennui does not weaken any one organ more than another, but that its evil effects are manifested in a deterioration of every organ and portion of the body and tissues at once, let us consider for a moment what health really is.

It was Emerson, I think, who said, "Give me health and a day, and I will make the pomp of emperors ridiculous."

There is a deal of truth underlying that sentence. To put it in my own homely way: if a young man, or a middle-aged one either, while spending a day in the country, with the fresh breezes of heaven blowing on his brow, with the larks a-quiver with song in the bright sunshine, and all nature rejoicing,—I tell you that if such an individual, not being a cripple, can pass a five-barred gate without an inclination to vault over it, he cannot be in good health.

Will that scale suit you to measure your health against?

Nay, but to be more serious, let me quote the words of that prince of medical writers, the late lamented Sir Thomas Watson, Bart:—

"Health is represented in the natural or standard condition of the living body. It is not easy to express that condition in a few words, nor is it necessary. My wish is to be intelligible rather than scholastic, and I should puzzle myself as well as you, were I to attempt to lay down a strict and scientific definition of what is meant by the term 'health.' It is sufficient for our purpose to say that it implies freedom from pain and sickness; freedom also from all those changes in the natural fabric of the body, that endanger life or impede the easy and effectual exercise of the vital functions. It is plain that health does not signify any fixed and immutable condition of the body. The standard of health varies in different persons, according to age, sex, and original constitution; and in the same person even, from week to week or from day to day, within certain limits it may shift and librate. Neither does health necessarily imply the integrity of all the bodily organs. It is not incompatible with great and permanent alterations, nor even with the loss of parts that are not vital—as of an arm, a leg, or an eye. If we can form and fix in our minds a clear conception of the state of health, we shall have little difficulty in comprehending what is meant by disease, which consists in some deviation from that state—some uneasy or unnatural sensation of which the patient is aware; some embarrassment of function, perceptible by himself or by others; or some unsafe though hidden condition of which he may be unconscious; some mode, in short, of being, or of action, or of feeling different from those which are proper to health."

Can medicine restore the health of those who are threatened with a break-up, whose nerves are shaken, whose strength has been failing for some time past, when it seems to the sufferer—to quote the beautiful words of the Preacher—the days have already come when you find no pleasure in them;

when you feel as if the light of the sun and the moon and the stars are darkened, that the silver cord is loosed, the golden bowl is broken, and the pitcher broken at the fountain?

No, no, no! a thousand times no. Medicine, tonic or otherwise, never, alone, did, or could, cure the deadly ailment called ennui. You want newness of life, you want perfect obedience for a time to the rules of hygiene, and exercise above all.

Now I do not for a moment mean to say that caravanning is the very best form of exercise one can have. Take your own sort, the kind that best pleases you. But, for all that, experience leads me to maintain that no life separates a man more from his former self, or gives him a better chance of regeneration of the most complete kind, than that of the gentleman gipsy.

Take my own case as an example. I am what is called a spare man, though weighing eleven stone odd to a height of five feet nine. I am spare, but when well as wiry and hard as an Arab.

I had an unusually stiff winter's work last season. On my 1,300-mile caravan tour I had assuredly laid up a store of health that stood me in good stead till nearly April, and I did more literary work than usual. But I began to get weary at last, and lost flesh. I slaved on manfully, that I might get away on my second grand tour, from which I have just returned, after covering ground to the extent of a thousand and odd miles. Well, I started, and as I took a more hilly route, the journey was more fatiguing for us all. We all weighed before starting; six weeks afterwards we weighed again; my coachman had increased one and a half pounds, my valet three pounds, while I, who underwent the greatest fatigue of the three, had put on five pounds. Nor was this all; my heart felt lighter than it had done for years, and I was singing all day long. Though not a young man, I am certainly not an old one, but before starting, while still toiling at the drudgery of the desk's dull wood, I was ninety-five years of age—in feeling; before I had been six weeks on the road I did not feel forty, or anything like it.

The first fortnight of life in a great caravan like the Wanderer is just a little upsetting; even my coachman felt this. The constant hum of the waggon-wheels, and the jolting—for with the best of springs a two-ton waggon will jolt—shakes the system. It is like living in a mill; but after this you harden up to it, and would not change your modus vivendi for life in a royal palace.

Now I would not dream of insulting the understanding of my readers by presuming that they do not know what the simple rules of hygiene which tend to long life, perfect health, and calm happiness, are. There is hardly a sixteen-year-old schoolboy nowadays who has not got these at his finger-ends; but, unfortunately, if we do not act up to them with a regularity that at length becomes a habit, we are apt to let them slip from our mind; and it is so easy to fall off into a poor condition of health, but not so very easy to pull one's self together again.

Let me simply enumerate, by way of reminding you, some of the ordinary rules for the maintenance of health. We will then see how far it is possible to carry these out in such a radical change of life as that of an amateur gipsy, living, eating, and sleeping in his caravan, and sometimes, to some extent, roughing it.

The following remarks from one of my books on cycling are very much to the point in the subject I am now discussing, and the very fact of my writing so will prove, I think, that I am willing you should hear both sides of the question, for I know there are people in this world who prefer the life of the bluebottle-fly—fast and merry—to what they deem a slow even if healthful existence. ("Health upon Wheels." Messrs Iliffe and Co, 98 Fleet Street, London.)

Good habits, I say, may be formed as well as bad ones; not so easily, I grant you, but, being formed, or for a time enforced, they, too, become a kind of second nature.

Some remarks of the author of "Elia" keep running through my head as I write, and for the life of me I cannot help penning them, although they in a certain sense militate against my doctrine of reform. "What?" says the gentle author, "have I gained by health? Intolerable dulness. What by early hours and moderate meals? A total blank."

I question, however, if Charles Lamb, after so many years spent in the London of his day, had a very great deal of liver left.—If he had, probably it was a very knotty one (cirrhosis) and piebald rather than healthy chocolate brown.

Now I should be sorry indeed if I left my readers to infer that, after a reckless life up to the age say of forty, forty-five, or fifty, a decided reformation of habits will so far rejuvenate a man that he shall become quite as healthy and strong as he might have been had he spent his days in a more rational manner; one cannot have his cake and eat it too, but better late than never; he can by care save the morsel of cake he has left, instead of throwing it to the dogs and going hot foot after it.

Every severe illness, no matter how well we get over it, detracts from our length of days: how much more then must twenty or more years of a fast life do so? With our "horse's constitution" we may come through it all with life, but it will leave its mark, if not externally, internally.

I am perfectly willing that the reader should have both the cons and the pros of the argument, and will even sit in judgment on the statements I have just made, and will myself call upon witnesses that may seem to disprove them.

The first to take the box is your careless, sceptical, happy-go-lucky man, your live-for-to-day-and-bother-to-morrow individual, who states that he really enjoys life, and that he can point to innumerable acquaintances, who go the pace far faster than he does, but who, nevertheless, enjoy perfect health, and are likely to live "till a fly fells them."

The next witness has not much to say, but he tells a little story—a temperance tale he calls it.

Two very aged men were one time subpoenaed on some case, and appeared in the box before a judge who was well-known as a staunch upholder of the principles of total abstinence. This judge, seeing two such aged beings before him, thought it a capital opportunity of teaching a lesson to those around him.

"How old are you?" he said, addressing the first witness.

"Eighty, and a little over," was the reply.

"You have led a very temperate life, haven't you?" said the judge.

"I've never tasted spirits, to my knowledge, all my life, sir."

The judge looked around him, with a pleased smile on his countenance. Then he addressed the other ancient witness, who looked even haler than his companion.

"How old are you, my man?"

"Ninety odd, your worship."

"Ahem?" said the judge. "You have doubtless led a strictly abstemious life, haven't you?"

"Strictly abstemious!" replied the old reprobate; "indeed, sir, I haven't been strictly sober for the last seventy years."

Diet.—Errors in diet produce dyspepsia, and dyspepsia may be the forerunner of almost any fatal illness. It not only induces disease itself, but the body of the sufferer from this complaint, being at the best but poorly nourished, no matter how fat and fresh he may appear, is more liable to be attacked by any ailment which may be in the air. Dyspepsia really leaves the front door open, so that trouble may walk in.

The chief errors in diet which are apt to bring on chronic indigestion are: 1. Over-rich or over-nutritious diet. 2. Over-eating, from which more die than from over-drinking. 3. Eating too quickly, as one is apt to do when alone, the solvent saliva having thus no time to get properly mingled with the food. 4. The evil habit of taking "nips" before meals, by which means the blood is heated, the salivary glands rendered partially inert, the mucous membrane of the mouth rendered incapable for a time of absorption, and the gastric juices thrown out and wasted before their proper time, that is meal-time. 5. Drinking too much fluid with the meals, and thereby diluting the gastric juices and delaying digestion. 6. Want of daily or tri-weekly change of diet. 7. Irregularity in times of eating.

Drink.—I do not intend discussing the question of temperance. 1. But if stimulants are taken at all, it should never be on an empty stomach. 2. They ought not to be taken at all, if they can be done without. 3. What are called "nightcaps" may induce sleep, but it is by narcotic action, and the sleep is neither sound nor refreshing. The best nightcap is a warm bath and a bottle of soda water, with ten to fifteen grains of pure bicarbonate of soda in it.

Coffee is a refreshing beverage.

Cocoa is both refreshing and nourishing, but too much of it leads to biliousness.

Oatmeal. Water drunk from off a handful or two of this is excellent on the road.

Cream of tartar drink. This should be more popular than it is in summer. A pint of boiling water is poured over a dram and a half of cream of tartar, in which is the juice of a lemon and some of the rind; when cold, especially if iced, it is truly excellent in summer weather. It cools the system, prevents constipation, and assuages thirst.

Ginger-ale or ginger beer is good, but should be taken in moderation.

Tonic drinks often contain deleterious accumulative medicines, and should all be avoided.

Cold tea, if weak, flavoured with lemon-juice, and drunk without sugar, is probably the best drink of the road. But let it be good pure Indian tea.

Baths.—The morning cold sponge bath, especially with a handful or two of sea-salt in it, is bracing, stimulating, and tonic. No one who has once tried it for a week would ever give it up.

The Turkish bath may be taken once a week, or once a fortnight. It gets rid of a deal of the impurities of the blood, and lightens both brain and heart. Whenever one feels dull and mopish, he should indulge in the luxury of a Turkish bath.

Fresh air.—The more of this one has the better, whether by day or by night. Many chronic ailments will yield entirely to a course of ozone-laden fresh air, such as one gets at the seaside, or on the mountain's brow. Have a proper and scientific plan of ventilating your bedrooms. Ventilators should be both in doors and windows, else one cannot expect perfect health and mental activity. Without air one dies speedily; in bad air he languishes and dies more slowly; in the ordinary air of rooms one exists, but he cannot be said to live; but in pure air one can be as happy and light-hearted as a lark.

Exercise.—This must be pleasurable, or at all events it must be interesting—mind and body must go hand in hand—if exercise is to do any good. It must not be over-fatiguing, and intervals of rest must not be forgotten. Exercise should never be taken in cumbersome clothing.

"Work," I say in one of my books, "is not exercise." This may seem strange, but it is true. I tell my patients, "I do not care how much you run about all day at your business, you must take the exercise I prescribe quite independently of your work." There are perhaps no more hard-working men in the world than the Scottish ploughmen—wearily plodding all day long behind their horses, in wet weather or dry; no sooner, however, has the sun "gane west the loch," and the day's work is done, than, after supper and a good wash, those hardy lads assemble in the glen, and not only for one, but often three good hours, keep up the health-giving games for which their nation is so justly celebrated.

Cooking.—Good cooking is essential to health. I do not care how plainly I live, but pray exercise the attribute of mercy. Let my steak or chop be tender and toothsome; my fish or vegetables not overdone, and oh! pray boil me my potatoes well, for without old pomme de terre life to me would be one dreary void.

Now let us see how far the rules of health may be carried out in a caravan like the Wanderer.

First comes early rising. You get up almost with the lark—you are bound to, for there is a deal to be done in a caravan; what with getting breakfast, having the carriage tidied and dusted, the beds stowed away on the roof, dishes washed, stove cleaned, carpets shaken, and pantry swept and washed, eight o'clock comes before you know where you are. And by the time your flowers are rearranged in the vases, and everything so sweet and tidy that you do not mind Royalty itself having a look inside, it will be pretty near nine o'clock, and the horses will be round, the pole shipped, the buckets slung, and all ready for a start. But then you will think early rising the reverse of a hardship, for did you not turn in at ten o'clock? and have you not slept the sweet sleep of the just—or a gentleman gipsy?

The first thing you did when you got up was to have a bath under the tent which your servant prepared for you. Oh that delicious cool sponge bath of a lovely summer's morning! If you do not join the birds in their song even before you have quite finished rubbing down, it is because you have no music in your soul.

But I mentioned a Turkish bath as a health accessory. Can that be had in a Wanderer caravan? Indeed it can. I have a portable one, and it does not exceed three inches in height, and when put away takes hardly as much space up as a pair of boots does.

The greatest cleanliness is maintainable in a caravan where regularity exists,—cleanliness of person, and cleanliness of the house itself.

As to regularity, this is one of the things one learns to perfection on a gipsy tour extending over months. There can be no comfort without it. Everything in its place must be your motto, and this is a habit which once learned is of the greatest service to one in more civilised life. For the want of regularity causes much worry, and worry is one of the primary causes of illness.

Fresh air.—You are in it all day. Now down in the valley among the woods, or breathing the balmy odours of the pine forests; now high up on the mountain top, and anon by the bracing sea-beach. And at night your ventilators are all open, without a chance of catching cold, so no wonder your sleep is as sweet and dreamless as that of a healthy child.

As to the weather, you are hardly ever exposed. The caravan does not leak, and if you are on the coupé you are protected by the verandah (vide frontispiece).

Exercise.—This you get in abundance, and that too of the most wholesome and exhilarating kind.

Food in the caravan.—Perhaps you have been living too freely before, and having too many courses; all this will be altered when you take to the road. Plainly you must live, and you will soon come to prefer a plain substantial diet.

The first result of your new mode of life—and this you will not be twenty-four hours out before you feel—will be hunger. It does not matter that you had a substantial breakfast at eight o'clock, you will find your way to the cupboard at eleven, and probably for the first time in your life you will find out what a delicious titbit a morsel of bread-and-cheese is. Yes, and I would even forgive you if you washed it down with one tiny glass of mild ale, albeit beer is not the best thing on the road.

At the midday halt you will have luncheon. You can drink your tea cold on the road or warm it in the spirit stove; and when settled for the night in some quiet and peaceful meadow, your servant will speedily cook the dinner, which has been put all ready in the Rippingille stove during the midday halt.

While this is being cooked, in the privacy of the saloon you can play the fiddle or discourse sweet music from the harmonium, or if tired lie on the sofa and read.

I have said that you must live plainly in a caravan. But the word plainly is a term. You may not have French dishes nor twenty courses, but I append extracts from bills of fare of caravan cookery, to show that diet is not necessarily a mere off-put in the Wanderer.

I must, however, premise that I myself did not always bother with so good a menu.

To begin with, here are my cook's general instructions:—

Always see that the stove is clean and in order. Wipe the tanks thoroughly dry, if any oil is perceptible upon them; trim the wicks, light them, turn down low, place in the proper grooves, and carefully follow instructions given with the stove. When set fairly in, regulate the light by observing the height through the sight holes. Brush out the oven, and then all is ready for a good day's work. All this will occupy very little time, one-tenth of that generally spent in lighting coal fires and trying to escape the dust and dirt the old-fashioned open range entailed. Next rinse out the kettle, fill with fresh water from the tap, place over one of the burners. Wash your hands, and then get all ready for breakfast. Cut rashers of bacon and slices of bread sufficient for the family requirements. Bring out the eggs, butter, pepper, salt; then the tea-caddy, coffee, etc, with their respective pots; plates, dishes, toast-rack, fish slice, teacup or small basin, and lay on the table near the stove, so that no time may be lost running about when the cooking begins. These instructions apply to all meals. First get the apparatus and material ready, and then begin to cook.

Breakfasts.

I. Toast, poached eggs, tea, coffee, or chocolate.

II. Toast, fried eggs and bacon, or mashed eggs, tea, etc.

III. Oatmeal porridge with butter and creamy milk, followed by a boiled new-laid egg and a rasher, with tea. N.B.—The butter is always the sweetest, and the milk the crème de la crème.

IV. Herrings, devilled melt and roe, toast, tea, etc, eggs bouillés.

V. Mock sausages, boiled eggs, and usual fixings.

VI. Finnan haddocks, poached eggs, and usual fixings. And so on ad libitum.

Eleven o'clock Snacks.

I. Bread or biscuit and cheese with a modicum of beer.

II. Bloater-paste or anchovy-paste, or buttered toast with cold tea.

III. Tongue and ham (potted), turkey and tongue, and fixings.

Luncheons.

The cold joints of yesterday, with hot potatoes, piquant sauces, and chutney; washed down with a cup of delicious chocolate or new milk.

Dinners.

I. Fried cutlets of fish; roast fowls; brown sauce, potatoes, greens, and bread; rice or golden pudding.

II. Spatch cock; minced meat, baked potatoes, green peas; custard.

III. Roast mutton, mashed turnips, potatoes; and fruit pudding.

IV. Rabbit stewed, game in season, vegetables; and sago pudding.

V. Beefsteak and onions, boiled potatoes, cauliflower; pudding.

VI. Salmon à la Reine; cold meat and salad; La Belle pudding.

And so on ad libitum, with wine or beer to suit the taste.

Suppers.

I. If required, a snack of anything handy.

II. Tomatoes forcés (tinned tomatoes if fresh cannot be had), cocoa, toast.

III. Macaroni cheese and toast.

IV. Eggs à la Soyer, toast; or a poached egg on toast. Salad, especially of lettuce, with a modicum of good beer or stout.

A cleverer cook than I could devise a hundred simple dishes for caravan cookery, but I do not think my menu is altogether prison fare.

Ailments Likely to be Benefited by Caravan Life.

I can, of course, only mention a few of these, and it must be distinctly understood that I am not trying to enforce the merits of a new cure. I am but giving my own impressions from my own experience, and if anyone likes to profit by these he may, and welcome.

I. Ennui.

II. Dyspepsia.
III. Debility and enfeeblement of health from overwork, or from worry or grief.
IV. Insomnia.
V. Chronic bronchitis and consumption in its earliest stages.
VI. Bilious habit of system.
VII. Acidity of secretions of stomach, etc.
VIII. All kinds of stomachic ailments.
IX. Giddiness or vertigo.
X. Hysteria.
XI. Headaches and wearying backaches.
XII. Constipated state of system.
XIII. Tendency to embonpoint.
XIV. Neuralgia of certain kinds.
XV. Liver complaints of a chronic kind.
XVI. Threatened kidney mischief.
XVII. Hay fever.
XVIII. Failure of brain power.
XIX. Anaemia or poverty of blood.
XX. Nervousness.

Some of the great factors in the cure of such complaints as the above by life in a caravan for a series of months would be, that perfect rest and freedom from all care which is so calming to shattered nerves, weary brains, and aching hearts. The constant and pleasurable change of scene and change of faces, the regularity of the mode of life, and the delightfully refreshing sleep, born of the fresh air and exercise, which is nearly always obtainable at night.

In concluding this chapter, let me just add that of all modes of enjoying life in summer and autumn I consider—speaking after a somewhat lengthy experience—caravan travelling the healthiest and the best.

THE CYCLE AS TENDER TO THE CARAVAN

"When the spring stirs my blood
With the instincts of travel,
I can get enough gravel
On the old Marlborough road."
Thoreau.

I begin to think, reader, that the plan of putting headlines or verses to chapters, although a very ancient, time-honoured custom, is not such a very excellent one after all.

The verses are written subsequently, of course, after you have finished the chapter, and the difficulty is to get them to fit; you may have some glimmering notion that, once upon a time, some poet or other did say something that would be apropos, but who was it? You get off your easy-chair and yawn and stretch yourself, then lazily make your way to the bookshelf and commence the search among your favourite poets. It is for all the world like looking for a needle in a bundle of hay, and when you do find it, it isn't half so bright as you thought it would be, only down you jot it in a semi-reckless kind of a way, feeling all the while as if you were a humbug, or committing some sort of a deadly sin.

If this good poet Thoreau had said,—
"When the spring stirs my blood
With the instincts of travel,
I can get enough exercise
On my Marlborough tricycle."
—Although not metre, it would have been to the point. But the poet did not, so there we are. Nevertheless, the Marlborough is the cycle I have bestridden during my tour this summer, and a sweet wee thing it is. In my

caravan tour of 1885 it was the Ranelagh Club I had as tender to the Wanderer, also a good one.

But really, without a cycle, one would sometimes feel lost in caravan travelling. The Wanderer is so large that she cannot turn on narrow roads, so that on approaching a village, where I wish to stay all night, I find it judicious to stop her about a quarter of a mile out and tool on, mounted on the Marlborough, to find out convenient quarters. Then a signal brings the Wanderer on.

Another advantage of having a tender is this. In narrow lanes your valet rides on ahead, and if there really be no room for a trap to pass us, he warns any carriage that may chance to be coming our way.

Take, for example, that ugly climb we had when passing through Slochmuichk, in the Grampians (see illustration). My valet was on ahead, round the corner and on the outlook for coming vehicles, and so had anyone hove in sight a probable accident would have been avoided.

Again, when passing through a town where board schools with their busy bees of boys are numerous, my valet, on the Marlborough tender, comes riding up behind, and accordingly the bees do not have a chance of sticking on to the carriage.

Tramps will, at times, get up and try the drawers behind, but whenever I see a suspicious gang of these worthless loafers, a signal brings the tender flying back, and thus robbery is prevented.

I had the utmost satisfaction once this year in punishing some country louts. Butler, my valet, was innocently riding on about a hundred yards ahead, and no sooner had he passed than the three blackguards commenced stone-throwing. They had no idea then the cycle belonged to the caravan. They had soon after though. I slid quietly off the coupé, whip in hand, and for several seconds I enjoyed the most health-giving exercise. Straight across the face and round the ears I hit as hard as I knew how to. One escaped Scot-free, but two tumbled in the ditch and howled aloud for mercy, which I generously granted—after I got tired. The beauty of the attack was in its suddenness, and those roughs will remember it to their dying day.

But the main pleasure in possessing a cycle lies in the opportunities you have of seeing lovely bits of scenery, and quaint queer old villages, and quaint queer old people, quite out of the beaten track of your grand tour. And it is a pleasure to have a long quiet ride through woods and flowery lanes, of a summer's evening, after having been in the caravan all day long.

Just let me pick one extract from a book I wrote last year, describing cycling in connection with my grand tour.

("Rota Vitae, The Cyclist's Guide to Health and Rational Enjoyment." Published by Messrs Iliffe and Sturney, 98 Fleet Street, London.)

The little work is really a bombshell, as ancient divines used to call their tracts, aimed at the senseless making of records by cyclists who go flying from one end of the kingdom to the other, and come back as wise as they went, and infinitely more tired.

Haddington and round it.

Everywhere you go around Haddington, you will be charmed with the character and beauty of the scenery, and its great variety.

Inland, are there not grand old hills and wild woodlands, lonely straths and glens, and splendid sheets of water? Is there not, too, the finest tree scenery that exists anywhere in Scotland? Yes! and the very wild flowers and hedgerows themselves would repay one for all the toil incurred in rattling over somewhat stony roads, and climbing lofty braelands. Then, towards the east, you come in sight of the sea itself—the ever-beautiful, ever-changing sea. Go farther east still, go to the coast itself, and you will find yourself among such rock scenery as can hardly be beaten, expect by that in Skye or the Orkneys. When tired of wandering on the shore, and, if a naturalist, studying and admiring the thousand-and-one strange objects around you, why, you may go and hobnob with some of the fisher folks—male or female, take your choice—they will amuse, ay, and mayhap instruct you, while some of the oldest of them will tell you tales of the old smuggling days, and life in the caves, that will heat anything you ever read in books.

If you should stay at Cockburnspath all night you will not forget to visit the seashore and the caves. Those caves have a history, too; they were connected with the troublesome times of "auld lang syne," and later still, they came in remarkably handy for bold smugglers, who, before the days of smart revenue cutters, made use of them as temporary storehouses when running a cargo on shore.

How lovely the sea looks on a summer's day from the hills around here! How enchanting the woods! How wild! How quiet! You will be inclined to live and linger among scenery such as this, book in hand, perhaps, on a bank of wild thyme and bluebells, and if you do notice some blue-coated bicyclist, with red perspiring face and dusty tout ensemble, speeding past on his way to John-o'-Groat's, how you will pity him! Farther west is the romantic Dunglass Dene, which you will visit without fail. Says Scott:

"The cliffs here rear their haughty head
High o'er the river's darksome bed;
Here trees to every crevice clung,
And o'er the dell their branches hung:
And there, all splintered and uneven,
The shivered rocks ascend to heaven;
Oft, too, the ivy swathed their breast,
And wreathed their garland round their crest;
Or from the spires bade loosely flare

Its tendrils in the summer air."

The most romantic parts of Scotland which may be visited by the caravannist, with his tricycle as tender, are:—

I. The counties of Barns, Hogg, and Scott (comprising all the space betwixt a line drawn from Edinburgh to Glasgow and the Tweed).

II. The Grampian Wilds.

III. The Perthshire Highlands.

IV. The Valley of the Dee.

V. The Valley of the Don.

VI. The sea coast from Edinburgh to Fraserburgh, and west as far as Inverness itself.

Coming south now to England, I must permit the tourist himself to choose his own headquarters. I shall merely mention the most healthy and interesting districts.

I. The Lake Country.

II. The Yorkshire District (most bracing and interesting).

III. The Peak District of Derbyshire.

IV. The Midland District.

V. The East Coasts.

VI. North Wales (centre, probably Bala).

VII. South Wales.

VIII. South Devon.

IX. South Cornwall.

X. Jersey (Saint Heliers).

I should also mention both Orkney and Shetland, these islands are healthy and bracing.

In both the last-named districts riding will be found practical, but boating excursions will rival the tricycle. Fishing and shooting, and walking among the moorlands and hills, combine to render a holiday in either the Orkneys or Shetland Islands a most enjoyable one.

Both at Kirkwall and Lerwick fairly good hotels are to be found, and respectable lodgings, while living is as cheap as anyone could desire.

NB—An ordinary-sized caravan can be taken by sea, but take my advice, never put it on board a train.

HINTS TO WOULD-BE CARAVANNISTS

"We live to learn ilka day,
The warld wide's the best o' skools,
Experience too, so auld folks say,
Is just the jade for teachin' fools."
Nemo.

I.

First catch your hare. That is, get your caravan.

"Oh!" I think I hear some one say, "I shall hire one." Take Punch's advice to people about to marry—"don't."

And the same advice holds good as regards secondhand caravans.

Mind, I do not say that you may not be able to meet with a good and clean one, but, woe is me, there is a chance of guests, in old caravans of the gipsy class, that you would not care to be shipmates with.

Besides, the woodwork may be bad, or "going," and there may be flaws in the springs, the wheels. The roof may leak, and a hundred and fifty other disagreeables be found out after you fairly start on the road.

I would as soon buy an old feather-bed in the east end of London as an old caravan.

Get your car then from a really good maker, one who could not afford to put a bad article out of hand.

I have neither object nor desire to advertise the Bristol Waggon Company, but it is due to them to say that having paid a fair price, I got from them a splendid article. But of course there may be other makers as good or better. I do not know.

II. Style of Build.

You may copy the Wanderer if so minded. I do not think that I myself, after two years on the road, could improve on her, except that the shutters are difficult to draw on and off, and ought to run upon castors.

However, few caravannists might care to have so long and large a chariot as mine; one about twelve feet long would serve every purpose, and be easily moved with one good horse. It would also be more easily drawn into meadows at night.

A caravan, both exteriorly and interiorly, is capable of an infinite amount of ornamentation. But I do not think a gentleman gipsy's carriage ought to, in any way, resemble that of a travelling showman, although it certainly should not be like a Salvationist's "barrow."

The entrance door may be at the side, or behind, as in the Wanderer.

The windows should be large and neat, and prettily curtained or upholstered. A caravannist is constantly being gazed at, and people will assuredly judge of your interior fittings by the taste and appearance displayed outside.

The Wanderer, with my books and furniture (all light) on board, weighs well-nigh two tons. Even for a pair of good-hearted horses, such as I possess, this is rather much, so that I should advise that a single horse caravan be not much over fifteen hundredweight.

The Wanderer is double-walled, being built of well-seasoned beautiful mahogany, and lined with maple, having an interspace of about one inch and a half. But double walls are really not necessary, and only add to the expense.

The body of the carriage might be made of Willesden waterproof paper, fastened to a framework of light strong wood. This remarkable paper keeps its shape in all weathers, and can be charmingly painted and gilded.

For a very light summer caravan the upper works might be painted Willesden canvas. Such a carriage, however, would hardly withstand the cold of winter.

The roof of the Wanderer is painted white. I am often asked, Is it not very hot in summer? But the answer is "No, because with the doors open there is always a delightful breeze." Then, wood being a conductor, and there being so much ventilation, as soon as the sun goes down the caravan becomes as cool as can be desired.

Upholstering and Furnishing.

A deal of taste can be shown in this. Everything most be of smallest possible dimensions.

A few favourite books should be taken, while magazines, etc, can be bought in towns and villages as you pass through. I have a fairy edition of the poets, my little ebony bookcase is a fairy one, and a good many other articles as well are of fairy dimensions also. Mirrors are tolerably heavy, but let in here and there in the panels, etc, they have a very nice effect, and make the caravan seem double the size.

Flower vases of different shapes and sizes may be almost everywhere. Flowers we can always get, and if the same kind hospitality be extended to every gentleman or lady gipsy that was lavished on me, his or her caravan will always be florally gay.

The coupé is easily convertible into a delightful lounge. I have a bag close at hand on the splashboard, where I keep the road-book or guide, the map of the county through which I am passing, and my pens, ink, pencils, and note-books. There is also on the coupé a brass-gilt little rack for holding my book or newspaper, as well as a minimum thermometer.

If a shower faces the caravan and is blown in under the verandah, or if the dust is troublesome, it is easy to retire into the saloon for a short time, and shut the glass door.

If you are at all handy with the pencil and...

—My vases, or blind or curtain one inch awry. Be gentle and firm with your valet, and he will soon come to see things as you do, and act in accordance with all your wishes.

The cooking-stove should be black-leaded, the tin things should shine like burnished silver, and every kitchen utensil be as bright and clean as a new sovereign.

What though your table be small, the viands plain? they are well put on, your delft is polished, and that flower in the vase, and those coloured glasses, look well on a spotless cloth.

The Cooking-Range.

Does it smell at all? I have often been asked that question. The reply is "No, not at all," and in October I light the range of an evening to warm the caravan.

When breakfast is wanted in a hurry, to ensure an early start, the cooking is done the night before, and the tea made and poured off the leaves into a large bottle, so that five minutes' time in the morning is sufficient to warm everything. The oil for the range is hung underneath in a can.

Underneath also are slung two buckets, a dog's food-can, and a dust-proof basket in which vegetables are carried, to be cleaned and made ready for cooking at the midday halt, and so prepared without delay when the bivouac is chosen.

Everything that can be done the evening before should be done—boot cleaning, knife polishing, filling cistern and filter, and preparing the range for immediate lighting.

The Provision Book.

This should be presented to you every morning at breakfast by your valet, who is to call your attention to the articles wanted, whether bread, butter, meat, vegetables, or groceries. Then the shopping is done in the forenoon as you pass through village or town, although many things are better and more cheaply procured at cottages.

An Early Start Desirable.

Make an early start and all will go well. On the other hand, if you laze and dawdle in the morning the day will be spoiled, luncheon will be hurried, and dinner too late.

Asking the Road.

This is the duty of your valet, who is on ahead with the tricycle. But do not trust altogether to him, but when any doubt exists ask yourself, and be sure that your informant really knows his right hand from his left. Remember that if a man stands facing you his right is your left.

Draymen, butchers, and waggoners, are the best men to enquire the state of the roads of, as regards hills, condition, etc.

I make a point of mingling in a kindly way of an evening with the villagers at the inns where my horses are stabled. I get much amusement sometimes by so doing. I meet many queer characters, hear many a strange story, and last but not least get well-ventilated opinions as to the best and nearest roads.

A caravannist must not be above talking to all kinds and conditions of men. If he has pride he must keep it in a bucket under the caravan. Never if possible get belated.

If you do, you are liable to accidents of all kinds. I have been run into more than once at night by recklessly-driving tipsy folks. Certainly it only slightly shook my great caravan, but capsized the dogcart.

While on the road, your coachman will for the horses' sakes keep on the best parts. Make room, however, wherever possible for faster vehicles that want to pass you. But whenever the drivers of them are insolent I laugh and let them wait; they dare not "ram" me. Ramming would not affect the Wanderer in the slightest, but would be rough on the rammer.

Stabling.

Stable your horses every night. Never think of turning them out. The horses are your moving power, and you cannot take too much care of them. See then that they are carefully groomed and fed, and stand pastern-deep in dry straw.

Civility.

This is a cheap article. Be civil to everyone, and you will have civility in return.

The Price of Stabling.

Make it a rule, as I do, to know exactly what you have to pay for your horses' accommodation. You will thus have no words in the morning, you will part in friendship with the landlord, who will be glad to see you when you return, while the ostler's good word can be bought cheaply enough.

Water.

Drink nothing but what has passed through the filter. I use one from the Silicated Carbon Company, and find it excellent.

Dangers of the Road.

These are nominal, and need hardly be mentioned. I carry a revolver which I seldom load; I have shutters that I seldom put up; and I often sleep with an open door. But I have a faithful dog. My most painful experience on the road this year I sent an account of to the Pall Mall under the title of "A Terrible Telegram."

"A few claret corks and an empty 'turkey and tongue' tin—nothing else will be left to mark the spot where the Wanderer lay." My friend Townesend gazed on the grass as he spoke, and there was a look of sadness in his face, which, actor though he be, I feel sure was not assumed. He had come to see the last of me and my caravan—the last for a time, at all events—to bid me good-bye and see me start. Parting is sweet sorrow, and I had spent a most enjoyable week at that delightful, quiet, wee watering-place, Filey, Yorkshire. I had lazed and written, I had lounged and read; my very soul felt steeped in a dreamy glamour as pleasant as moonshine on the sea; I had enjoyed the dolee far niente, book in hand, among the wild thyme on the sunny cliffs of Guisthorpe; for me, blades of dulse—the esculent and delicious rhodamenia palmata—culled wet from the waves that lapped and lisped among the Brigg's dark boulders, had been veritable lotus leaves, and, reclining by the mouth of a cave, I could readily believe in fairies and sea nymphs—ay, and mermaids as well. No letters to write, no bills to pay, no waiters to tip—for is not the Wanderer my hotel upon wheels?—and no lodging-house cat,—surely one would think a gentleman gipsy's life leaves little to be desired. And truly speaking, apart from that "terrible hill" which, day after day, seems ever on ahead of us, but which we always manage to surmount, caravanning in summer has but few drawbacks. So perfectly free and easy, so out-and-out happy is one's existence when so engaged, that he actually cares as little for the great current events of the day, or for the rise and fall of governments, as the whistling ploughboy does about the storms that rage in mid-Atlantic. Why then should that wretched little fraud, that so-called boon to the public, the sixpenny telegram, burst like a thunderstorm around my head, and tear my peace and joy to rags?

Listen, reader, and I already feel sore of your indulgence and sympathy. We left Filey on Monday forenoon, and after five days of toiling over the hills and wolds, found ourselves at Askern. Askern is a little spa and health resort, its waters are chemically similar to those of Harrogate, and useful in the same class of cases. The halt and maim and rheumatic come here, and those who seek for quiet and rest after months of drudgery at the desk's dull wood. Many more would come were the place but better known. On Friday night here the rain came down in torrents, but Saturday morning was fine, so I allowed both my servants to take an after-dinner trip to Doncaster. I would take an after-dinner nap. I was on particularly good terms with myself; I had had letters from home, I had done a good day's work, and presently meant to resume my writing.

"A telegram, sir!" A telegram? I took it and tore it open. A telegram always gives me momentary increase of heart-action, but this laconic message caused such pericardial sinking as I hope I shall never feel again. "Come home immediately, and wire the time you leave," so ran the terrible telegram. But, greatest mystery of all, it name from Mark-lane, and the sender was not my wife but "Hyde." I had never been to Mark-lane, and who is Hyde? But what dreadful calamity had happened to my home? My wife and bairnies live in Berks; but she must have gone to town, I thought, and been killed in the street, having but time to breathe my name and address ere closing her eyes for ever. Were she alive she herself would have wired, and not Hyde. There must be a mortuary at Mark-lane, and Hyde must be the dead-house doctor. I dashed my manuscript all aside, then rushed to the post-office and wired to Hyde for fullest particulars. There would be a train at four which would take me to London by 8:30.

Before I received the telegram my tongue was as red and clear as that of my Newfoundland dog's, in a moment it had become white and furred; there was a burning sensation in my throat, and my heart felt as big as a bullock's, and all these are symptoms of sudden shock and grief. But it was a time for action. In an hour the train would leave; 'twould seem a long, long hour to me. I packed my handbag with trembling hands, drew the shutters over all the windows of the Wanderer, determining to lock all up and board my valet at the hotel. Hurricane Bob, my dog, must have thought me mad, for I gave him the joint that had been meant for our Sunday's dinner; it would not keep till my return. Then I went and sat down in the post-office, and with thumping heart awaited Hyde's reply. How long the time seemed! How slowly the minute hand of the clock moved! My feelings must have been akin to those of a felon waiting the return of the jury and a verdict. The reply came at last, but only to deepen the mystery and my misery. No Hyde of Mark-lane could be found. I wired again, wired and waited for nearly another awful hour. Meanwhile my train had gone. The reader can judge of the state of my feelings, when at length the clicking needles informed the clerk that the first telegram was meant for another "Gordon Stables," of another Askarn, spelt with an "a" instead of an "e."

I did not know I had a double till now, because my name is so unusual. If I rejoiced in the name of John, and my patronymic were Smith, the marvel would be small, but the Gordon Stableses of that ilk are not dropped into this world out of a watering-can, so I do wonder who my double is, and sincerely hope that telegram has not brought him grief, but ten thousand a year.

I have no more to add. I trust if the reader does go on the road he will find a gipsy's life as happy and pleasant as I have done. Good-bye.

Printed in Great Britain
by Amazon

23089634R00123